Everyman, I will go with thee,
and be thy guide

LIUDPRAND OF CREMONA

The Embassy to Constantinople and Other Writings

Translated by
F.A. Wright

Edited by
John Julius Norwich

J.M. Dent
London
Charles E. Tuttle Co.
Rutland, Vermont
EVERYMAN'S LIBRARY

The Embassy to Constantinople and Other Writings first
published in Everyman in 1993
First published as *The Works of Liudprand of Cremona*
by George Routledge & Sons Ltd, 1930

© Introduction and chronology, J.M. Dent, 1993

Typeset at The Spartan Press Ltd, Lymington, Hants
Printed in Great Britain by The Guernsey Press Co. Ltd,
Guernsey, C.I.
J.M. Dent
Orion Publishing Group
Orion House
5 Upper St Martin's Lane
London WC2H 9EA
and
Charles E. Tuttle Co., Inc.
28 South Main Street
Rutland, Vermont
05071, USA

ISBN 0 460 87235 4

Everyman's Library
Reg. US Patent Office

CONTENTS

INTRODUCTION

The history of tenth-century Italy is not, it must be admitted, an altogether edifying one. The Carolingian Empire, which had been declining steadily ever since the death of Charlemagne, had effectively disintegrated with the deposition of Charles the Fat in 887; from that moment on the Italian peninsula – to any adventurer with sufficient power, ambition and lack of scruple to go after it – had been a prize ripe for the taking; and since its throne was now seen as the most obvious stepping-stone to that of the Empire itself, those who entered the lists were by no means confined to the local nobility, but regularly included kings and princes from neighbouring lands. To make matters worse, the Magyars were ravaging Lombardy, and in 924 had burnt its capital, Pavia; the coasts were subject to continual raids by the Saracens from Sicily, North Africa and, not least, from their pirate enclave at Le Frassinet – now La Garde Freinet – in Provence; while in Rome the local nobility had established complete control over the Church and had created what was known as the papal pornocracy, during which the See of St Peter sank to a level of decadence and debauch unparalleled before or since.

This was the world into which Liudprand – or Liuzo, to give him his Italian name – was born at Pavia, in 920 AD. He himself was a Lombard through and through, born of a noble and cultivated family closely associated with the government and administration. When he was seven, his father had been sent on a mission to Constantinople by Hugh of Arles, the former Count of Provence who had just seized the throne of Italy: a mission which, we are told, almost ended in disaster when the two fierce hunting-dogs with which Hugh had entrusted his ambassador as a present to the Emperor Romanus I Lecapenus made a violent attack on their new master, who narrowly escaped a nasty mauling.[1] Only a few years later we find young Liudprand as a singing pageboy at the court: he is said to have had a beautiful voice, and Hugh was passionately fond of music. The King's other pastimes were, regrettably, rather less innocent: and that curious combination of prudishness and prurience, which we find again and again in Liudprand's work, may well be the result of an adolescence spent in a court which was a byword for debauch and depravity, a lodestar to which all the loveliest courtesans in Europe came flocking.

Those years at the court of Pavia, whether Liudprand enjoyed them or not, certainly taught him a great deal about the ways of the world. They also enabled him to move at ease in royal circles, an accomplishment that would serve him in good stead during his later life. It is almost certainly a mistake, however, to conclude – as at least one writer has done – that they drove him, by the sheer disgust he felt for them, to take refuge in the Church. Among his many references to Hugh we find far fewer expressions of disapproval than we might normally have expected from a bishop; and there is no reason to think that his experiences at Pavia, however lurid they may have been, left any serious scars. To the intelligent, educated and ambitious young nobleman of those days (and his later writings leave us in no doubt that Liudprand was all three) the Church offered the quickest road to promotion and preferment: surely we need seek no other reason for a perfectly natural decision – and one which, incidentally, was to prove amply justified by his subsequent career.

Hugh's own fortunes were less happy, for he had fallen under the spell – whether political or erotic, or both, it is hard to say – of the infamous Marozia, Senatrix of Rome, mistress, mother and grandmother of Popes. In 928 this sinister figure had had her mother's lover, Pope John X, strangled in the Castel Sant' Angelo in order to instal her son by her former paramour, Pope Sergius III – after three years during which a couple of nonentities kept the throne warm for him while he grew to manhood. Five years later she took Hugh as her second husband, he having defamed his mother, blinded his half-brother and quite possibly murdered his wife in order to marry her; and the two would certainly have seized the Western Empire had not Alberic, Marozia's son by her first marriage, engineered a popular revolt against them. She was thrown into a dungeon of the Castel Sant' Angelo, where she spent the rest of her life. Hugh managed to escape, but from that moment his power began to decline: after 945 the effective ruler of Italy was Berengar, Marquess of Ivrea.

By this time Liudprand was a deacon at Pavia, and when Berengar began to look about for an intelligent and efficient confidential secretary he must have been an obvious choice – although, as he himself admits,[2] his mother and step-father had to pay dearly to ensure his appointment: the Marquess never gave anything away for nothing. His notorious parsimony came once again to the fore in 949 when, wishing to send another embassy to Constantinople, he made it clear that any ambassador he chose would be required to travel at his own expense. Fortunately Liudprand's step-father (who had himself led a diplomatic mission to the Bosphorus seven years before) decided that the sum required was a small enough price to pay for the prestige and experience that would be gained – to say nothing of the golden opportunity to acquire some knowledge of Greek – and supplied his stepson with all he needed. On 1 August 949 Liudprand set off down the Po on his first diplomatic mission.

Infuriatingly for us, he gives no hint of its object. He does report, on the other hand, that an ambassador from Otto the Great, a rich merchant of Mainz named Liutefred, was travelling to Constantinople at the same time: the two actually found themselves boarding the same ship in Venice. It therefore seems likely that Berengar's main purpose was to make his presence felt and to ensure that as ruler of Italy he would be party to any understanding reached between Byzantium and the Western Empire. Such was his meanness, however, that whereas the imperial envoys had brought magnificent presents for the Emperor, he had sent only a letter – 'and that', sniffs Liudprand, 'was full of lies'. The embarrassed envoy had no option but to produce the gifts that he had intended to offer the Emperor on his own account and to pretend, most reluctantly, that they came from his master – whom, incidentally, he never forgave. Of these presents, by far the most mysterious are the four *carzimasia*;[3] why, one wonders, should these luckless youths have been so sought after – particularly by Constantine Porphyrogenitus, whose sexual tastes seem to have been entirely normal and who already enjoyed a limitless supply of slaves of every kind?

Apart from this little *contretemps*, Liudprand's embassy was (unlike his second mission, nineteen years later) a considerable success. He was accorded an official audience by the Emperor – being duly astonished by the famous golden tree and its mechanical songbirds with which Constantine loved to impress his guests – and was later received rather less formally at a banquet, where an acrobatic cabaret amazed him even more. Not until the early summer of 950 did he return to Italy, and to the master whom by now he cordially despised. At that time Berengar's star was still rising – on the death of Hugh's son Lothair a few months later he was to arrange the election of himself and his son Adalbert as joint Kings of Italy but his unpopularity grew with every day that passed, and before long the exodus began: a steady stream of voluntary exiles no longer prepared to tolerate his avarice and greed – let alone the cruelty of his odious wife Willa – most of them crossing the imperial frontier to the north and finding their way to the court of the German King, Otto of Saxony.

Among them was Liudprand. At first he hated his 'Babylonian captivity' which must, he knew, endure for as long as Berengar remained in power; but by 958 or thereabouts he had caught the eye of Otto, on whose behalf he seems to have paid a second visit to Constantinople two years later. He was certainly in Otto's train when in August 961, responding to an appeal from the unspeakable Pope John XII,[4] Otto swept down into Italy, put Berengar to flight and rode on to Rome where, on 2 February 962 at St Peter's, the Pope crowned him Emperor. He then set about posting his partisans, both clerical and lay, in key positions, appointing Liudprand to the bishopric of Cremona.

It was to be another two years before Otto was able finally and firmly to establish his rule. In 963 he first took Berengar and his wife prisoner and sent them captive to Bamberg, where they died three years later; then, in December of that same year, he deposed Pope John – who had predictably turned against him – and engineered the election in his place of a layman, who took the name of Leo VIII. John managed to return briefly to power in February 964; but he died in May, and in June Leo resumed the pontifical throne. Thus at last the *Regnum Italicum* was united with the German Kingdom under the Roman imperial aegis, and Charlemagne's Empire was reborn.

Throughout these crucial years, Liudprand remained at his master's side. By this time he had made himself indispensable to the Emperor not only in all his Italian involvements – in which he served as his interpreter and his chief adviser on local affairs – but also, as a Greek speaker, in his dealings with Byzantium. When in June 968 Otto decided to send another embassy to Constantinople to arrange a dynastic marriage between his son (the future Otto II) and a Byzantine princess, he turned naturally to the Bishop of Cremona. Liudprand's report on this journey, the so-called *Relatio de legatione constantinopolitana*, is the most enjoyable – as well as the most malicious – account ever written of a diplomatic mission to the Eastern Empire; but if he has little good to say of it, this is hardly surprising in view of the difficulties with which he had to contend – the chief of which lay in the unusually abrasive personality of the Emperor himself.

On Liudprand's earlier mission he had got on splendidly with Constantine Porphyrogenitus, for whose sophisticated and scholarly mind any Western intellectual probably had considerable appeal. Nicephorus II Phocas, on the other hand, was a harsh and narrow-minded soldier who lived a life of formidable asceticism and had no interests outside the army and his religion. To him, the Bishop of Cremona was everything most abhorrent: a dangerous heretic, a smooth-tongued trickster – made still more untrustworthy by his fluent Greek – and, worst of all, the representative of a German adventurer who had had the audacity to usurp his own imperial title, whereas it was well known to every right-thinking person that the Roman Empire was one and indivisible, with its seat at Constantinople.

To Liudprand, however, such considerations seem never to have occurred. All he knew was that nineteen years before, as the emissary of a mere Marquis, he had been politely and respectfully received; now, a plenipotentiary of the Emperor of the West, he was treated with extreme discourtesy and lodged in conditions of appalling discomfort. He describes his tribulations in considerable detail, making no attempt to put a good face on them: it was not, he tells us, until 2 October – four nightmare months after his arrival – that

I left the city that was once so rich and prosperous and is now such a starveling, a city full of lies, tricks, perjury and greed, a city rapacious, avaricious and vainglorious. My guide was with me, and after forty-nine days of ass-riding, walking, horse-riding, fasting, thirsting, sighing, weeping and groaning, I arrived at Naupactus . . .

Nor were his sufferings even now at an end. He was delayed by contrary winds at Naupactus, deserted by his ship's crew at Patras, unkindly received by a eunuch bishop and half-starved on Leucas and subjected to three consecutive earthquakes on Corfu, where he later fell among thieves. He was conscious, too, that his mission had been an abject failure. Relations between East and West were if anything even more strained than they had been when he left Italy; indeed, before he was back in Cremona the two Empires were actually at war again. And the imperial marriage seemed further away than ever.

It was, in fact, nothing of the kind. Nicephorus died in 969. His successor, John Tzimisces, was only too pleased to put an end to the five-year quarrel with Otto by forging an indissoluble link between the two Empires; and it was at his invitation that an embassy under the Archbishop of Cologne arrived in Constantinople in the last days of 971 to collect a Byzantine princess named Theophano – probably Tzimisces' niece, rather than the daughter of Romanus II as was formerly supposed – and to bear her back to her imperial bridegroom. As to whether Liudprand was a member of this embassy or not, scholarly opinion is still divided. It seems, however, more than likely. Fluent Greek speakers were, after all, rare in the West; and even though a mere bishop might not have been considered of sufficiently exalted rank to head a mission entrusted with the safety of a future Empress, it would have been surprising to find a man of his experience and knowledge omitted altogether.

Moreover, there is a cruious story given in a collection of ancient sources known as *Italia Sacra* and published in Venice in the early eighteenth century. The story itself, which concerns the acquisition of Liudprand of the body of St Hymerius for the Cathedral at Cremona, need not concern us here; but it ends with the words: 'soon afterwards the needs of the imperial service took him to Constantinople, whence he never returned'. If we accept this evidence – and there is no reason why we should not – Liudprand must have died on the Bosphorus, presumably in January 972, before the mission returned with Theophano to the West. We can only hope that he was by then to some extent reconciled to the city in which he had been so abominably treated less than four years before.

This book contains translations – by F.A. Wright, Professor of Classics at London University, and first published by Messrs Routledge in 1930 – of the only three works which can be attributed with any certainty to Liudprand of Cremona: the *Liber de Rebus Gestis Ottonis*, the *Antapodosis* and the *Relatio* referred to above. The first of these, despite its title, covers only one episode of Otto's reign, albeit an extremely important one – his deposition of Pope John XII – and from its abrupt ending we can be virtually certain that it was originally part of a much longer and fuller work. It makes riveting reading – after all, it is not every day that we see a Pope accused of simony, sacrilege, fornication and drunkenness – and we can only regret the loss of the rest.

The *Antapodosis* – the word actually means 'repayment', but here it has the sense of 'revenge' and has rather surprisingly been translated by Prof. Wright as 'Tit-for-Tat' – is essentially a brief history of Germany, Italy and Byzantium between 887 and 949, written by Liudprand expressly to get his own back on the hated Berengar.[5] It is much the longest of his writings, and is divided into six books. The first three are mostly concerned with events which occurred before his birth, and it is only in Books IV and V that we meet Berengar and Willa – who, in view of the author's stated purpose, get off surprisingly lightly. This, however, is probably only because the *Antapodosis*, like the *Liber*, is incomplete, suddenly – and infuriatingly – breaking off in the middle of Book VI, half-way through Liudprand's description of his first embassy to Constantinople. Once again, we should be almost certainly wrong to blame the author. We know that he began it in 958, and that it was still in progress in 962; but at that time he had another ten years to live, and it seems hard to believe that he simply stopped work on it, leaving the events of his most successful mission only partially recorded and his principal object barely achieved at all.

And so we come to the *Relatio de legatione constantinopolitana*, the most famous – as well as the most entertaining – of the three. Several other sources tell us about the reign of Nicephorus Phocas, but none bring Constantinople to life in the way that Liudprand does; and the fact that this particular journey was from his point of view an unmitigated disaster – on his departure he even had to suffer the confiscation of the five lengths of sumptuous purple cloth that he had bought to adorn his cathedral in Cremona – makes the *Relatio* if anything even more enjoyable. In his own original introduction to these translations, Professor Wright goes so far as to suggest that it also explains 'why it was that there was so little real intercourse between Constantinople and Western Europe during medieval times. It is plain', he continues,

that Liudprand and his companions cordially disliked Byzantine food, Byzantine drink, Byzantine dress and Byzantine manners; that they were not allowed to ride on horseback through the streets seemed to them an insult; that the palace in which they were lodged admitted the air freely was an intolerable hardship. Byzantine splendour they thought extravagance, Byzantine simplicity meanness.

There may be some truth in this view; surely, however, the professor overstates his case. First of all, medieval Constantinople received a steady flow of Westerners: diplomatists, merchants, pilgrims and scholars, most of whom – judging from such contemporary accounts as we possess – were lost in admiration for the city and (religious differences apart) the civilization it enshrined. Second, there is no evidence that Liudprand's reactions on his first embassy were anything but highly favourable. It was only on his mission to Nicephorus that he was badly treated, and there can be little doubt that he was a genuine victim of the Emperor's galloping xenophobia and suspicion of all things Western – even if he did allow his resentment to colour every word that he wrote.

This tendentiousness is one of Liudprand's two greatest faults as a writer, matched as it is only by his quite astonishingly lackadaisical approach to hard historical fact:

In his *Antapodosis* we have a difficulty in obtaining a firm foothold for history amid the crumbling and quaking mass of rancorous, if often contemporary, gossip which Liudprand loves to heap up. Of noble birth, bred at King Hugh's court, and once Berengar II's secretary, he was in the best position to give accurate and full information, but he had a soul above documents. It is hardly his fault that he depended on oral tradition for all events before his own time, for there seems to have been no Italian chronicle for him to use, but he evidently made no record at the time and when he wrote rested wholly on a memory which rejected dates and political circumstances and was singularly retentive of amorous scandal however devoid of probability.[6]

Finally, a word about his extraordinary style. Liudprand was a scholar and a linguist, and is determined that we should know it. In the first five books of the *Antapodosis*, there are no less than fourteen occasions on which he lapses for no particular reason into verse, using six different metres. He also has a passion for quotations – scriptural, patristic and classical – the more obscure the better. Finally – and extremely irritatingly – he cannot refrain from interlarding his Latin with Greek words, phrases and sometimes whole sentences. In the translations that follow, Professor Wright has – perhaps wisely – ignored the verse, and has given sources for the quotations. For the Greek interpolations he has, however adopted the curious course of translating them into French. This, he readily admits,

gives a result which is neither as striking nor as humorous as the original. However, it has been used here in default of anything better; and those readers who find my French *pas très idiomatique* must remember that Liudprand's Greek is in the same predicament.

Such readers will, I fear, be many; but they should also try to imagine the magnitude of the task Professor Wright set himself, and be grateful that he managed it at all. Today, but for his efforts, only a handful of scholars would ever have heard of the Bishop of Cremona; and the rest of us would have been deprived of the companionship of one of the few medieval writers who had a sense of humour, who loved scandal and a bit of gossip – and who could never resist a good story. Liudprand made history fun; would that there were more like him.

John Julius Norwich
26 October 1992

Notes

1 *Antapodosis*, III, 23.
2 *Antapodosis*, V, 30.
3 *Antapodosis*, VI, 6.
4 'We read, with some surprise, that the worthy grandson of Marozia lived in public adultery with the matrons of Rome; that the Lateran Palace was turned into a school for prostitution; and that his rapes of virgins and widows had deterred the female pilgrims from visiting the shrine of St Peter lest, in the devout act, they should be violated by his successor.' Gibbon, *The Decline and Fall of the Roman Empire*, Chapter 49.
5 *Antapodosis*, III, i.
6 *Cambridge Medieval History*, Vol. III, chap. vii.

ANTAPODOSIS
Tit-for-Tat

CONTENTS

BOOK 1

In the name of the Father and the Son and the Holy Ghost, here begins the book *Antapodosis*, Tit-for-Tat, repayment to the kings and princes of part of Europe, written by Liudprand, deacon of Pavia, *en captivité*, an exile in foreign lands, and dedicated to Recemund Bishop of Elvira in Spain.

BOOK 1

Ch. 1. To the reverend Lord Recemund, Bishop of Elvira, full of all sanctity, Liudprand, the unworthy deacon of Pavia, sends greetings. For two years, dearest father, through lack of skill I have postponed compliance with your request, when you urged me, as one who did not depend on doubtful hearsay but had the sure knowledge of an eye-witness, to set down the doings of the emperors and kings of all Europe. The following considerations deterred me from beginning the task; firstly, my own complete lack of eloquence, and secondly, the thought of my critics' jealousy. These men, swollen with superciliousness and rendered sluggish by much reading, possessed, as the wise Boethius says, of a fragment of Philosophy's robe and imagining that they have the whole garment, will jeer at me and cry: 'Our predecessors have already written so much that soon there will be fewer readers than there are books.' And then they will quote the line from the play:—'Nothing can be said to-day, sirs, which has not been said before.'

To their yelpings I make this reply. Lovers of learning are like men sick of the dropsy: as these thirst the more ardently the more water they drink, so students, the more they read, the more eagerly seek after new knowledge. Let students then, when they are wearied by the difficult perusal of Cicero's wit, find recreation in these outpourings of mine. For, if I am not mistaken, just as the eyes are dazzled and blinded by the sun's rays, unless some substance intervenes to cloud their pure brilliancy, so in the case of our academic, peripatetic and stoic philosophers the mind is weakened by the constant study of their doctrines unless it finds refreshment in the useful humours of a comedy or in the delectable histories of heroic men. If the accursed rites of the pagans of old are thought worthy of description in books, although, so far from being helpful, they are dangerous even to hear about, why should we pass over in silence the campaigns of such great commanders as Caesar and Pompey, Hannibal, his brother Hasdrubal and Scipio Africanus, generals of glorious renown, worthy all of equal praise? In the case of these men, when we tell of their righteous deeds we can proclaim the goodness of Our Lord Jesus Christ; when we tell of their errors we can remind men of His saving and correcting hand.

Let no one be disturbed if I insert in this poor record the doings of some weak kings and effeminate princes. Almighty God, the Father the Son and the Holy Ghost, is ever one and ever just. Justly does He overwhelm the wicked, as the reward of their crimes; justly does he exalt the virtuous, as the reward of their good deeds. True, I say, is the promise made to the saints by Our Lord Jesus Christ: 'Beware of him and obey his voice, and I will be an enemy unto thine enemies, and an adversary unto thine adversaries, and mine Angel shall go before thee.' The voice of wisdom, which is Christ, cries out also by the mouth of Solomon:— 'The whole world shall fight for him against the foolish.' That this is happening now every day even those who are asleep understand. I will give one example from the many that exist, and keeping silence myself will allow the town of Fraxinetum to speak, a place which, as all are aware, lies on the borders of Italy and Provence.

Ch. 2.   I imagine, my lord, that you are well acquainted with Fraxinetum and know it better than I do, since you have the information of those who are tributary to your king Abdereha-men. But for the benefit of the general reader, I will say here that it has the sea on one side, and on all others is protected by a close undergrowth of cactus. If anyone gets into this entanglement, he is so impeded by the winding brambles, and so stabbed by the sharp points of the thorns, that he finds it a task of the greatest difficulty either to advance or to retreat.

Ch. 3.   But by the mysterious, and since it cannot be otherwise, by the just judgement of God, a band of some twenty Saracens, who had sailed from Spain in a small boat, was forced by contrary winds unwillingly to land here. These pirates, disembarking under cover of night, entered the manor house unobserved and murdered – a grievous tale! – the Christian inhabitants. They then took the place as their own, and made Moor's Mount which adjoins the manor a stronghold against attacks from their neighbours. For their protection they encouraged the cactus to grow even taller and thicker than before, so that now if any one stumbled against a branch it ran him through like a sharp sword. Finally all access to the hill except by one very narrow path became impossible. Relying therefore upon this difficulty of approach they started stealthy raids on all the neighbouring country, and sent messengers back to Spain to bring over more of their comrades. They praised the land and declared that the people were of no account; and so in answer to this invitation a fresh band, not more than a hundred men, arrived to test the truth of their tale.

Ch. 4.   Meanwhile the people of Provence close by, swayed by envy and mutual jealousy, began to cut one another's throats, plunder each other's substance, and do every sort of conceivable mischief. But inasmuch as one faction by itself was not able to satisfy upon the other the demands of jealous indignation, they called in the help of the aforesaid Saracens, men who were as perfidious as they were cunning, and in company with them proceeded to crush their neighbours. Indeed, not satisfied with murder, they turned the whole fertile land into a desert. But let us see what good their envy did them. Envy, as a certain author says, is always just, and of it he writes:

> Envy its own just retribution brings
> And stabs its harbourer with poisoned stings.

In trying to deceive, Envy is itself deceit's victim; in endeavouring to quench others, its own fire is put out. Do you ask what happened? The Saracens, who in themselves were of insignificant strength, after crushing one faction with the help of the other, increased their own numbers by continual reinforcements from Spain, and soon were attacking everywhere those whom at first they seemed to defend. In the fury of their onslaughts they exterminated the whole people and left no survivors, so that all the neighbourhood began to tremble. As the prophet says: 'One man chased a thousand, and two put ten thousand to flight.' How was that? 'Because their God sold them and the Lord shut them up.'

Ch. 5. At this time the city of Constantinople was ruled by Leo Porphyrogenitus, son of the Emperor Basil and father of the present Emperor Constantine who is now happily on the throne. That stout fighter Simeon was governor of Bulgaria, a Christian but a bitter enemy of his neighbours the Greeks. The Hungarians, from whose savage cruelty almost all peoples have since suffered, but who now by the mercy of the most holy God and the might of our invincible king Otto, as I shall relate more fully, do not even dare to mutter in fear, were at that time unknown to all of us. They were cut off by the difficult barriers generally known as 'the closures,' and were not able to make their way out either to the south or to the west. At this same date the most mighty king Arnulf, who had succeeded Charles surnamed the Bald, was overlord of the Bavarians, the Swabians, the Teutonic Franks, the Lotharingians and the bold Saxons; but he was vigorously opposed by Centebald Duke of the Maravani. The two emperors Berengar and Wido were fighting for the throne of Italy. Formosus Bishop of Porto was recognized as Pope of Rome, supreme and universal. Let me now relate, as briefly as I can, what happened in the days of these several rulers.

Ch. 6. Leo, the most pious emperor of the Greeks, of whom we have made mention above, father of the present emperor Constantine Porphyrogenitus, had at that time secured peace everywhere and exercised over the Greeks a just and righteous dominion. I call him Porphyrogenitus, not because he was born in the purple, but because he was born in the palace called Porphyra. And since the subject has come up, let me set forth what I have heard of the circumstances of his birth.

Ch. 7. The august emperor Constantine, from whom the city of Constantinople gets its name, ordered *ce palais*, this palace, to be built and called it Porphyra. His intention was that the successive rulers of his noble family should see the light of day first here, and that all the offspring of his line should be called by the glorious title of Porphyrogenitus. Some people therefore say that our Constantine, son of the emperor Leo, is his descendant. But the truth of the matter is this.

Ch. 8. The august emperor Basil, the present emperor's grandfather, was born of a humble family in Macedonia. Under the compelling yoke of *pauvreté*, that is, of poverty, he came down to Constantinople, and was for a time servant to an *abbé*, that is, an abbot. The then emperor Michael went one morning to pray in the monastery where he was serving, and seeing that he was exceptionally comely called the *abbé*, the abbot, and asked him to give him the lad. He then took him off to the palace and made him his chamberlain; and in a little time he became so powerful that everyone called him the second emperor.

Ch. 9. Almighty God is ever just, even when He visits His servants with a heavy hand. He did not allow the emperor Michael to keep his sanity all his life; but His purpose was that the mercy of His kindness above might equal the severity of His punishment below. We are told that Michael in his mad fits frequently sent off his dearest friends to be beheaded. But when he returned to his senses he would ask for them again, and unless they were forthcoming would order that their executioners, who had only obeyed his commands, should be put to death. His servants accordingly became alarmed, and when he ordered an execution they did not put it into effect. This happened several times to Basil, and finally his intimates gave him – O shame! – this advice – 'The king's orders may some day be carried out, if he gives them to your enemies, and not to your friends. You had better kill him yourself first, and take the imperial sceptre.' Under the compulsion of fear, and beguiled by desire of rule, Basil carried out their suggestion without delay. Michael was murdered and Basil became emperor in his place.

Ch. 10. A short time afterwards Our Lord Jesus Christ appeared to him in a vision, holding the hand of his former master, the emperor, whom he had killed, and addressed him thus:– '*Pourquoi avez-vous tué votre mâitre l'empereur?*' 'Why did you

kill your master the emperor?' Awakened by the words he realized
that he had been guilty of a heinous crime, and collecting his
thoughts considered earnestly what he should do. Finally, comforted by our Lord's acceptable promise of salvation, given by the
mouth of His prophet, that on the day when the wicked man
turneth from his wickedness he shall be saved, he made confession
with tears and groans and acknowledged himself a miserable
sinner, the guilty shedder of innocent blood. He also followed
wise advice and made friends to himself of the mammon of
unrighteousness, helping them in this world with temporal
subsidies that their prayers might release him later from the
everlasting fires of hell. Moreover he built near the palace a
wonderful and costly church facing eastwards, which men now
call 'La nouvelle église,' 'The new church,' and dedicated it to the
archangel Michael, that mighty prince of heaven, whom the
Greeks call general of the celestial host.

Ch. 11. It would not be out of place to insert in this humble
record two incidents in which the son of this Basil, the august and
famous emperor Leo, was concerned: for they are well worth
relating and are also laughable. The city of Constantinople, which
was formerly called Byzantium and is now called New Rome,
stands in territory surrounded by warlike peoples. On the north it
has the Hungarii, the Pizenaci, the Chazari, and Rusii sometimes
called by another name Nordmanni, and the Bulgarii who live too
close for harmony. On the east come the Bagdae, and on the
south-east the inhabitants of Egypt and Babylonia. To the south
lies Africa and the island of Crete, its own too near neighbour and
perpetual foe. The other tribes in this quarter of the globe, the
Armenians, Persians, Chaldaeans and Avasgi have been reduced
to subjection.

   Now the inhabitants of this city, as they surpass the races we
have mentioned in wealth, so also surpass them in wisdom. As a
precaution against attacks from the neighbouring peoples it is
their custom to post armed soldiers each night at every point in the
city where two, three, or four roads meet and assign to them the
task of keeping watch and ward. If after dark the guard catch any
one roaming about the streets, their orders are to arrest him at
once and give him a whipping: he is then to be fettered, kept under

close watch in prison, and brought up for public trial the next day. By this method the city is not only protected from foreign enemies but is also secured against highway robbery.

One day his majesty the emperor Leo determined to test the fidelity and trustworthiness of the guards, and so when night fell he left his palace unattended and turned his steps to the nearest guard post. As soon as the soldiers sighted him he pretended to be alarmed and made as though to run away: they at once caught hold of him, and asked him who he was and where he was going. 'I am just an ordinary man,' he said, 'and I was on my way to have a woman.' 'Very well,' the guards replied, 'you shall have a good thrashing first, and then we will keep you under lock and key till to-morrow, with irons on your legs.' *Pas si vite, mes frères*' – which being interpreted is – 'Nay, brothers, not so quick', said the emperor. 'Take what I have on me and let me go my way.' He then handed them twelve gold pieces and was at once set free. So passing along he came to the second post, where he was arrested as before, and again escaped, at the price this time of twenty gold pieces. At the third post, however, things were different: this time he was not allowed to go on making payment: all his money was taken from him, he was soundly pommelled and thrashed, put into heavy irons, and thrust into prison to appear before the judge on the morrow.

When the soldiers had gone away the emperor called to the jailer and said: '*Mon ami*' – which means 'My friend' – 'do you know the emperor Leo?' 'How could I know him,' replied the man, 'when I do not remember ever having seen him properly? Certainly I have gazed at a distance once or twice, when he has appeared in public, but I could not get close, and it seemed to me then that I was looking at a wonder of nature rather than at a human being. It would be more to the purpose for you to be thinking how to get out of here with a whole skin rather than to ask such questions as that. Fortune is not so kind to you as she is to him: *vous êtes en prison, il est sur son trône d'or*; you lie in prison, he sits upon his golden throne. I had better fetch some heavier irons, these are too light; then you will not have time to think about the emperor.' 'Enough,' cried Leo, 'I am his majesty the emperor himself: deuce take the hour when I left my place of honour in my palace!' At that the jailer, thinking that he was telling lies:— 'Do you expect me to believe that you are the emperor, a dirty rogue like you who squanders his substance with loose women. Since your education in astrology has been neglected, I will give you a little savoir on that subject. *Ecoutez moi*. At this moment Mars is in triangle, Saturn faces Venus, Jupiter is square, Mercury is unfavourable to you, the Sun is as round as a wheel, and the Moon is on the jump: bad luck threatens you and is near at hand.' 'To prove that my words are true,' replied the emperor, 'as soon as they give the morning signal and it is safe for us, come with me to the palace and you will see that the omens then will be more favourable. If you do not find that I am welcomed there as emperor, you may kill me on the spot. Murder itself is not a worse crime than to say I am emperor if it is not the truth. Perhaps you are afraid of getting into trouble over this: may God do this to me and worse, if you are not rewarded rather than punished.'

The jailer at last was convinced, and when the morning signal was given, he went with the emperor, as he had suggested, to the palace. On their arrival his companion was received with every sign of respectful admiration, so that the jailer almost sank into the earth with astonishment. The high court dignitaries ran up before his eyes, showered compliments upon the emperor, took off his shoes for him, and bustled about doing various acts of service, while the poor man thought that he had better die at once. 'Consult the stars again', said the emperor to him, 'and if you can declare correctly what luck will attend your arrival here, you will prove that you have a real knowledge of the augural art. But tell me first, pray, what is this sudden sickness that has made you turn so pale?' 'Clotho, queen of the Fates', replied the jailer, 'is ceasing now to spin for me; Lachesis refuses to trouble to twist the wool; Atropos, the most cruel of the three, her fingers on the distaff, is only waiting for your majesty's verdict to draw the threads together and break my life. As for my pale face, the reason for it is that my vital force has gone from my head and drawn the blood with it to the lower parts of my body.' At that the emperor with a smile replied:— 'Take your vital force back, and with it this four pound bag of gold coins: as for myself, do not say a word to anyone except that I got away from prison.'

He then ordered that the guards who had let their prisoner go, and the others who had beaten and jailed him, should be brought into his presence. On their appearance he said to them:— 'While you were keeping guard and watch over the city did you at any time come across any thieves or fornicators?' Those who had taken the bribe said that they had seen nothing: the others, who had beaten and jailed him, replied:— '*Votre sacre majesté*', that is, 'Your sacred majesty gave orders that if your guards came across anyone roaming in the streets after dark, they were to arrest him, give him a thrashing, and put him in jail. In obedience to your commands therefore, most reverend lord, last night we arrested a fellow who was intending to scour the brothels, and after we had whipped him we put him under lock and key, so that we might bring him before your sacred majesty.' 'Quick,' said the emperor, 'let him be produced: my imperial authority demands instant obedience.' The men hurried off at once to fetch their prisoner, and when they were told that he had escaped they returned half-dead to the palace. They made their report to the emperor, who took off his cloak and showed them the cruel marks of their blows:— '*Venez ici, n'ayez pas peur*,' said he; that is — 'Come here and do not be afraid. I myself am the man whom you flogged and who you think has escaped from prison. I am quite sure and certain that it was not your emperor but your emperor's enemy that you intended to cudgel. As for these men who let me go, not thinking I was the emperor but knowing that I was a robber who threatened my life, it is not only my majesty's wish, it is my definite command, that they be beaten till they are at death's door and then be deprived of all their goods and banished from the city. To you others I give both money from my purse and also the property of these pernicious rogues.'

What wisdom Leo displayed your paternal excellence will be able to appreciate. After that day his men kept diligent watch and even in the emperor's absence thought of him as present with them. He never had occasion again to go down from his palace and the guard duty was faithfully performed.

Ch. 12. Another prank which this emperor played I think it foolish to veil in silence. The palace at Constantinople is guarded by numerous companies of soldiers in order to secure the emperor's safety, and every day a considerable sum of money is spent upon these men's pay and rations. Now it happened once that twelve of these guards were resting in one room from the heat of the day during the siesta hour, when it was Leo's custom to wander about the palace. On this occasion, when the twelve men I have mentioned had abandoned themselves to Lethean slumber, the emperor came into the room, artfully opening the door latch with a small piece of wood. But one trickster can trap another. Eleven of the men were really asleep: the twelfth was awake although he made a pretence of snoring, and with his face covered by his arms he carefully watched what the emperor was doing. Well, the emperor came in and seeing that the soldiers were all asleep put a pound bag of gold coins into each man's bosom. He then went out again quietly and shut the door behind him, expecting that when the men woke up they would congratulate each other upon their gains and wonder how on earth they got there. But as soon as he had gone, the one soldier who was awake jumped up, took the bags of gold from the sleepers, and stored them in his wallet. Then he went quietly to sleep.

In the afternoon the emperor, anxious to know the issue of his prank, bade the twelve guards to appear before him and addressed them thus:– 'If any one of you has been frightened or cheered by a dream vision, my authority bids you declare it. Moreover if any man on waking saw any strange sight, I order you to reveal that also.' To this the soldiers replied that they had seen nothing (as indeed was the truth) and surprised at the emperor's order 'silent stood with faces set intent'. Leo, however, thought that it was not out of ignorance but from cunning that they were keeping silence, and flying into a passion threatened them with dreadful punishments if they did not speak. Thereupon the one man of the company who knew the truth put on a very humble and suppliant tone of voice and addressed the emperor:– '*Votre gracieuse majesté*', that is 'Your gracious majesty, I do not know what these men saw; I myself had a most delectable dream; I only wish it would come often. I dreamed, while my comrades, unfortunately for them, to-day were really asleep, that I was awake, and, as it were, not asleep at all. And lo and behold, your Imperial Grandeur secretly opened the door, as it were, and entering quietly put a pound bag of gold in each of my comrades' bosoms. In my vision I saw your majesty go out again while my comrades were still asleep, and jumping up at once for joy I took the bags of gold from the eleven sleepers and stored them in my wallet where there was only one. I did not want them to go beyond the ten Commandments and be just eleven, but to join with mine and make twelve in memory of the twelve apostles. May it please you, august emperor, this vision up to now has not frightened me but rather made me cheerful. I hope your majesty will not prefer another interpretation for it. It is a well known fact that I am *un prophète et vendeur des songes*, that is, a prophet and dream pedlar.' At this the emperor burst into a loud guffaw, and admiring the fellow's skill and caution said at once: 'I have never heard before that you were *un prophète et vendeur des songes*, a prophet and a dream pedlar. But it is plain from what you say that you are a prophet, and you have not beaten about the bush! You could not have the power of keeping awake or the skill to draw auspices, unless it were given you by divine grace. So whether your interpretation is true – as I hope and believe – or false, *aussi que Lucien*, that is, as Lucian tells us of a man, that in his sleep he found a great treasure, but when the cock woke him there was nothing there; in either case, anything you saw or noticed or discovered, you may regard as yours.' With what confusion these words filled the sleepers and with what joy they filled the watcher, anyone can easily imagine if he puts himself in their place.

Ch. 13. Meanwhile, Arnulf, the strongest ruler among the northern peoples, found himself unable to overcome the vigorous resistance offered him by the aforesaid Centebald duke of the Maravani. Accordingly he broke down – O grievous tale! – the strong barriers which, as we have said before, are usually called the closures and called in the Hungarians to help him, a people greedy, reckless, ignorant of Almighty God, acquainted with every sort of crime, only eager for carnage and rapine. I use the word 'help' but I should rather say ruin, for when Arnulf soon afterwards died these Hungarians proved themselves a deadly danger both to his people and to all the other nations in the south and west. What happened? Centebald was beaten, subdued and forced to pay tribute: but he was not the only one. How blind was King Arnulf's desire for power! How cruel and accursed did that day prove! The bringing down of one weak man brought down sorrow upon all Europe. How many women were left widows, how many fathers made childless, how many virgins debauched, how many of God's priests and people taken prisoners, how many churches laid waste and lands left desolate! And all this the result of blind ambition! Have you not read, pray, the words of truth: 'What is a man profited, if he shall gain the whole world and lose his own soul? or what shall a man give in exchange for his soul?' If the stern verdict of the Judge of Truth did not dismay you, the common ties of humanity might have given pause to your mad desires. You were but a man among men, exalted indeed in rank, but like to others in nature. Lamentable and piteous is our condition. Beasts, birds and reptiles, separated though they be from us by reason of their intolerable fierceness or deadly venom – the basilisk, for example, the asp, the rhinoceros and the griffin-creatures whose very aspect seems to threaten death to all – live among themselves in peace and harmony, for they have the same origin and are endowed with the same disposition. Man, how-ever, formed in the likeness and resemblance of God, instructed in God's law, possessed of reason, so far from delighting to love his neighbour, would use all his strength in hating him. Let us see then what John, not John who you will, but the glorious virgin, admitted to the secrets of heaven, to whom as a virgin Christ upon the cross commended the Virgin, His mother; let us see what he said about such men:– 'Whosoever hateth his brother is a murderer: and ye know that no murderer hath eternal life abiding in him.'

But let us return to our subject. After defeating Centebald, duke of the Maravani, Arnulf settled himself peacefully in his kingdom. The Hungarians for their part surveyed the country, and while they waited for his end, were already, as was afterwards made plain, devising mischief in their hearts.

Ch. 14. Meanwhile Charles, surnamed the Bald, king of Gaul, exchanged this present life for death. In his lifetime two noble and powerful princes from Italy had been his vassals, one named Wido, the other Berengar. These men, you must know, were cemented by such close bonds of friendship that they had undertaken on oath to support each other's appointment in the event of their surviving Charles. Wido was to become ruler of Roman France so called, Berengar was to have Italy. But the ways of friendship, which in divers manners joins the human race together in a partnership of affection, are uncertain and unstable. In some cases a previous recommendation induces men to enter into friendly relations; in other cases the link is some similarity of business, trade, profession, or military operations. But with all such ties, as they come into existence from varying associations of profit, pleasure and necessity, so they are severed immediately any occasion of divergence intervenes. And there is one kind of friendship which has been proved by many examples to be always short lived. Those whose friendship is based on a partnership in conspiracy can never maintain for long an unbroken harmony of purpose. The cunning enemy of mankind uses all his energy and skill to break friendship's bonds and make men traitors to their own sworn oath. And if some simple soul asks me 'Is there then no real friendship?' I should answer that real harmony and friendship can only exist when morals are pure and men are of the same purpose and virtuous life.

Ch. 15. It happened that both these men, Wido and Berengar, were absent when King Charles' funeral took place. But as soon as Wido heard of his death he set out for Rome without consulting the Franks and was anointed there as ruler of all France, the Franks in his absence electing Oddo as king. As for Berengar, at Wido's suggestion, in accordance with their sworn agreement, he set himself up as ruler of Italy, and Wido made his way back to France.

Ch. 16. But as he was passing through Burgundy and about to enter Roman France so called, he was met by some Frank messengers who said they were on their way back and that Oddo had been unanimously chosen as king. 'We were tired of waiting for you,' they declared, 'and we could not do without a king any longer.' It is said however that the real reason why the Franks did not elect Wido as king was as follows. As he was nearing Metz, which is the strongest and most famous city in Lothar's realm, Wido sent his steward forward to prepare for him a regal banquet. The bishop of Metz, as is usual with the Franks, offered to provide a sumptuous feast, but in reply to his hospitality the steward said: 'If you will only give me a horse to ride on, I will guarantee that a third of these dainties satisfy King Wido.' At that the bishop: 'It is not fitting for a man to rule over us as king if a cheap ten shilling dinner suffices him.' The result was that the Franks threw Wido over and elected Oddo in his place.

Ch. 17. Wido was greatly disturbed by the message given by the Frank envoys and was soon in a turmoil of thought. There was the kingdom of Italy, which he had promised under oath to Berengar, and there was the Frankish throne, which he now clearly realized he could not secure. He wavered between the two for a time, and finally, unable to be king of the Franks, he decided to break the oath he had sworn to Berengar. He accordingly collected as large an army as he could – he had some connections among the Franks – and marched hastily into Italy. There he made confident overtures to the people of Camerino and Spoleto, his kinsmen, and although they had supported Berengar's cause secured their desertion by gifts of money; and so began active hostilities.

Ch. 18. The forces of both parties assembled near the river Trebia, five miles from Piacenza, and prepared for civil war. In the ensuing battle many fell on either side, and finally Berengar took to flight and Wido triumphed.

Ch. 19. After a few days, however, Berengar quickly gathered together a fresh force, and gave Wido battle once more on the broad plain of Brescia. The carnage was again terrific, and again Berengar escaped by flight.

Ch. 20. Being unable to withstand Wido with his inferior numbers, Berengar now asked help from King Arnulf, who was, as we have said, a very potent monarch, promising that if by the help of his valour he should beat Wido and win the kingdom of Italy he and his people would serve him as his vassals. Allured by these high promises King Arnulf sent his son Centebald, whom he had had by a concubine, with a strong army to his assistance, and the joint forces marched with all haste on Pavia. Wido, however, had protected the little stream called Vernavola, which flows on one side of Pavia, with a palisade and detachments of soldiers; and so this river barrier prevented either army from making an attack upon the other.

Ch. 21. Twenty-one days passed, as we have said, and neither side was able to do any damage. One of the Bavarians every day used to taunt the Italians with cowardice and cry out that they knew nothing of horsemanship. Finally, as a crowning insult, he leapt into their ranks, knocked a spear out of one man's hand, and returned triumphantly to his own camp. Accordingly Hubald, father of Boniface who later on in my time became marquess of Camerino and Spoleto, anxious to wipe out this insult to his people, put on a shield and went out to meet the aforesaid Bavarian. This latter, remembering his previous triumph and rendered all the bolder thereby, hastened gladly forth against him in careless anticipation of another victory. Wheeling his horse he now urged him fiercely forward, now tugged at the reins and threw him back. Meanwhile Hubald came straight on. When they were within striking distance of each other, the Bavarian wheeled his horse round as usual and began to turn him this way and that, circling in confused windings and hoping by this method to baffle Hubald's attack. But as he retreated, intending on his return to deal a frontal blow at Hubald, his opponent spurred his horse vigorously forward and pierced the Bavarian with his lance before he could turn round, the weapon going through the shoulder blades to the heart. Hubald then took the Bavarian's horse by the bridle and left the man's body stripped of its armour in the middle of the river. So having avenged the insult offered to his people he returned merrily in triumph to his own side. This exploit certainly caused considerable alarm among the Bavarians and equally inspired the Italians with confidence. The Bavarians indeed held a council of war, and as Wido offered him some pounds of silver Centebald retired to his own country again.

Ch. 22. Berengar saw his bright prospects thus clouded over, and in company with Centebald again approached the mighty King Arnulf as a suppliant, promising if he would help him, that he would put himself and all Italy, as he had undertaken to do before, under his control. Arnulf once again was allured by these high promises and entered Italy with a very large army, Berengar acting as his shield bearer, a guarantee of his undertaking and a pledge of his fidelity.

Ch. 23. Verona welcomed him gladly and he then marched on Bergamo. The people there trusted to, or rather were deceived by, their strong fortifications and refused to come out against him. He accordingly pitched his camp and took the city by a vigorous assault, cutting down and butchering the defenders. As for the Count of Bergamo, a man named Ambrose, he had him hung before the city gate in his finest clothes, sword, belt and armlets complete. This punishment struck terror into every city and every prince. When people heard of it, both ears tingled.

Ch. 24. The people of Milan and Pavia were indeed so alarmed by the news that they could not endure to wait for his arrival, but sent an embassy to him promising to submit to his orders. He therefore sent Otto, the mighty duke of Saxony — grandfather of our most glorious and invincible King Otto, who is still alive and happily reigning over us — to defend Milan, and himself marched straight to Pavia.

Ch. 25. Wido, not being strong enough to withstand his attack, began to retreat on Camerino and Spoleto. The king pursued him vigorously without delay, taking by force any city or castle that offered resistance. There was indeed no fortress, however strong by nature, that was competent to resist the king's valour. What wonder, seeing that mighty Rome herself, queen of cities, was unable to withstand his attack! The Romans refused him a peaceful entrance, and so he called his troops together and addressed them thus:

Ch. 26

> My braves, upon whose arms the gold is worn
> Wherewith yon weaklings useless books adorn:
> Chiefs famed in war, now all your courage show
> And let your martial rage fresh strength bestow.

No Pompey have we here, no Caesar bold
Whose sword subdued our ancestors of old.
The British born took all true sons of Rome
To his new city and his Eastern home.
These men know well the fishing rod to wield;
They have no strength to raise the flashing shield.

Ch. 27.   Fired by these words the heroes despise life in their desire for glory. Protecting themselves with shields and wicker coverings they rush in serried bands to storm the walls. They had furthermore prepared a number of military engines, when in the midst of the turmoil under the people's eyes it happened that a little hare, frightened by the din, started to run towards the city. The soldiers, as is their wont, chased the poor creature furiously, and the Romans thinking they were rushing to the attack flung themselves from the walls. The assailants, seeing them in retreat, piled their packs and horses' saddles against the walls and mounted over the heaps that they thus made. One division found a beam of wood fifty feet long and with it battered down one of the gates, storming into that part of Rome which is calledLeonine, where the precious body of Saint Peter, chief of the apostles, rests. Thereupon the other districts across the Tiber under compulsion of fear bowed their neck to Arnulf's dominion.

Ch. 28.   At this time the Romans were cruelly tormenting their very reverend Pope Formosus, at whose exhortation Arnulf had made his way thither. Therefore when he entered the city to avenge the wrongs done to the Pope, Arnulf gave orders that a number of the Roman princes who came in haste to greet him should be beheaded.

Ch. 29.   The cause of the quarrel between Pope Formosus and the Romans was as follows. At the death of Formosus' predecessor, there was a certain Sergius, deacon of the church at Rome, whom a certain section of the people elected as Pope. Another influential body however were keenly desirous to appoint this Formosus, who was then bishop of Porto and a man of real sanctity, well versed in all God's teachings. So at the moment when Sergius ought to have been ordained as vicar of the apostles on earth, Formosus' faction drove him from the altar with loud and insulting cries, and made their candidate Pope in his stead.

Ch. 30. Sergius then made his way into Tuscany to get the help of the powerful marquess Adalbert. In this he finally succeeded, and later on, Formosus being then deceased and Arnulf dead in his own country, Adalbert drove out the Pope who had been appointed after Formosus' death and gave his place to Sergius. Thereupon the fellow, who was an impious wretch and ignorant of sacred doctrine, issued orders that the body of Formosus should be exhumed and that the corpse dressed in priestly raiments should be set upon Peter's chair, while he proceeded to taunt it thus: 'Seeing that you were bishop of Porto, why were you so inflated with ambition as to claim the world-wide see of Rome?' After satisfying his spite in this manner, he stripped the body of its sacred vestments, cut off three of its fingers, and threw it into the Tiber. He then deposed from their positions all the priests whom Formosus had ordained, and performed a second ordination service himself. How wrong his conduct was, reverend father, you can judge by this fact. Those men who received the apostolic greeting or benediction from Judas, the betrayer of Our Lord Jesus Christ, before the time of the betrayal, were not deprived of their offices after the betrayal had taken place and Judas had hanged himself, except in some cases where they had disgraced themselves by scandalous living. The benediction, which Christ's servants receive, comes not from him who is seen but from Him whom no eye can behold. 'Neither is he that planteth any thing, neither he that watereth; but God that giveth the increase.'

Ch. 31. What authority and what sanctity Pope Formosus possessed we may infer from the following incident. His body was found by some fishermen and carried to the church of Saint Peter, chief of the apostles, where as it lay in its coffin the images of certain saints came to life and saluted it with every sign of respectful veneration. This story I have frequently heard from some of the most reverend men in Rome. But let us leave this now and return to the order of our narrative.

Ch. 32.   Though King Arnulf had achieved his desire he did not cease hostilities against Wido, but setting out for Camerino laid siege to a certain castle, called 'Strong' by name as it was strong by nature, where Wido's wife was then living, Wido himself being in some obscure hiding place. This Strong Castle, so well named, he surrounded with entrenchments and proceeded to bring up such siege engines as were necessary. Wido's wife was caught in a trap from which all hope of escape seemed impossible, and so with snakish cunning she began to look about for some way to compass Arnulf's death. She secured an interview with one of the king's intimates, and after giving him some handsome presents asked him for his help. The man declared that this was impossible, unless she surrendered the place to his master; but she persisted in her entreaties, not only promising him pounds of gold but actually presenting them to him on the spot. She finally begged him to give the king his master a certain draught to drink which she showed him, one that would not do any harm but would soften the king's cruel temper. As a proof of her words she gave the drink in his presence to one of her servants, who, after standing in sight for an hour, left the room apparently unharmed. At this point I may quote Virgil's true saying:—

> Accursed thirst for gold, to what fell crimes
> Dost thou not force men's hearts?

Well, the man took the deadly draught from her and departing in haste gave it to the king. Arnulf drank, and immediately fell into so profound a sleep that for three days the din of his whole army could not waken him. It is said that his friends tried to rouse him, now by shouting and now by shaking his body, but that though his eyes were open he could neither feel anything nor utter any articulate words. He lay devoid of understanding and such sounds as he made were more like the lowing of oxen than human speech. These happenings, of course, brought about the retirement of his whole army, and fighting ceased.

Ch. 33.   I believe that it was by the just verdict of God's stern judgement that Arnulf came upon this miserable fate. While his power was prospering and increasing everywhere, he attributed his success to his own merits and rendered not to Almighty God the honour that is His due. God's priests were dragged off to prison, holy virgins were raped, married women were violated. Fugitives found no shelter even in the churches; God's house was made into a market, a place of rioting, of foul gestures and merry songs. Women actually came there – O shameful crime – and publicly offered themselves to men.

Ch. 34. Arnulf then returned slowly home, a very sick man, and King Wido came slowly after him. As he was crossing over Monte Bardone, on the advice of his counsellors he decided to put out Berengar's eyes and himself rule Italy at his ease. One of Berengar's kinsmen however, who was a familiar intimate of Arnulf, heard of the plan and informed Berengar without delay. So the intended victim handed over to another the lamp, which it was his duty to hold before the king, and made his escape with all speed to Verona.

Ch. 35. From that time everyone in Italy regarded Arnulf with scorn and contempt. On his arrival at Pavia there was a fierce outbreak, and so many of his men were killed that all the sewers – or as they call them 'cloacae' – in the city were choked with corpses. Unable to get through Verona he decided to return by Hannibal's old road, that called Bardus, over the Great St Bernard, and made his way to Ivrea where the marquess Anscar, who had urged the citizens to revolt, was then living. Arnulf swore solemnly that he would not leave the town until the people brought Anscar into his presence. Anscar, however, was a very timid person, in all repects like the man of whom Virgil speaks:–

> A champion with his tongue, and free of purse,
> But cold his hand in war.

and so he crept from the castle and hid in some rocky caves near the city wall. He did this in order that the citizens might lawfully assure Arnulf that Anscar was not in the town. The king therefore accepted their oath and proceeded on his way.

Ch. 36. When he arrived at his own country he died of a disgusting malady. He was cruel tormented by the tiny worms that are called lice and expired in agony. It is said that these worms bred so fast that no doctor's care could diminish their number. Whether in requital for his heinous crime of letting the Hungarians loose he was punished by a double affliction, as the prophet says, or whether from his earthly penalty he achieved forgiveness in the world to come, we may leave to the wisdom of Him, concerning whom the Apostle says:— 'Judge nothing before the time, until the Lord come, who both will bring to light the hidden things of darkness, and will make manifest the counsels of the hearts, and then shall every man have praise of God.'

Ch. 37. This justice of God brought the grief of widowhood upon Wido's wife, who had brought death upon Arnulf. For as Wido was following close upon Arnulf's retreat, he departed from his life near the river Taro. As soon as Berengar heard of his death he came in haste to Pavia and took the throne by force of arms. But Wido's faithful supporters, fearing lest Berengar should avenge the wrongs they had done him, and relying on the fact that the Italians always prefer to have two kings, so that they may keep the one in check by threatening him with the other, set up as king the dead Wido's son, a young man called Lambert who was an accomplished youth and of very warlike character. Very soon the people began to flock to his side and abandon Berengar. He marched on Pavia with a large force and Berengar, unable through lack of numbers to check him, retired to Verona and remained there in peaceful seclusion. After a short time however Lambert's strictness made him unpopular with the princes, who sent envoys to Verona asking Berengar to come to their support, and endeavoured to drive Lambert from the throne.

Ch. 38. Furthermore in the course of the next five years Manfred, the wealthy count of Milan, broke out into open war against him and not only held his own city of Milan but cruelly ravaged the surrounding districts that were still loyal to Lambert. But the king did not allow his violence to go unpunished and often reflected upon the word of the Psalmist:— 'When I shall have the time, I will give just judgment.' So after a little while he had Manfred convicted and put to death on a capital charge; a verdict which struck terror into the hearts of all the Italians.

Ch. 39. About the same time Adalbert, the illustrious marquess of Tuscany and a powerful count named Ildeprand tried to stir up a fresh rebellion against him. Adalbert was a man of such influence that among all the princes of Italy he alone had the title of the 'Rich'. His wife was a woman named Berta, mother of the Hugh who was king in my time, and it was at her instigation that he started his wicked plot, collecting an army with count Ildeprand and marching resolutely on Pavia.

Ch. 40. Meanwhile King Lambert, who knew nothing of all this, was busy hunting at Marengo, about forty miles from Pavia. He was in the middle of the forest, and the marquess and count with a large but unreliable Tuscan army were just crossing Monte Bardone, when he received news of how things stood. Being a man of firm courage and vigorous strength he could not endure to wait for his soldiers to assemble, but gathered together about a hundred men who were on the spot, and hastened off at full speed to meet the assailants.

Ch. 41. He had just reached Piacenza when he heard that his enemies had pitched camp near the river Stirione close to the stronghold where lies the precious body of the sacred and venerable martyr Domninus. Not knowing what the coming night was to bring they had drunk deep and after some foolish diversions abandoned themselves to slumber, some snoring loudly, others, who had taken too much, vomiting in their sleep. The king, who was both bold and sagacious, fell upon them in the dead of night, stabbing them to the heart before they could wake, and cutting their throats while they still yawned in their dreams. At last he came to the heroes who were the leaders of this host. It was not one of their own company but the king himself who told them of the glorious deed, and sheer terror prevented them, I will not say from fighting, but even from running away. Ildeprand, it is true, managed to slip off, but Adalbert was left hiding in the place where the beasts were tethered. There he was found and brought before the king, who at once addressed him thus:— 'Your wife Berta, methinks, prophesied with true Sibylline inspiration, when she undertook by her skill to make you either a king or an ass. She would not or, as is more probable, she could not make you a king, and so, in order to keep her word, she turned you into an ass and drove you into the stable with the herds of Arcady.' Thereupon the others with Adalbert were taken, put in chains, carried to Pavia, and delivered there into custody.

Ch. 42. After this success Lambert again betook himself to the chase of Marengo, leaving the fate of the prisoners to be settled by the decision of the princes. Ah would that his hunting had had wild beasts and not kings as its quarry! It is said that while he was chasing boars with his horse on a loose rein, he fell and broke his neck. But I would not say that it were correct to attach credence to this account. There is another story of his death which is constantly repeated and seems to me more probable. Manfred, Count of Milan, whom I mentioned just now, on being sentenced to capital punishment for his crimes against the state and the king, left one son Hugh as heir to all his property. Lambert, seeing that the youth was of conspicuous beauty and surpassing courage, tried to assuage the bitter grief caused by his father's death by showering favours upon him, and admitted him to the privilege of his intimate friendship. So, while Lambert was hunting at Marengo – there is a very large and beautiful wood there which is especially suitable to the chase – it happened that while the rest of his followers were scouring the thickets in the hunt, the king was left alone with this Hugh in a coppice. They were waiting for the boar to pass, but as he did not appear the king at last grew weary of the long delay and fell asleep for a while, leaving the traitor, in whom he trusted, to keep watch and ward over him. While he sat there alone Hugh, the king's guardian, or rather the king's betrayer and murderer, began to think again of his father's death and to forget all the kindness that Lambert had shown him. He did not consider that his progenitor had been justly put to death; he did not fear to break the oath he had sworn to his king; he did not blush to be called successor to Judas, who betrayed Our Lord Jesus Christ; what is worse, he did not tremble at the everlasting punishment that would be his fate. No; he took a big piece of wood and with a great effort broke the sleeper's neck. He was afraid to use his sword lest he should be plainly revealed as a murderer, and his trick was so far successful that as there were no sword cuts but plain marks of bruises against wood, when the body was found it was believed that the king had fallen from his horse and broken his neck. For many years the truth was hidden; but when in process of time Berengar gained the throne and held it firmly without opposition, Hugh himself betrayed the crime of which he had been guilty, and so the words of the prophet-king were fulfilled:— 'The sinner is praised in the desires of his heart, and doing iniquity he is blessed.' But he could not have done otherwise, since it is Truth itself that says: 'There is nothing hidden that shall not be revealed, nothing secret that shall not be made known.'

Ch. 43. After these things had thus happened King Berengar was honoured with the king's dignity he had held before, but now in fuller measure: marquess Adalbert and the others were sent back to their own lands.

Ch. 44. I would fain, dear father, write of the death of this great king with tears, I would fain shed tears over my writing. In him was to be found an honest probity of character, a pure and awe-inspiring strictness. His body was graced by the bright vigour of youth, his mind adorned by the grave sanctity of age. He evidently gave more glory to the state than the state gave to him. If swift death had not snatched him away, he was one who might have followed in the path of the Roman Empire and subdued the whole world in his forceful sway.

CONTENTS

BOOK 2

BOOK 2

Ch. 1. After the vital warmth had deserted Arnulf's limbs and left his body lifeless, his son Louis was unanimously elected to the throne. But the death of the great king was as clearly known to the Hungarians close by as it was to the inhabitants of the whole world, and the day of that joyful event was to them more pleasant than any festivity, more precious than any treasure. Why need I say more?

Ch. 2. In the first year after Arnulf's death and his son's succession, the Hungarians collected a large army and laid claim to the territory of the Maravani, a people in whom Arnulf had thought to find a support against their attacks. They also seized the land of the Bavarians, destroyed their castles, burned their churches, massacred their people, and, to make themselves more and more feared, drank the blood of those whom they had slain.

Ch. 3. Accordingly King Louis, seeing the cruelty of these enemies and the havoc they were making among his own people, so fired the hearts of all with apprehension that if any one by chance failed to serve in the war which he proceeded to wage against them, there was nothing left for him to do but to hang himself. Against Louis' great army an innumerable multitude of the villainous Hungarians hastened to advance. No man ever more ardently desired a drink of cold water than these cruel savages longed for the day of battle. Indeed their only joy is in fighting. In the book which deals with their origin I read that 'as soon as a child is born his mother makes a cut on his face with a sharp knife, so that he may learn to bear the pain of wounds

before he has received nourishment from the breast'. This
assertion is rendered credible by the wounds they inflict on their
own live flesh as a sign of grief when their kinsmen are dying. *Ce
gens sacrilège et impie*, that is, this ungodly and impious race shed
blood, it appears, instead of tears. King Louis with his army had
just reached Augsburg, a city on the borders of Swabia, Bavaria
and eastern France, when he heard of their unexpected, or rather
undesired, proximity. Accordingly next day the two armies met
on the plains of the river Lech, by their extent well suited to the
work of Mars.

Ch. 4.   And so it came about that before 'Aurora left Tithonus'
saffron bed' the Hungarians, thirsting for murder and eager for
the fray, fell upon the others, namely the Christians, while they
were still yawning with sleep. Some indeed were awakened by
arrow points before they heard the cries of battle; others were
transfixed in their beds, and were not roused either by the din or
by their wounds: their life had gone before their slumber ended.
On both sides a furious battle started, and the Turks retiring in
feigned retreat caused great havoc by the fierce fire of their *flèches*,
that is, of their arrows.

> When great Jehovah veils the golden light
> Of Phoebus with his clouds and draws dark night
> Athwart the heavens, swiftly all around
> The lightnings play and fast the thunders sound.
> Then tremble they whose trade it is to turn
> Black into white and fear themselves to burn
> In levin fire, conscious of their sins,
> So swift, so fast, when once the fight begins,
> The foemen's arrows hurtling in the air
> Pierce breastplates through and leave each quiver bare.
> And as the cruel hail on cornfields falls,
> Or rattles on the roofs of lordly halls,
> So fall the sword strokes on the helms beneath,
> So arrows send the brave to mutual death.

By this time Phoebus sinking in the sky marked one hour after
noon and the war god was still smiling upon Louis' side, when the
Turks with their wonted cunning set an ambush and feigned to

retreat. As the king's men, deceived by the trick, rushed boldly forward, the troops in ambush fell on them from every side and the victors found themselves in a moment vanquished and slain. The king himself, conquered now instead of conqueror, was filled with dismay, the reverse being all the more serious because it was so unexpected. You could have seen the woods and fields strewn with corpses, the rivers and water channels running red with blood, while the neighing of horses and the blare of bugles increased the terror of the fugitives and cheered on the assailants to fresh efforts.

Ch. 5. Though the Hungarians thus achieved their desire, their native villainy was not satisfied even by this dreadful massacre of Christians. To glut their perfidious rage they scoured the kingdoms of Bavaria, Swabia, France and Saxony, burning everything as they went. No one could withstand their onset, unless protected by the natural or artificial strength of fortifications, and for some years every one here had to pay them tribute.

Ch. 6. At the time of this onset a certain Adalbert – I am not referring to an ordinary person, but to the great hero of that name – was maintaining a fierce feud against the government in his castle of Bamberg. King Louis frequently collected all his forces and attacked him, but the hero, so far from staying near his castle, as most men would have done, marched out from his fortifications for some distance and took the initiative in attack. The king's soldiers at first did not comprehend how bold he was, and thought to go ahead, entice him from the castle in a preliminary skirmish, and kill him before the king arrived. But Adalbert was not only acquainted with this manoeuvre, but was fed up with it, and had already advanced so many miles that his enemies never realized he could have got so far until his fierce sword point thirsty for blood was actually at their throat. For about seven years the hero Adalbert carried on hostilities in this fashion, and at last Louis saw that he could only overcome his bold resistance by trickery. He therefore called in Hatto, Archbishop of Mainz, and asked him what he had better do. To that Hatto, who was well versed in every sort of guile, replied: 'Do not trouble yourself. I will soon relieve you from these embarrassments. I will arrange that he shall come to you: you must see that he does not go back again.' Then with the same confidence as had often before snatched success for him from disaster, he made his way to Bamberg, pretending to be in sympathy with Adalbert, and on his arrival addressed him thus:— 'Even if you thought there was no after life, you would be acting wrongly in persisting in rebellion against your liege lord, especially as your conduct is quite unreasonable. You are so passionate and high spirited that you do not understand the love that is felt for you by everyone, and most of all by the king. Trust me now and take my advice: I give you my oath that you may without hesitation leave your castle and return to it again. Even if you do not believe my priestly word, you can at least trust my solemn oath. I will guarantee to bring you back to this castle safe and sound, in the same state as I will now lead you out.'

Accordingly Adalbert, beguiled, or rather betrayed, by this honey sweet talk, agreed to accept Hatto's assurance on oath and at once invited him to dinner. Hatto however, mindful of the trick which he meant in a moment to play, said that he could not possibly dine with him there that day, and hastily prepared to take his departure. Adalbert took him by the hand and escorted him for a little way, and as soon as Hatto saw that he was outside the castle, he said:— 'I am sorry now, my noble lord, that I did not take your advice and refresh myself with some food, for I have a long journey in front of me.' Thereupon Adalbert, never suspecting what danger and disaster lurked for him beneath these simple words, replied:— 'Let us go back, my master: you must not injure your health by too prolonged a fast: take at least a little refreshment.' To this Hatto agreed and went back to the castle the same way as he had let him out, still holding his hand as he retraced his steps. They then took a hasty meal together, and setting out again arrived that same day at the king's camp.

When the news spread that Adalbert had come on a visit to the king, the whole place was filled with shouting and uproar. Louis, no little rejoiced at his appearance, at once called his lords together and bidding them prepare to sit in judgement thus addressed them: 'What havoc Adalbert has wrought, in the past seven years, what harm he has done, what distress of rapine and conflagration he has brought upon us, we know only too well; it is not a matter of report, but of painful experience. Therefore I now await your judgement and ask you what shall be his reward, to pay for these his glorious deeds.' The court unanimously decided that in accordance with the laws of the kings of old Adalbert was adjudged guilty of high treason and should be beheaded. As he was being dragged off in chains to execution, he looked Hatto in the face and cried:– 'You yourself will be guilty of perjury, if you allow me to be put to death.' But Hatto replied: 'I promised that I would take you from your fort and bring you back again safe. I saw that I had fulfilled my promise when I led you out by the hand and led you back again at once safe and sound.' Adalbert sighed to think that he had discovered the trick too late, and grieving over his mistake followed the executioner as unwillingly as he would have been glad to go on living, if he had been allowed.

Ch. 7.　After a few years then, since there was no one in the east or south-east of Europe able to resist the Hungarians – for they had by this time forced the Bulgarians and the Greeks to pay them tribute – they took the opportunity to visit the peoples of the south and west and try their strength upon them also. They got together an army so huge that it defied numbering, and swooped down upon hapless Italy. They pitched their tents, or rather the miserable rags that served them for shelter, near the river Brenta, and then sent out scouts for three days to discover the lie of the country and how many or how few people were living in it. On their return they got the following report:– 'This plain has a number of hills in it, and is bounded on one side, as you see, by rugged and fertile mountains, on the other by the Adriatic: there are also some strongly fortified towns. We do not know whether the people are good or bad fighters, but it is obvious that their numbers are very large. We do not advise an attack with our present small force. There are, however, some reasons which urge us to battle; our habit of victory, for example, our courage, our knowledge of warfare, and above all the wealth before us which we so ardently desire, wealth such as we have never seen or hoped to see in any part of the world. If you ask us for our opinion, we suggest that we now return home – it is not a very long or difficult journey and can be accomplished in ten days or less – and come back here again next spring, when we have got together all the bravest warriors of our nation. Then we shall strike terror into these people both by our courage and by our numbers.'

Ch. 8. As soon as they heard this the Hungarians returned to their own country and spent the rough winter months in making armour, sharpening weapons, and training their young men in military exercises.

Ch. 9. The sun had not yet passed from the sign of the Fishes into that of the Ram, when with an army huge beyond all counting they made their way into Italy. They passed through the strong cities of Aquileia and Verona, and arrived unchecked at Ticinum, a town which is now known by the more glorious name of Pavia. King Berengar, who had never before even heard the word 'Hungarian', could not contain his surprise at this strange and wonderful exploit, and at once sent round letters and messengers to the peoples of Italy, the Tuscans, the Volscians and the men of Camerino and Spoleto. He ordered them all to assemble in one place, and so got together a force three times as strong as that of the Hungarians.

Ch. 10. Berengar, seeing this great host assembled, was inflated with pride and attributed his triumph over the enemy not to God but to his own strength. He stayed himself in a small town with a few attendants, and gave himself up to pleasure. Why need I say more? As for the Hungarians, when they saw his huge army, they were filled with consternation and could not decide what to do. They were afraid to fight; they could not run away. Finally, after long wavering, flight seemed preferable to battle, and they swam across the river Adda pursued by the Christians, making the passage in such haste that many of them were drowned in the crossing.

Ch. 11. Thereupon they wisely sent envoys to the Christians, offering to give up all the booty they had gained if they might be allowed to return home in safety. This request – O lamentable tale! – the Christians insultingly rejected, and began to look about for chains to bind the Hungarians rather than for swords to kill them. The heathens, therefore, being unable to appease the

Christians' fury, determined to follow their original plan and seize the opportunity to escape by flight.

Ch. 12.   Continuing their retreat they got to the broad plains round Verona, where the Christian vanguard fell upon their rear. A skirmish took place in which the heathen were victorious: but as a stronger force of their enemies was coming up, they remembered what they had meant to do, and resumed their journey.

Ch. 13.   The Christians and the idolaters arrived together at the river Brenta, for the Hungarians' horses were too weary to allow them to go further. The two armies therefore faced one another, separated only by the waters of the above named stream. The Hungarians by this time were in a mortal panic and undertook to surrender furniture, captives, arms and horses, keeping only one animal for each man to return. To back up their petition, they undertook, if the Christians would allow them to depart alive, that they would never again enter and would give up their sons as pledges of their word. But alas! the Christians, swollen with deceitful pride, thought that the heathens were already beaten and answered them back with threats. *Leur réponse*, that is, their reply was as follows:– 'If we were to accept gifts of surrender from surrendered dead dogs and enter into any treaty, even such a madman as Orestes would swear on his life that we were out of our senses.'

Ch. 14.   The Hungarians were driven to despair by the failure of their envoys, and collecting their bravest fighters began to comfort each other with mutual exhortations like these:– 'Since there is nothing worse that can happen to men than the ruin which faces us to-day, inasmuch as entreaties are useless and flight is impossible, while submission means death, why should we fear to rush upon our enemies' swords and pay for death with death? Is it not better to make fortune, not our own cowardice, responsible for our end? To fall fighting like men is not to die, but to live. Let us leave our *heritage*, that is, our inheritance of fame to our descendants, even as we received it from our fathers. We ought to trust ourselves and our own experience at least, for we have often defeated a superior force with greatly inferior numbers. A host of weaklings is a mere crowd led out to the slaughter. The War God slays the fugitive and protects the stout fighter. These men, who have shown no pity to our supplications, do not know or understand that victory is a good thing but excessive triumph is odious.'

Ch. 15. After having cheered their hearts with these words of encouragement they arranged a triple ambush, and crossing the river rushed straight upon the middle of the enemies' line. Most of the Christians wearied by the long delay caused by these negotiations, had got down from their horses and were taking a meal in camp; and the Hungarians came down upon them with such speed that in some cases their swords actually transfixed the food in their gullets. In other cases flight was impossible, since their horses had been scared away, and without their steeds they were left easy victims. To increase the disaster the Christians suffered from their mutual discords. Some of them not only refrained from attacking the Hungarians, but panted to see their neighbours slain, thinking in their perverse folly that they themselves would rule without restraint, provided that their neighbours were overthrown. So by refusing to help their neighbour's needs and by rejoicing in his ruin they brought destruction upon themselves. The Christians finally fled, and the heathens pursued them savagely; for since their proffered gifts had not won them mercy, they now in their turn refused to listen to supplications. The flight became a butchery, and the whole realm was scoured by the Hungarians' merciless fury. No one ventured to withstand their approach unless he was behind strong walls. Indeed at this time their valour was so irresistible that while one section of them was plundering Bavaria, Swabia, France and Saxony, another host was laying waste all Italy.

Ch. 16. However, it was not their own valour that won them these triumphs. The word of the Lord is true, it is more enduring than earth and heaven, it cannot be changed: even as by the mouth of the prophet Jeremiah it threatens all peoples in the person of the house of Israel, saying:— 'Lo, I will bring a nation upon you from far: it is a mighty nation, it is an ancient nation, a nation whose language thou knowest not, neither understandest what they say. Their quiver is as an open sepulchre, they are all mighty men. And they shall eat up thine harvest and thy bread, which thy sons and daughters should eat: they shall eat up thy flocks and thine herds: they shall eat up thy vines and thy fig trees: they shall impoverish thy fenced cities, wherein thou trustedst, with the sword. Nevertheless, in those days, saith the Lord God, I will not make a full end with you.'

Ch. 17.   At this same time King Louis died, and Conrad, a man of Frankish origin and an energetic and skilful warrior, was unanimously chosen to fill the throne.

Ch. 18.   Under him the most powerful princes were these: Arnold of Bavaria, Bruchard of Swabia, Everard the powerful count of France, and Giselbert duke of Lorraine. Among them also was Henry, the illustrious and powerful duke of the Saxons and Turingians.

Ch. 19.   In the second year of his reign the princes mentioned above, and especially Henry, rose up in rebellion against the king. Conrad however, by his vigorous wisdom and undaunted courage had the better of them, and they returned again to their allegiance. Arnold for his part was so frightened that, taking his wife and children with him, he fled to the Hungarians, and stayed with them so long as the breath of life was in Conrad's body.

Ch. 20.   In the seventh year of his reign Conrad knew that the time had come for him to be summoned into God's presence. He therefore called the princes to him, Henry alone being absent, and addressed them thus:— 'As you see, the time is near at hand when I shall be called from the corruptible to the incorruptible, from mortality to immortality. Therefore I beg you now again and again to pursue peace and harmony one with the other. When I leave this life let no desire for rule, no ambition for empire, fire your hearts. Elect Henry, the wise duke of the Saxons and Turingians, as king, and make him your liege lord. He is a man rich in wisdom, abounding in severity, and of righteous judgement.' After saying this he bade his attendants bring out his regal crown, not one of plain gold, such as distinguishes a prince of any rank, but one adorned, or rather weighed down, with most precious jewels, together with his sceptre and royal robes. Then, in spite of his weakness, he poured forth these words:— 'By these regal ornaments I appoint Henry as my heir and successor to my regal dignity. I advise, nay more I beg you, to render him all obedience.' His death followed soon after these instructions, and compliance with them followed his death. As soon as he had expired, the princes took the crown and the royal vestments to Henry, and told him everything that Conrad had said in due order.

Conrad at first had modestly declined the high position of king, and even when he accepted it he never showed any personal ambition. If his rule had not been so abruptly ended by death —

> Pale death that with impartial foot
> Knocks at the rich man's tower, the poor man's cot

he would have been one whose glorious empire would have extended over many nations of our universe.

Ch. 21. At this same time Arnold, returning with his wife and sons from Hungary, was welcomed with every mark of honour by the Bavarians and the eastern Franks. Indeed not only was he welcomed, but strongly urged by them, to become king. Accordingly King Henry, seeing that everyone was obedient to his rule and that Arnold alone was inclined to resist him, collected a strong army and set out for Bavaria. Arnold heard of this, and not having the patience to wait for his arrival in Bavaria gathered together such forces as he could and hastened to meet him; for he certainly had the ambition of becoming king himself. But when they were within an ace of being forced into fighting, King Henry, like a wise man and God fearing king, reflected on what irreparable harm a conflict might do either side, and sent a messenger to Arnold inviting him to a private conference. Arnold thought that he summoned him to a single combat, and so he came alone to the appointed place at the appointed hour.

Ch. 22. As he came in haste to meet him King Henry addressed him thus:

Why madly strive against the Lord's decree?
The people wills that I their king should be,
By ordinance of Christ in whom consists
The universe nor hell itself resists.
He strikes down mighty monarchs from their throne
And sets the humble there, that they may own
God's favour through the years and to Him raise
Perpetual songs of gratitude and praise.
Why thirst in cruel rage for Christian blood?
Why thus assuage the stings of envy's mood?
Be sure of this: were you the people's choice
I more than any should with truth rejoice.

So by the fourfold grace of his oratory, which was both copious and brief, both compact and flowery, wise King Henry succeeded in appeasing Arnold, and then returned to his own people.

Ch. 23. Arnold reported the king's speech to his partizans and got from them *cette réponse*, that is, this reply:— 'There is a saying of the Wise Man, nay a saying of Wisdom herself, which runs thus:— 'By me kings reign and wise men decree justice. By me princes rule.' And there is one of the Apostle: 'Who doubts that the powers that be are ordained of God? Whosoever resisteth the power, resisteth the ordinance of God.' In choosing Henry all the people could not have been of one mind, if he had not been chosen before the foundation of the world by the Trinity which is one God. If he proves a good man, we ought to love him and praise God in him; if bad, we must bear him with resignation. For subjects often by their own deserts bring it about that their rulers are a burden rather than a guidance. It seems to us only right and just, however, that if you agree with the rest and consent to Henry as king, he for his part should take your rank and wealth into consideration, and assuage your natural resentment by granting you some special privilege that your predecessors did not possess. We suggest that the bishops of all Bavaria be put under your authority and that you shall have the power, when one bishop dies, of ordaining his successor.' Arnold agreed with this wise and excellent advice, became a vassal of King Henry, and was honoured by him with the gift of all the bishoprics in Bavaria.

Ch. 24. About the same time the Hungarians heard of the death of King Conrad and the succession of Henry to the throne. They therefore held a conference and addressed to one another these arguments: 'It may be that a new king will wish to follow new laws. Let us therefore gather together a large force, and go up and investigate the position, and find out whether King Henry means to pay us the tribute that he owes us. If – as we do not believe – he is different from the other kings, let us lay his kingdom waste with an endless series of massacres and conflagrations. We will not occupy the land of the Bavarians immediately: we will take the territory of the Saxons first, where Henry himself is king. Then if – as we do not expect – he should try to get an army together, it will not be able to reach him in time either from Lorraine or from France or from Swabia or from Bavaria. Moreover the land of the Saxons and the Turingians can be easily ravaged, inasmuch as it has no mountain defences, nor any of the protection that fortified towns afford.'

Ch. 25. King Henry was laid up with a serious illness when he was informed of the Hungarians' near approach. He scarcely waited for the report to end, but sent off messengers at once through Saxony, bidding every man who could come to him in five days under pain of death. Before the time had expired a strong army had assembled; for it is the laudable and praiseworthy custom of the Saxons to allow no male above the age of thirteen to shirk military service. Thereupon the king, weak in body but strong in spirit, found enough vigour to mount his horse and collecting his forces round him fired their fury for the fray by this address:

Ch. 26.

> Famous in war were the Saxons of old.
> Lions in battle their own they did hold,
> Even when Charles the whole world had subdued
> And every land with red carnage embrued.
> E'en that great victor the Saxons defeated;
> And if before his next rush they retreated,
> That was God's kindness who willed that our nation
> Should have its share of the Christian salvation.

Now 'tis the heathenish Turks who attack,
Men who know nothing of Christ, and alack!
Hate God's own church, and would force us to pay
Money as ransom ere they march away.
Up then, my heroes, and enter the fight,
Show to the foe your invincible might.
Pay them no tribute, but let the knaves know
Death is the gift they shall carry below,
And, when their reckoning with you they tell,
Count their doubloons in the red fires of hell.

Ch. 27. The King seeing that his exhortations had fired his men for the fray, called for silence and once again touched by the breath of divine inspiration added these words: 'The deeds of the Kings of old and the writings of the holy fathers suggest to us what we ought to do. It is not hard for God to defeat a great host with a small company if the faith of those who desire victory deserves it: a faith, I mean, not only of professions but of works, not only of the lips but of the heart. Let us pray then and according to the psalmist offer up our vows; I first, who seem to be foremost in rank and position. Let the heresy of Simony, hated by God and condemned by the blessed Peter, chief of the apostles, which up to now has been rashly maintained by my predecessors, be altogether banished from our realm. Love of unity will then bind together those whom the devil's cunning has separated!'

Ch. 28. The King was desirous of saying more to the same effect when a flying messenger rushed in with news that the Hungarians were at Merseburg, a castle on the borders of the Saxons, Turingians and Slavonians. He added that they had taken a huge company of women and children prisoners and had killed an immense number of men; for they had declared, in order to strike terror into the Saxons, that they would leave no one over ten years of age alive. The King's firm courage, however, was not dismayed, but he urged his men all the more vehemently to battle, telling them it was their bounden duty to fight for their country and meet a glorious end.

Ch. 29. Meanwhile the Hungarians were questioning their captives to find out if they were bound to attack. Being assured that otherwise their success was impossible, they sent out scouts to see if it was true. These men set out at once and came in sight of King Henry with a huge army close to the above mentioned town of Merseburg. They scarcely had time to return to their men and tell them of the enemies' approach: indeed it was the King in person, not a messenger, who gave them warning of attack.

Ch. 30. The battle began immediately. From the Christians' ranks on all sides was heard the holy, and wondrous cry 'Kyrie eleison' 'Lord have mercy upon us': from the heathen came the foul and diabolical shout 'Hui hui.'

Ch. 31. Before the beginning of the engagement Henry had given his men this sagacious and practical advice: 'When you are hastening forward to the first skirmish, let no one of you try to get ahead of his comrades just because he has a swifter horse. Cover yourselves on one side with your bucklers, and catch the first flight of arrows on your shields: then rush at them at full speed as furiously as you can, so that before they have time to fire a second volley they may feeel the blows of your swords upon their heads.' The Saxons accordingly, remembering this practical advice, advanced in level line. No one used his horse's speed to get in front of his slower neighbour, but covering themselves on one side with their shields, as the king bade them, they caught the enemies' arrows on them and rendered them harmless. Then, according to their wise leader's command, they rushed at full speed upon the foe, who groaned and gave up the ghost before they could shoot again. So, by the kindness of God's grace, the Hungarians found flight preferable to battle. Their swiftest horses then seemed sluggish to them: their gorgeous trappings and bright shields appeared a burden rather than a protection. They threw aside their bows, flung away their arrows, tore off their horses' trappings, that nothing might check their speed, and thought of nothing but precipitate flight. But Almighty God, who had stripped them of courage for the fray, denied them any chance of escape. The Hungarians accordingly were cut to pieces and put to flight, the great throng of their prisoners was released, and the voice of lamentation changed to songs of joy. This memorable and glorious triumph the king celebrated in the upper room of a house at Merseburg *par un tableau*, that is, by a picture, so that you can now see the battle, not as it might have happened, but as it actually occurred.

Ch. 32. While this was going on the Italians almost unanimously by messengers invited a certain Louis, a man of Burgundian descent, to come to them, drive Berengar from the throne, and take the power himself.

Ch. 33. The instigator of this foul crime was Adalbert, marquess of Ivrea, to whom Berengar had given his daughter Gisla in marriage. By Gisla Adalbert had a son, whom he called after his grandfather, and he, he, I repeat, is the present Berengar, under whose monstrous tyranny all Italy is now groaning, the man whose foul tricks have forced the rest of the world to destroy rather than to assist our poor country. But enough on that subject. Let us return to our narrative.

Ch. 34. This same Adalbert was a man of thoroughly bad character, a source of danger to all honest folk. In the days of his hot youth he had been wonderfully pious and liberal, so much so indeed that if a poor man met him on his return from the chase and wanted something which he could give, he would at once hand him the horn which hung by a gold fastening from his neck, and later buy it back from him at its full value. But afterwards he got so bad a reputation that grown men as well as children sung the following lines about him; and they were well deserved. They sound better in another language, so let us give them thus:

> Adalbertus est cohortis
> Comes validus et fortis.
> Ensem longum tenet, idem
> Regi parvam tenet fidem.

The meaning of the lines is that Adalbert has a long sword but little sense of loyalty.

Ch. 35. At the instigation of his fellow men and of some other Italians, the above mentioned Louis came into Italy. As soon as Berengar heard of his approach he marched against him, and when Louis saw Berengar's large army and his own small force, under compulsion of terror he promised with an oath that no offers would ever tempt him into Italy again, if he were then allowed to return unharmed. His expulsion was the easier in that Berengar at this time by lavish gifts had secured the loyal support of Adalbert, the powerful marquess of Tuscany.

Ch. 36. But after a little time had elapsed the Adalbert in question took offence against Berengar; and his wife Berta, mother of Hugh who in my time became king of Italy, sedulously fostered his grievance. The result was that the princes of Italy, after consultation with Adalbert, again invited Louis to claim the throne. Louis' ambition made him forget his oath and he came at once in hot haste.

Ch. 37. Berengar, seeing that Louis was being supported both by the princes of Italy and the princes of Tuscany, set out for Verona. Louis, however, with the Italians, did not cease to pursue him and finally drove him even from Verona and subdued the whole realm.

Ch. 38. After this it seemed good to Louis that as he had seen all parts of Italy he should also pay a visit to Tuscany. He accordingly left Pavia and set out for Lucca, where he was received by Adalbert with great pomp and hospitality.

Ch. 39. So when Louis saw whole companies of well equipped soldiers standing about in Adalbert's palace, and noticed the expenses that his display of power involved, he was seized with jealous envy and said privately to his followers:– 'This fellow might well be called not marquess but king; in nothing but the name is he my inferior.' Adalbert got to know of this, and when his wife Berta, who was a shrewd woman, heard of it also, she not only induced her husband to renounce his allegiance to Louis but persuaded the other Italian princes to follow his example. As a result, when Louis arrived at Verona on his return journey, and suspecting no danger had taken up his quarters there without hesitation, Berengar bribed the city guards at dead of night and passed through the gates with a strong force of fearless followers.

Ch. 40. As the Tiber runs through Rome, so the river Adige runs through Verona. Over it a huge marble bridge has been built, of wonderful size and workmanship. On the left, or northern, bank the city is protected by a high steep hill, so that even if the right hand side is occupied by an enemy, it is possible to offer a manful resistance on the left. On the summit of the hill there stands a church of most costly structure, consecrated in honour of Saint Peter, the chief of the apostles, and here Louis, owing to its picturesque position and strong defences, was staying.

Ch. 41. Berengar, as we have said, entered the city by night without Louis' knowledge, and crossing the bridge with his men reached his enemy just as dawn was faintly breaking. Louis, awakened by the shouts and clamour of the soldiers, inquired what was the matter, and then, realizing his danger, took refuge in the church, no one except one of Berengar's men knowing where he had gone. This fellow determined not to betray his hiding place, but fearing lest his comrades might come upon it and reveal it and then Louis be put to death, he went himself to Berengar and addressed him thus: 'Since God has deemed you so worthy that He has now put your enemy into your power, it is your duty to honour His precepts, or rather His commands. He has said: "Be ye merciful, as your Father also is merciful. Judge not, and ye shall not be judged: condemn not, and ye shall not be condemned."' Berengar, who was not devoid of cunning, realized that the man knew where Louis was hiding, and so he deceived him with this sophistical answer:— 'Do you imagine, blockhead, that I wish to kill a man, nay more, a king, whom the Lord has put into my hands? When God put King Saul in David's power, had not that righteous man the opportunity to slay him and yet refused to use it?' The soldier was induced by these words to point out the place of Louis' retreat, and the latter was thereupon dragged out and brought before Berengar where the king rebuked him thus:— 'How long, Louis, will you abuse our patience? Can you deny that occasion in the past, when you were so hemmed in by my forces and my careful guard that you could not move a hand against me? And did I not then listen to the voice of pity, which you did not deserve, and let you go free? Have you realized, I say, that you are a prisoner, caught in the meshes of your own perfidy? You assured me, you know, that you would never set foot in Italy again. I grant you your life, for I promised it to the man who betrayed you; but not only do I order, but I insist, that you be deprived of your sight.' His commands were fulfilled; Louis was blinded, and Berengar again became master of the realm.

Ch. 42. Meanwhile the mad rage of the Hungarians, unable to find vent in Saxony, France, Swabia and Bavaria, spread itself without resistance over all Italy, Berengar doing his best to win their friendship as he could not rely on the loyalty of his own soldiers.

Ch. 43. The Saracens also, who, as I have said, were living at Fraxinetum, after ruining Provence, extended their savage raids to the northern districts of Italy close by, and finally, after sacking several cities, came to Acqui, a town about forty miles from Pavia, which gets its name from the wonderful square baths that have been built there. The whole country accordingly was in a panic, and no one waited for the Saracens to approach unless he had a perfectly sure refuge.

Ch. 44. At this same time another band of Saracens sailed from Africa to Italy and laid hands on Calabria, Apulia, Benevento and almost all the cities belonging to the Romans, so that in every place the Romans held but one half, these Africans the other. Indeed they established a fort on Mount Garigliano, where they kept in security their wives, children and captives, and all their goods and chattels. No one coming from the west or north to make his prayers on the thresholds of the blessed apostles was able to get into Rome without being either taken prisoner by these men or only released at a high ransom. Indeed although our poor Italy was hard pressed by the ravages of the Hungarians and the Saracens from Fraxinetum, no fury, no pestilence was so destructive as these Africans proved to be.

Ch. 45. It is said that the occasion of their leaving Africa and coming to Italy was as follows. When the august emperors Leo and Alexander left this mortal life, Romanos, as I shall relate in fuller detail, was joint ruler at Constantinople with Constantine, son of the emperor Leo, who is still alive amongst us. The usual thing happened in the first year of Romanos' reign: an attempt at rebellion was made by some of *les orientales*, that is, by some of the eastern peoples. As a further result, while the emperor's troops were occupied in quelling this revolt, Apulia and Calabria, two countries which were then part of his dominions, also rebelled against him. With a large army already in the east, the emperor could not spare any great force for Italy, and he therefore at first merely summoned the rebels to return to their former allegiance. They flatly refused to do anything of the sort, and the emperor in a rage sent messengers to the African king, offering him money and begging him with the help of his brave soldiers to subdue Apulia and Calabria for him. Thereupon the African sent a huge fleet and army across to Italy, and by force of arms brought these two districts once more beneath the emperor's control. But when the time came for the Africans to leave Calabria, they wheeled northwards in the direction of Rome, and for their own security laid claim to Mount Garigliano, and also captured many strong cities in fierce fight.

Ch. 46. Our Lord Jesus Christ, co-eternal and consubstantial with the Father and the Holy Ghost, whose mercy fills the earth, who wishes no man to perish, but all men to be saved and come to knowledge of the truth, lest that be lost which God foreordained before the world was made, when He created man after all other creatures, to make use of them and be their master, man whom at the end of time He who is true man and true God, not two but one, redeemed by the shedding of His blood – Our Lord, I say, invites some men by kindness to love Him and cherish their native land, while in other cases He uses the compulsion of fear. He seeks not His own glory, for He can get no benefit from our goodness – as the prophet testifies saying:– 'Thou needest not my goods' – nor derive any harm from our badness, but He desires to help us. So, as kindness had proved in vain, He willed for the moment to chastise us with terror in this fashion. But finally, lest the Saracens should insult too long and say – 'Where now is their God?' God turned the hearts of the Christians and filled them with an even greater desire for fighting than that which they had felt for flight.

Ch. 47. At this time John of Ravenna occupied the venerable see of Rome, having obtained the papacy by a crime that outraged all law, human and divine. The circumstances were as follows.

Ch. 48. A certain shameless strumpet called Theodora, grandmother of the Alberic who recently passed from this life, at one time was sole monarch of Rome and – shame upon us even to say the words! – exercised power in the most manly fashion. She had two daughters, Marotia and Theodora, and these damsels were not only her equals but could even surpass her in the exercises that Venus loves. Marotia, as the result of shameful adultery, became the mother by Pope Sergius, whom we have mentioned above, of the John who after the death of John of Ravenna won his way to the papacy; by the marquess Alberic she had another son, the Alberic who in our days made himself prince of Rome.

Now the see of Ravenna, an archbishopric held only second in importance to the papacy of Rome, was then in Peter's hands. John, who afterwards became Pope, was one of his church clergy and was frequently sent by him to Rome with official messages of due respect to his apostolic superior. Theodora, who, as I have declared, was a quite shameless harlot, saw the young man, and at once was all on fire with lust to possess him. So inflamed was she by his handsome person that not only did she offer herself to him as his mistress, but forced him to comply with her desires again and again. While this shamelessness was going on, the Bishop of Bologna died and John was elected in his place. Just before the day of his consecration Peter the Archbishop of Ravenna passed away, and at Theodora's instigation John abandoned his see at Bologna and filled with vaunting ambition broke all the laws of the holy Fathers and claimed the Archbishopric as his own. He therefore came to Rome and soon afterwards was ordained Bishop of Ravenna. Then a little time elapsed and God summoned the Pope who had illegally ordained him. Thereupon Theodora, with a harlot's wanton naughtiness, fearing that she would have few opportunities of going to bed with her sweetling if he were separated from her by the two hundred miles that lie between Ravenna and Rome, forced him to abandon his archbishopric at Ravenna, and take for himself – O monstrous crime! – the papacy of Rome. This was the man then, and this was the way in which he became Vicar of the holy apostles, when the Africans, as I began by saying, were wreaking such cruel havoc on Benevento and the cities near Rome.

Ch. 49. It happened meanwhile that one of the African soldiers, as the result of some wrong done to him, deserted and came to Pope John and under divine inspiration addressed him thus:– 'If you were wise, lord bishop, you would not allow your people and your country to be so cruelly mangled by the Africans. Pick out some young men, nimble and quick of foot, who will obey me readily as master, teacher and general. No one of them must carry anything except one shield each, one javelin, one sword, some simple clothes and a small quantity of provisions.'

Ch. 50. Sixty youths answering to his description were found and handed over to him, and with them he hastened to attack the Africans, hiding by the side of the narrow roads which they used. So on several occasions when the Africans were returning from a raid, the young men sprang out from their ambush with a fierce cry upon them, and taking them unawares and off their guard cut them down with but little difficulty. A shout from the lips and a blow from the hand were simultaneous, nor were the Africans aware of what was happening, or who were their assailants, until they found themselves transfixed by their javelins. Finally several other bands of Romans, encouraged by news of these successes, routed the Africans in different parts of the country, and at last the enemy, worn down by this clever policy, gave up their plans and left the Roman cities alone, only keeping Mount Garigliano as a place of refuge.

Ch. 51. When John was made pope, as we have said, a certain Landolf, an energetic man and skilful in all military exercises, was the illustrious prince of Benevento and Capua. As the Africans were doing great damage to the state, Pope John consulted this noble prince Landolf and asked him what he had better do in regard to this African business. When the prince got this message, he sent envoys to the Pope with the following reply: 'My spiritual father, this is a matter that requires careful consideration and a bold policy. Send therefore to the emperor of the Greeks, for these fellows are continually ravaging his territory this side of the sea just as they do ours. Invite the people of Camerino and Spoleto also to help us, and under God's protection let us all then begin a vigorous campaign. If we win, let the victory be imputed, not to our host, but to God: if the Africans beat us, let it be put to the account of our sins and not to cowardice.'

Ch. 52.   As soon as the pope heard this he sent off messengers to Constantinople, humbly asking the emperor for assistance. The latter, being a righteous and God fearing man, without delay sent off a fleet with an army on board, which passed up the river Garigliano and joined forces with Pope John, Landolf the powerful prince of Benevento, and the people of Camerino and Spoleto. A fierce battle then followed, from which the Africans, seeing that the Christians were the stronger, retreated to the summit of Mount Garigliano and contented themselves with blocking all the narrow paths up it.

Ch. 53.   The Greeks this same day pitched their camp on that side of the hill where the ascent was steeper and opportunities for retreat more available. They then kept a close watch on the Africans to prevent them from escaping, and by daily assaults caused them considerable loss of men.

Ch. 54.   Day by day the Greeks and the Latins continued their attacks, and finally by God's grace not a single African remained; they were all either slain by the sword or taken alive. In this fighting some faithful believers saw the figures of the two apostles Saint Peter and Saint Paul, and we are confident that it was owing to their prayers that the Christians obtained the victory and the Africans were put to flight.

Ch. 55.   At this time Adalbert, the powerful marquess of Tuscany, died and his son Wido was appointed by King Berengar marquess in his place. However, Adalbert's wife Berta, after her husband's death, exercised as much authority with her son as Adalbert himself had possessed. By cunning, lavish gifts, and the pleasant exercises of the nuptial couch, Berta secured a number of loyal supporters. Consequently, when a little later she with her son was taken prisoner and confined in Mantua, her friends refused to surrender her cities and castles to King Berengar, but held them firmly for her and soon afterwards released her and her son from prison.

Ch. 56. This lady by common report had three children by her husband: Wido, whom we have mentioned above; Lambert, who is still alive but blind; and one daughter Ermengarde, her mother's doughty rival in the sweet delights of Aphrodite, whom she married to Adalbert marquess of Ivrea on the death of his first wife, Gisla daughter of Berengar and mother of the King Berengar now alive. Ermengarde had one son named Anscar, and my next book will describe what marvellous courage and boldness he possessed.

Ch. 57. At this same period Adalbert, the king's son-in-law, marquess of Ivrea, and Odelric count of the palace, a man of Swabian descent, together with the rich and energetic count Gislebert and Lampert Archbishop of Milan, joined with some of the other Italian princes in a rebellion against Berengar. The cause of their revolt was as follows. When the time came for Lampert after his predecessor's death to be ordained Archbishop of Milan, Berengar, contrary to the rules of the Holy Fathers, claimed from him a large sum of money, and after his own demands had been satisfied sent in a further account, stating the sums still due to his chamberlains, his porters, the guardians of his peacocks, and even his poultry men. Lampert was so inflamed with desire to become archbishop that he paid all that the king demanded; but how it pained him to do so you will understand by what follows.

Ch. 58. At that time the above mentioned Odelric, count of the palace, was Berengar's prisoner, and on Lampert's appointment the king entrusted him with the care of his captive until he should decide what to do with him. Lampert however had not forgotten

the amount of money he had paid for his bishopric, and soon
began to discuss the king's irreligious conduct with his charge.

Ch. 59.   A few suns had set when Berengar sent a messenger
ordering Odelric to appear before him. The bishop's reply, as is
well known, was couched in these ironical words:– 'Assuredly I
ought to be deprived of my holy office, if I hand over any man to
one who intends to cut his throat.' The messengers saw that this
refusal to surrender to the king a man whom he had entrusted to
him meant nothing else but open rebellion, and therefore on their
return they made their report in the line from Terence's play:

> If you want it kept securely, hand it over, pray, to him.

Ch. 60.   At this time King Rodulf held sway over the haughty
Burgundians, his great power having been further increased by his
marriage with Berta, daughter of Bruchard the mighty duke of
Swabia. The Italians accordingly now sent messengers to him,
asking him to drive Berengar from the throne.

Ch. 61.   In the middle of their negotiations, however, it happened that without their knowledge a body of Hungarians arrived
at Verona, whose two leaders Dursac and Bugat were close
friends of Berengar. Marquess Adalbert, Count Odelric, Count
Gislebert, and several others were in the mountains near Brescia,
fifty miles from Verona, holding secret meetings to arrange for
Berengar's downfall, when the king sent to the Hungarians,
asking them, if they loved him, to fall upon his enemies. The
Hungarians, who were, as ever, eager for battle and thirsty for
blood, at once agreed. Berengar provided them with a guide who
took them by an unusual route, so that they came upon the
conspirators from the rear and attacked them so quickly that they
had no time to put on armour or snatch up a sword. Many were
captured, many were killed; Count Odelric, who defended
himself manfully, being among these latter, while the Marquess
Adalbert and Gislebert were taken alive.

Ch. 62.   Adalbert was no great man of war, but he was
excessively clever and shrewd. When he saw the Hungarians

bursting in on every side and knew there was no hope of escape, he threw away his belt and golden armlets and any other ornaments of value, and dressed himself up in a soldier's rough coat, so that the Hungarians might not recognize him. Accordingly, when they laid hands on him and asked him who he was, he said that he was a soldier's batman, and prayed them to take him to the neighbouring town of Calcinate, where, he declared, his parents would pay ransom for him. Not being recognized he was taken to the town, and handed over at a very low figure, the actual purchaser being one of his own vassals, a man called Leo.

Ch. 63.   Gislebert for his part was recognized, and after being scourged and put in chains was dragged before Berengar half naked. He had no drawers on and only a short tunic, so that when he fell down hastily on his face at the king's feet the whole company almost died with laughter to see his testicles plainly revealed. King Berengar, however, loving piety as always, listened again to the voice of mercy, although Gislebert did not deserve it, and instead of gratifying the people's wish by returning evil for evil, he had him taken to a bath at once and supplied with rich raiment, and then allowed him to depart, with these words: 'I demand no oath from you. I leave you to your own sense of loyalty; for you know that if you injure me you will have to render account to God.'

Ch. 64.   Gislebert then returned to his own estates and immediately forgot the kindness he had received. As envoy from Adalbert, the king's son-in-law and the others who had joined in the rebellion, he went to persuade Rodulf to come into Italy, and within a month succeeded in his purpose. Rodulf arrived, and obtaining universal support left Berengar nothing but Verona in the whole realm, which he himself forcefully governed for the next three years.

Ch. 65.   Seeing that a man in the course of twelve hours is now satisfied with himself and now dissatisfied, now loves a thing and now hates it, how is it possible that he should always consistently please all men? So before those three years had passed, while some people thought Rodulf a good king, others considered him a

tyrant. The result was that one half of the realm desired Rodulf for
ruler, the other half preferred Berengar. They therefore prepared
for civil war on a wide scale, and since Wido, Bishop of Piacenza,
supported Berengar's faction, they made ready for battle near
Fiorenzuola, twelve miles from Placentia.

> A week had passed in fair July
> Since its tenth day was born,
> And lo! the clouds of civil strife
> Darkened the gloomy morn.
> The sun had scarcely shown his light
> When clarions called each man to fight.
>
> Father slays son – O cruel fate!
> A son his father slays.
> A grandsire lifts the murderous sword
> And ends his grandson's days.
> The Furies fan the flame of strife
> As brother takes his brother's life.
>
> King Berengar speeds through the host;
> King Rodulf with fierce blade
> Wreaks havoc in the crowded ranks,
> As when the corn is laid
> By some black storm with sickle keen;
> And ruin reigns where peace has been.

Ch. 66.   King Rodulf had given his sister Waldrada, a lady who
is still alive and of high repute both for her beauty and her
wisdom, to the powerful Count Boneface, who later in my time
became marquess of Camerino and Spoleto. In company with
Count Gariard he collected a force and came to Rodulf's
assistance; but as he was as shrewd as he was bold, he preferred to
lie in ambush with his men and to await results rather than
encounter the first shock of battle. Rodulf's forces were almost all
in retreat and Berengar's soldiers at the signal of victory were
taking the opportunity to collect the spoils, when Boneface and
Gariard suddenly rushed from their ambush, and routed the
victors the more easily because their attack was so unexpected.
Gariard spared a few of the enemy, striking them with his spear

shaft rather than the blade; but Boneface was merciless and caused fearful havoc in their ranks. He was soon able to sound the signal of victory, and Rodulf's retreating forces having now joined him, they pursued Berengar's men together and forced them to take to flight. Berengar then retired to his wonted shelter in Verona; and in this carnage so great was the number of the slain that even to-day fighting men in this district are scarce.

Ch. 67.   After this success Rodulf subdued the whole realm by force of arms, and coming in haste to Pavia addressed his assembled forces thus:– 'Since by the kindness of heaven's favour it has been granted me to conquer my enemies and secure the throne, it is my desire to commend my realm of Italy to your loyal protection and to visit my old home in Burgundy.' To this the Italians answered: 'If that seems good to you, we are ready.'

Ch. 68.   After Rodulf's departure the people of Verona listened to bad advice and plotted treacherously to take Berengar's life. The instigator of this cruel crime was a certain Flambert, to whose son the king had acted as sponsor at the baptismal fount, thus sharing paternity with the father. Berengar became aware of the plot, and the day before he met his end he summoned Flambert to him and said these words:

Ch. 69.   'If there were not so many good reasons for affection between you and me, then perhaps I might believe what I hear about you. People tell me that you are plotting against my life: but I give no credence to their tales. I want you to remember that every increase of fortune and position you have had would have been impossible had it not been for my kindness. Therefore you ought to be grateful, and let me rest on the throne secure of your affection and loyal support. I think that no man has ever shown such care for his own fortunes and welfare as I have shown for your advancement. All my wishes have centred on that one object, all my exertions, cares and efforts, all my thoughts for the state. Be sure of this: if I see that you remain loyal, my own life will not be so dear to me as the pleasure I shall feel in pious gratitude.'

Ch. 70. When the king had ended thus, he handed him a heavy golden cup and added: 'As a pledge of welfare and affection, drink the contents and accept the container.' After that draught Satan truly and without doubt entered into the other, as it is written of Judas who betrayed Our Lord Jesus Christ: 'After the sop Satan entered into him.'

Ch. 71. Forgetful of the past and present favours he had received Flambert spent a sleepless night urging the people to murder the king. He, for his part, followed his usual custom and took up his lodging, not in the palace which could have been defended, but in a pleasant cottage near the church. Moreover, as he suspected no mischief, that night no guards were set.

> The crowing cock had clapped his wings,
> And loud the brazen bell
> Rang out for men to rise from sleep,
> Casting off slumber's spell,
> And come to God's own house and raise
> To heaven the morning song of praise.
>
> The king was kneeling in the church
> Praying to Him who gave
> This life to men and bade us seek
> A realm beyond the grave;
> When lo! the door was opened wide
> And Flambert waiting stood outside.
>
> A crowd was with him who had come
> In haste their lord to kill.
> The king rose quickly at the noise
> Suspecting naught of ill,
> And when he saw the signs of war
> Cried out to Flambert from afar:—
>
> 'Good sir, what means this turmoil here?
> What seeks this armèd throng?'
> The other answered:— 'Have no fear.
> They would not do you wrong.
> Their aid against those rogues they bring
> Who plot this day to slay their king.'

So trustfully to them he came
Expecting help to find.
Then swift the murderer raised his spear
And smote him from behind.
Down falls the king, and as he falls
Upon God's gracious mercy calls.

Ch. 72. How innocent was the blood these men shed, how perverse their villainy, I need not declare. The stone before the church door with its blood marks is plain evidence to all who pass by. However much they are washed and scrubbed, those stains can never be wiped away.

Ch. 73. Berengar had brought up with all care in his household a youth of heroic character named Milo, a young man well worthy of history's praise. If the king had listened to his advice, he would not have met this so unhappy fate; unless indeed all this was the result of God's providence and could not be altered. Certainly on the night when Berengar was betrayed Milo had brought in soldiers and proposed to have a force on guard for the night. The king however, deceived by Flambert's promises, not only would not have a guard set but strictly forbade Milo to take any precautions. But though he was not able to protect the king in his absence, Milo, like a faithful upright servant not forgetful of the kindness he had received, soon found means to take signal vengeance on his assassin. Three days after the murder he laid violent hands on Flambert and his accomplices, and had them all hanged. There were indeed in Milo manly virtues of high excellence and of them at the proper time I will speak, if God so pleases and life be granted to me.

CONTENTS

BOOK 3

BOOK 3

Ch. 1. I do not doubt, reverend father, that the title of this work causes you some surprise. You say perhaps: 'Since it sets forth the deeds of illustrious men, why is it called *Antapodosis* ('Tit-for-Tat').' My answer is this: The aim and object of this work is to reveal, declare and stigmatize the doings of this Berengar, who now is not king but rather despot of Italy, and of his wife Willa, who because of her boundless tyranny is rightly called a second Jezebel, and because of her insatiate greed for plunder a Lamia vampire. Such shafts of falsehood, such extravagance of robbery, such efforts of wickedness have they gratuitously used against me and my household, my kinsmen and dependents, as neither tongue avails to express nor pen to record. Let this present page then be to them antapodosis, that is, repayment. In return for the troubles I have endured I will unveil to present and future generations their *sacrilège infâme*, that is, the abominable impiety of which they have been guilty. But my book will also be repayment for the benefits conferred upon me by men of sanctity and repute. Of all those whose deeds are recorded, or are worth recording, in history, there are few or none – except only this accursed Berengar of course – for whose kindness the fathers and sons of my family have not to render hearty thanks. Finally, that this book has been written *en captivité*, that is, in my captivity and sojourning abroad, my present exile shows. I began it at Frankfort, a place twenty miles from Maintz, and I am pushing on with it to-day in the island of Paxo, nine hundred or more miles from Constantinople. But let me return to my subject.

Ch. 2. After the death of King Berengar and during Rodulf's absence the mad rage of the Hungarians under Salard's leadership extended through all Italy. Finally they surrounded the city of Pavia with earthworks, and pitching their tents in a circle round the town cut off all exit. The citizens, owing to their past sins, could not resist them in battle nor were they able to appease them by gifts.

Ch. 3.

Now Phoebus passing from the sign of rain
Had to the Zodiac's entrance come again,
And Aeolus to melt the mountain snows
With all the fury of the March wind blows;
When lo, the fierce Hungarians on him call
And fling their torches o'er the city wall.
The breezes spread the flames, nor are the foe
Content with that: on every side they go,
And as the townsfolk from the burning flee
They send them down to death in impious glee.
Our fair Pavia falls consumed in fire,
And Vulcan rising high in windy ire
Through all the city runs his deadly race
And grips our churches in his fierce embrace.
Children fall lifeless at their mothers' sides,
And maids unwed who now shall ne'er be brides.
Even the novices, that sacred band,
Must share the ruin of their native land,
And our good pastor dies in his dear town,
As Bishop John to all the people known.
The gold that we in chests had stored away,
Lest any strangers on it hands should lay,
Runs through the sewers, mixed with mud and mire.
Our fair Pavia falls consumed in fire!
Bright silver bowls to molten metal turn;
The very corpses in the graveyard burn;
Jasper and topaz, beryls, sapphires bright,
Melt in the heat and vanish from men's sight.
The merchants now for gold feel no desire.
Our fair Pavia falls consumed in fire!

Not e'en the Ticinus avails to save
The ships that ride upon its crystal wave;
Their bilges blaze. And soon, ah woe the day!
Our fair Pavia in fire has passed away.

This happened in the year of Our Lord nine hundred and twenty four and in the twelfth indiction period, at nine o'clock in the morning of the twelfth of March, that being the sixth day of the week. I earnestly pray all those who saw that conflagration, and all those who read of it here, to give that disaster the honour of pious remembrance.

Ch. 4. But the sword of the righteous and almighty Lord, of whose judgements and mercy the prophet sings together and whose mercy fills the world, did not rage against us to the end. For though Pavia was burning in punishment for her sins, she was not delivered over into the hands of her enemies. So the words of the prophet king are fulfilled:– 'Will the Lord cast off for ever? And will He be favourable no more? Is His mercy clean gone for ever? Doth His promise fail for evermore? Hath God forgotten to be gracious? Hath He in anger shut up his tender mercies? Selah.' And again another prophet says: 'In wrath remember mercy.' Therefore it was that those of the people who survived the fire offered a stout resistance to the Hungarians and at the end could sing joyfully with the prophet:– 'This is a change wrought by the hand of the Highest.'

Ch. 5. A further help and assistance to us was the intercession in glory of Saint Syrus, our holy father and famous master, whose relics lie in the aforesaid town. It was to fulfil his prophecy that the city of Pavia was brought so near to falling and then was set free by God's mercy. Saint Hermagoras, a disciple of Mark the evangelist, sent Syrus to preach the gospel at Pavia, and the holy father, filled with the spirit of prophecy, honoured her with the following presage:

Ch. 6. 'Rejoice, O city of Pavia, and be glad, for exultation shall come to thee from the mountains without. Thou shalt be called not least among thy neighbouring cities but full of plenty.'

In order that this prophecy might win firmer credence, he that same hour announced the fall of the well known city of Aquileia in these words: 'Woe to thee, Aquileia! Thou shalt fall into the hands of impious men, and thou shalt be destroyed, nor shalt thou be rebuilt and rise again.' That these warnings were fulfilled the plain evidence of our eyes shows. Aquileia, once a great and wealthy city, was taken by Attila, the impious king of the Huns, and completely demolished, nor does there seem at present any chance of its revival. Pavia, however, as the saint predicted, is still called and seen to be a land of plenty. Not only does she surpass her neighbours in wealth but she outshines cities far away. Why mention other places, when glorious Rome herself, the best known city in the world, would be inferior to Pavia if she did not possess the precious relics of the blessed apostles? It is plain therefore that Pavia was saved by the intercession of our patron Saint Syrus who honoured her with so true and precious a prediction. To conclude, after burning Pavia and collecting much booty from all Italy, the Hungarians returned to their own land.

Ch. 7. At this time, Adalbert marquess of Ivrea being now dead, his wife Ermengarde, daughter of Berta and Adalbert marquess of Tuscana, held the chief authority in all Italy. The cause of her power, shameful though it be even to mention it, was that she carried on carnal commerce with everyone, prince and commoner alike.

Ch. 8. About the same time King Rodulf returned from Burgundy to Italy and seized the throne left vacant by Berengar's death. Soon, however, all Italy was in a turmoil of strife. Ermengarde's beauty in this corruptible flesh roused the fiercest jealousies among men; for she would give to some the favours she refused to others. In consequence, the rich archbishop of Milan and some others supported Rodulf, but Ermengarde had so many rebels on her side that they stoutly prevented the king from entering Pavia, the chief city of the realm.

Ch. 9. So King Rodulf collected a force and marched thither, pitching his camp a mile from the town just where the Ticinus and the mighty Po join. Virgil sings the praises of that great river, calling him 'Eridanus, king of rivers' and 'the horned ruler of Hesperia's streams'. Ermengarde thereupon with her usual cunning sent the following letter by night across the river to the king:

Ch. 10. 'If I had wished your ruin, you would have been crushed long ago. Were I but to give my consent, all your men are eager to abandon you and give me their enthusiastic support. You are in such a position that you would have been taken prisoner and put in chains long ago if I had agreed to their proposals.' Not only did the king believe this message but he was so frightened by it that he sent back an envoy to say that he would do whatever she advised. Then things moved quickly. The next night King Rodulf left his army, left his tent, left his bed unslept in, and unseen by the guards stepped on board a boat and hurried off to Ermengarde.

Ch. 11. So in the morning when the soldiers walked round the king's tent they found that all was quiet inside. His captains arrived and were filled with wonder why the king was sleeping at such a strange hour. As once the eunuchs tried to wake Holophernes, so now they tried to wake him by shouting: but he, like Holophernes, made no reply. At last they burst into the tent, only to find that there was nothing there. Some cried that he had been kidnapped, others that he had been murdered: no one could possibly suppose that he had turned deserter. As they wavered between surprise and doubt, news came that Rodulf was on the point of attacking them with their enemies. At this they were seized with consternation and began to retreat with such speed that, if you had seen them, you would have said they were flying rather than running.

Ch. 12. When they reached safety in Milan Archbishop Lampert with every one's consent sent a message to Hugh, the powerful and prudent count of Provence, begging him to come to Italy, drive Rodulf from the throne, and take the kingship himself. Hugh had for a long time been making frequent experiments, to see if he could possibly win the Italian throne. Indeed in the days of the aforesaid King Berengar he had come into Italy with a large force. But he had found that his time was not yet, and Berengar had driven him off in rout.

Ch. 13. Finally Rodulf, not being able owing to the disloyalty of his supporters to overcome his aforesaid enemies, went to Burgundy and proposed to Bruchard duke of Swabia, whose daughter he had married, that he should come to his help. Bruchard immediately collected his forces and set out for Italy with Rodulf; and on their arrival at Ivrea he addressed him thus:

Ch. 14. 'It seems not unsuitable that I myself should go to Milan under pretext of an embassy. I shall thus have the opportunity to reconnoitre the town, and find out the people's inclinations.' He accordingly set out, and on his arrival at Milan, before entering the city, turned aside to pray in the church of the precious saint and martyr Laurence. His real object, people say, was not to offer up petitions but something quite different. As the church is near the city and built of wonderfully costly materials, it is said that he meant to make a stronghold of it and had determined to shut up within its walls not only the chief men of Milan but many of the Italian princes. As he was coming out and was riding near the city walls, he addressed his men in their own, that is, in the German language, thus: 'If I do not make all the Italians use one spur instead of two and spoil the look of the mares they ride, my name is not Bruchard. As for the strength and height of these walls, in whose protection they trust, I snap my fingers at them. By one thrust of my spear I will fling my enemies dead from the rampart.' He said this because he thought that none of his enemies there knew the German language. But unfortunately for him there was a man there, a humble fellow in rags, who was acquainted with that tongue; and he immediately informed Archbishop Lampert of what he had heard. The latter, who was a man of shrewd wit, concealed his suspicions and evil intentions from Bruchard and gave him a very honourable reception; among other things allowing him, as a special privilege, to hunt the stag in his private park, a favour which he never granted to any but his greatest and dearest friends. Meanwhile, however, he invited all the princes of Pavia and some of the Italians as well to come and put Bruchard to death. Then he kept him at Milan until he thought that all those who were to kill him had assembled.

Ch. 15. Accordingly Bruchard at last left Milan and the same day reached Novara. He stayed there the night and arose at dawn to proceed to Ivrea, when suddenly the hosts of Italy appeared and fell upon him. He did not hasten to attack them, as a man of valour should, but attempted to escape. And since, according to the words of Saint Job, his destined end could not be avoided, and a horse is a treacherous safeguard, his mount fell into the ditch that surrounded the city walls and flung him to earth. The Italians at once rushed upon him and stabbed him to death with their spears. His followers, seeing this and having no other means of escape, took refuge in the church of Saint Gaudentius confessor of Christ; but the Italians filled with rage and indignation at Bruchard's threats, broke down the church doors and killed everyone they found there even at the altar.

Ch. 16. When Rodulf heard of this he left Italy and made his way in hot haste to Burgundy. Meanwhile Hugh, count of Arles and Provence, had taken ship and was hastening across the Gulf of Lyons to Italy. God, who wished him to be king of Italy, sent him favourable winds and soon brought him to Alphea, that is, to Pisa, the chief town of the province of Tuscany, of which Virgil sings – 'Pisa of Alphean origin'.

Ch. 17. On his arrival he was met by an envoy from John of Ravenna, Pope of Rome. Envoys from almost all the Italians were also there who invited him earnestly to reign over them. As he had for a long time desired this, he went in haste to Pavia and there was unanimously called to the throne. Soon afterwards he went to Mantua, where Pope John met him and concluded a treaty of alliance.

Ch. 18. At this time Berta, mother of King Hugh, died, and her son Wido by Adalbert, who had married the Roman harlot Marozia, took possession of the march of Tuscany.

Ch. 19. King Hugh was a man of no less learning than boldness, as strong in courage as he was in cunning, a worshipper of God and a lover of those who loved our holy religion, anxious in relieving the needs of the poor and solicitous for the welfare of the church: clerics and scholars he not only loved but treated with signal respect. But all these high qualities were marred by the way he yielded to the allurements of women.

Ch. 20. He had married a princess named Alda, a German Frank by descent, who had borne him a son called Lothair. He had also had at that time by a noble lady called Wandelmoda a son Hubert, who is still alive and is known as a powerful prince in the province of Tuscany. Of Hubert's exploits we will speak, with God's favour, in the proper place.

Ch. 21. When Hugh had thus been made king, being a prudent man he sent envoys all over the world to seek the friendship of kings and princes. He did this to many, but he was especially anxious to win the support of the famous King Henry, who, as we said above, was then ruling over the Bavarians, the Swabians, the Lotharingians, the Franks and the Saxons. He had also subdued the countless Slav tribes and made them tributary. Moreoever he was the first king to subjugate the Danes and make them his vassals. As the result of all this his fame had spread among many nations.

Ch. 22. While King Hugh was thus seeking the friendship of the neighbouring kings and princes, he was also anxious to make his name known to the Greeks in distant lands. At that time they were ruled by the Emperor Romanos, a man well worthy of praise and remembrance, generous, courteous, wise and pious. To Romanos Hugh sent my father as envoy, choosing him because of his upright character and powers of witty speech.

Ch. 23. On my father's arrival, among the other gifts that King Hugh had sent for the Emperor Romanos he led forward two dogs, of a breed that had never been seen before in that country. As soon as they appeared before the emperor they became furious and would have bitten him severely if they had not been restrained by force. I imagine that when they saw his strange dress and the Greek hood that covered his face they thought he was a monster not a man.

Ch. 24.   My father was received by the emperor with signal marks of honour. And this was not so much due to the novelty of his arrival nor the splendour of the gifts he brought, but rather to the fact that on his arrival at Salonica some of the Slavs, who were in revolt against Romanos and were plundering the district, made an attack upon him. By God's grace many of them were killed and two of their chiefs were taken alive in the fighting. When my father brought his prisoners into the emperor's presence, Romanos was excessively pleased and gave him a handsome present, so that he returned to his master King Hugh rejoicing. A few days after his return, however, he was taken ill and went into a monastery, where a fortnight after assuming the monastic dress he died and passed away to the Lord, leaving me, a young child, behind him.

But since I have mentioned the Emperor Romanos, it seems not out of place to insert here an account of his origin and how he made his way to the imperial dignity.

Ch. 25.   In the reign of Leo father of the present Constantine, the Emperor Romanos, although he was *pauvre*, that is, poor, was regarded by everyone as *un homme utile*, that is, as a useful fellow. He was then an ordinary sailor in the emperor's pay serving with the fleet. On several occasions *en bataille*, that is, in battle he rendered services that were *très utiles*, that is, very useful; and finally as a reward his superior officer *donna lui le rang de capitaine*, that is, gave him the rank of captain. One night he went out to reconnoitre the Saracens' position and came to a place where there was a marsh and a thick bed of reeds. At that moment it happened that a fierce lion leaped out from the rushes, and driving a herd of deer into the marsh, seized one of them and proceeded to satisfy on it his ravenous hunger. *Romanos, entendant le vacarme, était très effrayé*, when Romanos heard the noise he was very frightened; for he thought it was a band of Saracens who had sighted him and meant to kill him in an ambush. So the next day he got up *très matinal*, that is very early in the morning, and upon examining the ground discovered the lion's footprints and realized *sur le champ*, that is, immediately what had happened. As the lion was still lurking in the reeds Romanos ordered his men to set them alight with Greek fire, which can only be extinguished by acid. Now in the middle of the reeds there was a raised piece of ground thickly overgrown where the lion took refuge and escaped the flames; for the wind, blowing in the opposite direction, prevented the fire from reaching that spot. When the flames had gone out, Romanos accompanied by a single attendant and carrying only a sword in one hand and a cloak in the other went over all the ground and searched it thoroughly to see if he could find the lion's bones or any other sign of him. He could not find anything and was on the point of returning when he was taken with a fancy to investigate why the hillock had so strangely escaped being burned. So the two men sat down close to it and were talking about something or other when the lion heard them; he could not see them, since his eyes were blinded *par la fumée*, that is, by the smoke. Therefore, wishing to assuage on them the furious anger which the fire had kindled in his breast, the monster crept to the place where he heard voices and with a swift leap landed between them. The servant was panic stricken, but not so Romanos. Determining that 'though the whole world in ruin fall, the crash should strike him undismayed', he flung the cloak he was carrying in his hand between the lion's fore paws. While the beast was tearing at the stuff as though it were a man, Romanos got behind him and using all his strength thrust his sword right through the place where his buttocks joined. As his legs were thus severed and separated one from the other, the lion could not stand and fell in a heap. After having thus killed the lion Romanos looked round for his servant, and seeing him lying some way off half-dead on the ground raised his voice and called loudly to him. The fellow made no reply, and so Romanos went to him and kicking him with his foot cried, '*Lève-toi, pauvre misérable; n'aie pas peur*', that is, 'Get up, you poor miserable, and don't be afraid.' At that the servant got up; but when he saw the monstrous bulk of the lion he could scarcely breathe for admiration. Indeed *tout le monde merveilla au fait de Romanos*, that is, every one was astonished when they heard of Romanos' exploit. And so not long afterwards, as a reward for this glorious deed and for his other services, the emperor gave him the rank of admiral and ordered that *tous les bateaux*, that is, all the ships should be under his control and obey his orders.

Ch. 26. Finally, Leo, the most pious emperor of the Greeks, of whom we have made mention above, paid the debt of mortal life, and trod the path of all human flesh, leaving as his heirs his brother Alexander and his only son Constantine, who is still alive and happily reigning, he being then an infant *ne pouvant pas parler*, that is, not able to talk. As guardians of the palace and his private estate he appointed, as is the custom there, the eunuch who held the office of High Chamberlain and Focas commander in chief of the land forces. To Romanos, who was not a man of high birth but was of signal courage, he gave the post of Lord High Admiral of the fleet. Alexander died soon after his brother and left the little Constantine sole emperor. Now when the great emperor Leo departed from this life to go to Christ, the aforesaid Focas, commander-in-chief of the land forces, had led an army against Simeon king of the Bulgarians and by force of arms prevented his projected advance on Constantinople. Romanos, for his part, being a man of some shrewdness, when he heard of the death of the two emperors Leo and Alexander, got together a body of men from the fleet and collecting his ships made his way to a little island near Constantinople, almost within sight of the imperial palace. He himself, however, never crossed the water and refrained from paying the customary homage to the little emperor who had been born in the purple. This conduct of his caused no small dismay and alarm to the eunuch chamberlain and all the chief men in Constantinople. They therefore sent messengers and enquired the reason of his strange action, asking why he did not pay a visit to the monarch and render him the homage that was his due. Romanos replied that he had avoided the palace because he feared for his own life; and he added that if the chamberlain and the other lords did not come to see him and guarantee him his life and position, he would very soon join the king of the Saracens in Crete, and would help him with all his might to subdue the Greek realm. How cunningly this was said the issue will declare. Well, as we have mentioned, the terrified princes, little guessing that a snake was lurking for them in the grass, came in all confidence to see him, anxious and willing to do all that he wanted. But Romanos, following out his clever plan, as soon as they arrived, had them bound and stowed away in the hold, while he himself, free now from all apprehension, hastened with a numerous band of followers to the city. He there purged the palace of all whom he suspected to be against him and put his own partizans in their place. Governor, superintendents, patricians, accountants, head-steward, lord of the chamber, chamberlains, knights of the sword of all three classes, and sea-lord were now everyone creatures of his own appointment. Finally, to secure the success of his plans completely, he won the affections of Zoë, the little emperor's mother, and was admitted to her intimate favours. All the city was crowned with garlands, and Romanos everywhere was hailed as 'Father of the emperor'.

Ch. 27. General Focas, who himself ardently desired to have that title, heard of what Romanos had done when he was fighting against the Bulgarians and on the point of triumphing over the enemy. So dismayed and indignant was he at the news that he flung down the standard of victory, abandoned his pursuit of the foe, and retiring himself from the field compelled his men to do the same. The Bulgarians, cheered on by Simeon, plucked up courage, and soon were successfully attacking the very army from which just now they had fled in rout. The carnage among the Greeks was prodigious; so prodigious indeed that many years later the battle field still seemed full of bones.

Ch. 28. The aforesaid General Focas then returned in all haste to Constantinople, meaning to break his way into the palace and become 'Father of the Emperor' by force and not by fraud. But as Horace says:

> Brute force devoid of wisdom falls
> By its own weight: but if we blend
> Vigour with wisdom, heaven calls
> Our strength to some great end.

And so it was that the general was taken prisoner by Romanos and had both his eyes put out. The Bulgarians for their part gained a great increase in strength, and they repaid the Greeks two-fold by ravaging their country.

Ch. 29. According to common report their king Simeon was *un demi-Grec*, that is, half a Greek, and in his boyhood was taught at

Byzantium the rhetoric of Demosthenes and the logic of Aristotle. Later on, people say, he abandoned his literary studies and assumed the dress of a monk. But he soon left the calm retreat of a monastery for the storms of this world, and beguiled by desire of kingship preferred to follow in the footsteps of the apostate Julian rather than in those of Saint Peter, the holy keeper of the keys of heaven. He had two sons, one called Bojan, the other Peter, this latter being still alive and now ruling over the Bulgarians. It is said that Bojan was such an adept in the art of magic that he could suddenly turn himself before men's eyes into a wolf or any other beast you pleased.

Ch. 30. The same year that Romanos gained the title 'Father of the Emperor', he married his daughter Helena to his master, the little Emperor Constantine Porphyrogenitus. This latter name means, as I have said before, not 'born in the purple', but born in the Porphyra palace. And since the topic has come up, it may not be out of place to set forth again what I have heard about the birth of this Porphyrogenitus. You will find the previous passage in the first book of this history, from the sixth to the tenth chapter.

Ch. 31. The august Emperor Constantine, from whom the city of Constantinople gets its name, ordered *ce palais*, this palace, to be built and called it Porphyra. His intention was that the successive rulers of his noble should here first see the light of day, and that all the offspring of his line should be called by the glorious title of Porphyrogenitus. Some people therefore say that our Constantine, son of the Emperor Leo, is his descendant. But *la verité de son naissance*, that is, the truth about his birth is as follows.

Ch. 32. The august Emperor Basil, the present emperor's grandfather, was born of a humble family in Macedonia and under the compelling yoke of poverty came to Constantinople where he took service with a certain *abbé*, that is, abbot. The then emperor, Michael, went to the monastery, where he was serving, to offer up prayer, and seeing that he was exceptionally comely called the abbé and asked him to give him the lad. He then took him to the palace and made him his chamberlain; and in a little time he became so powerful that everyone called him the second emperor.

Almighty God is ever just, even when He visits His servants with a heavy hand. He did not allow the emperor to keep sane all his life; but His purpose was that the mercy of His kindness above might equal the severity of His punishment below. We are told that Michael in his mad fits frequently sent off his dearest friends to be beheaded. But when he returned to his senses he would ask for them again, and unless the condemned men were forthcoming their executioners were themselves put to death. His servants accordingly became alarmed, and when he ordered an execution they did not put it into effect. This happened several times to Basil, and finally, his partizans gave him – O shame! – this advice:– 'The king's mad order may some day be carried out designedly, if he gives it to your enemies and not to your friends. You had better kill him first and take the imperial sceptre.' Under the compulsion of fear, and beguiled by desire of rule, Basil carried out this suggestion at once. Michael was murdered and Basil became emperor.

Ch. 33. A short time afterwards Our Lord Jesus Christ appeared to him in a vision, holding the hand of his former master, the emperor, whom he had murdered, and addressed him thus: 'Basil, why did you kill your master here, the emperor Michael?' When he awoke he realized that he had been guilty of a heinous crime, and collecting his thoughts began to consider what he should do.

Ch. 34. Accordingly, comforted by our Lord's acceptable promise of salvation, given by the mouth of His prophet, that on the day when the wicked man turneth from his wickedness he shall be saved, he made confession with tears and groans, and acknowledged himself a sinner, the shedder of innocent blood. He also followed good advice and made friends to himself of the mammon of unrighteousness, helping them here with temporal subsidies that their prayers might release him later from the everlasting fires of hell. Moreover he built near the palace a wonderful and costly church facing eastwards in honour of the archangel Michael, whom the Greeks call general of the hosts of heaven. The church itself is called by some people *la nouvelle église*, that is, the new church; by others *la neuf*, because the clock that marks the office hours always strikes nine.

Ch. 35. Now in the second year after Romanos received the title of 'Father of the Emperor', he called the princes to him and addressed them thus: 'Princes of the Roman state, since on your advice I have received the title of "Father of the Emperor", and furthermore share in the loyalty due to our holy emperor by reason of his marriage to my daughter Helen *des yeux verts*, that is, of the green eyes, I think it only right that I should show upon my person some outward mark of my imperial rank and wear some article of dress that would be to all men a sign of my position.' Accordingly the people decided and it was unanimously decreed that since he was a person of such distinction and by marriage had set on the throne his daughter Helen *des bras blanc*, that is, of the white arms, he should wear the red leather shoes which are there reserved for the emperor. But even that did not satisfy him. After a year had elapsed and his power had become more assured, he addressed the princes again as follows: 'Since it has been decided by your unanimous verdict that I should wear the imperial shoes, I thank you, *très nobles héros*, that is, most noble heroes, for your good will and authority. It seems to me that this is *un don précieux*, that is, a precious gift; but on careful consideration I also think that when I walk abroad I look like an actor or mime, who paints himself in gay colours to raise an easy laugh from the crowd. Indeed I make myself as well as other people smile, for I seem to wear shoes of the imperial pattern and a head dress like that of the common people. "Could there be better farce than this or mime more humorous?" Therefore, either give me the crown or else take away the imperial shoes which make me a common laughing stock.'

This was plain enough, and his words were backed up by the irresistible power of his position. Accordingly by universal consent he was given the crown without having to forfeit the distinction of the shoes. Let no one wonder at his wisdom, but let him from the depth of his heart give praise to God, who lifteth up the oppressed and looseth the prisoners, in whose hand is a cup, and the wine is red; it is full of mixture; and from this to that he poureth out of the same.

Ch. 36. Romanos was of humble origin, an Armenian by birth, and had never thought that he would be admitted to the royal court, much less hold the imperial sceptre. But what says the prophet Hannah? 'The Lord maketh poor and maketh rich: he bringeth low and lifteth up. He raiseth up the poor out of the dust and lifteth up the beggar from the dunghill, to set them among princes and to make them inherit the throne of glory: for the pillars of the earth are the Lord's.' Therefore to the one God, immortal and invisible, be honour and glory world without end. Amen.

Ch. 37. When Romanos finally became emperor, he made his son Christopher, who had been born before his accession, joint ruler with himself; and after he had taken control of the empire his wife bore him a second son named Stephen. Later on she conceived a third time and bore a son who was called Constantine. All these sons Romanos made emperors contrary to human and divine law, and gave his first born Christopher precedence over his rightful master, the emperor Constantine Porphyrogenitus. This he did openly, and when they walked *en procession*, that is, in public procession to Santa Sophia, or at the palace of Blachernai, or at the feast of the Holy Apostles, Romanos with his first born Christopher went in front, Constantine Porphyrogenitus and his other two sons followed behind. With what wrath the Just Judge visited this conduct His subsequent vengeance will show; for soon afterwards Christopher died. And so Constantine Porphyrogenitus commended himself altogether to the Lord's care and spending his leisure in prayer and reading gained a livelihood by the work of his hands. He certainly was a skilful artist, and *ses tableaux*, that is, his paintings were very fine.

Ch. 38. At this same period Simeon of Bulgaria began to press the Greeks very hard. Accordingly Romanos arranged a marriage between the daughter of his son Christopher and Simeon's son Peter, who is still alive. He thus checked the fierce attacks that

Simeon had begun and allied him to himself by a treaty of friendship. As a result the bride changed her name to Irene, which means peace; because of her agency peace was firmly established between the Bulgarians and the Greeks.

Ch. 39. At this period Walpert and Everard Gezo were men of great influence in Pavia and acted as judges there. The reason of Walpert's power was that he had made his son Peter bishop of the rich diocese of Como, and had married his daughter Roza to Gilbert, count of the palace. At that time however both Peter and Gilbert were dead. The people of Pavia were in the habit of coming to him, and arguing all their disputes and law cases in his presence. The aforesaid Everard Gezo had a share of his power, as he was united to him by ties of marriage, and was regarded as a man of weight. Gezo however disgraced his high position by his infamous conduct. He was over-ambitious, greedy, envious, seditious, a corrupter of law, and careless of God's precepts: and these ways God did not allow to go unpunished. Not to make too long a story, Gezo was in all respects like Catiline, and as the Roman tried to murder Marcus Tullius Cicero, the consul and defender of the state, so Gezo plotted to bring King Hugh to death. One day, when Hugh, suspecting no danger, was staying at Pavia with a few attendants, Gezo planned to raise a revolt and fall upon him. Walpert, however, was not of such a violent disposition, and by his intervention the attempt was postponed.

Ch. 40. Still, even these men were checked in their wild schemes by the honeyed blandishments of King Hugh's eloquence. When he was told that a revolt was brewing and that the conspirators were gathered at Walpert's house, he sent envoys to them and addressed them in this language:– 'Why, my brave comrades, are you so strangely wrath with your liege lord and king? If anything has been done that displeases you, there is time to put it right. Even a late reformation will put an end to censure, especially when the delay has not been caused by wilful indifference.' This message considerably appeased their anger, and Gezo was left in a minority of one. He still persisted in his naughtiness, and did his best to get the others to fall upon the king and put him to a shameful death. But by the dispensation of God, his evil purpose was not carried into effect. The messengers accordingly returned to the king and told him all that they had seen and heard.

Ch. 41.   King Hugh then craftily pretended to regard all this as of no importance, and leaving Pavia hastened to a spot some considerable distance away, where by means of messengers and letters he bade his vassals assemble. Among those who came to him was the powerful count Samson, Gezo's bitter enemy. When Samson saw the king he addressed him thus:— 'I have noticed that you are disturbed by the disloyal plot that recently was hatched against you in Pavia. If you listen to me and take my advice, the rebels will be caught in their own snare. It would not be easy to find a man who can suggest a better plan than mine, and I am sure that none will be more advantageous to yourself personally. But there is one thing I ask for. When by my help you have caught the gang, give Gezo with all his goods and chattels into my hands.' On the king consenting to this, he added:— 'Leo Bishop of Pavia is known to be no friend to Walpert and Gezo, and they oppose him in every way they can. You know that it is the custom when the king is on his way to Pavia for the more important citizens to meet him outside the city. Tell the bishop secretly that you are coming to Pavia on a date that you will fix, and instruct him to have all the city gates locked after these fellows have come outside to meet you, and to keep the keys under his own charge. Then, when we begin to arrest them, they will not be able to escape back to the city nor have any help to hope for from the city.' This plan was put into effect. The king came to Pavia at the fixed time, the conspirators came out to meet him, and the bishop gladly carried out his instructions. The king gave orders for them all to be arrested, as he had been advised, and Gezo was handed over to Samson, who put out both his eyes and cut off the tongue which had spoken blasphemy against the king. How happy would it have been if Gezo, besides being blinded, had been rendered dumb for all time! But, shame upon it! though his tongue was cut off he did not lose the power of speech; and the loss of his eyes, according to the Greek story, actually prolonged his life, so that up till to-day he has been a constant source of mischief and calamity.

A merry story in the frivolous Greek fashion, giving the reason why blind men are long lived, may be inserted here. It runs as follows. '*Zeus et Héra se disputèrent au sujet de l'amour, pour savoir si c'etait l'homme ou la femme qui éprouve le plus grand plaisir à la copulation. Ils posèrent alors la question à Tirésias, fils d'Ebros. Celui-ci avait déjà pris successivement les deux sexes, après qu'il avait foulé un serpent aux pieds. Il prononce alors contre Héra, et celle-ci en colère le rendit aveugle. Mais Zeus lui accorda de vivre pendant de longues années et que tout ce qu'il dirait serait de vraies prophéties.*' The translation is this. 'Zeus and Hera argued about love, whether it was the man or the woman who got the greater pleasure from coition. They put the question to Tiresias, son of Ebros; for he, after treading on a snake, had been changed from one sex to the other. He pronounced against Hera, and the goddess in anger made him blind. But Zeus gave him long life and the power of prophecy for ever.'

But let us return to our subject. Gezo, as we have said, was mutilated in body and deprived of all his possessions. Most of his confederates were handed over to guards and put in prison. Walpert the next day was beheaded and his immense treasures seized. Cristina his wife was arrested and cruelly tortured to make her reveal his hidden wealth. From that day not only in Pavia but in all parts of Italy men's fear of the king increased, and Hugh was not treated as a nonentity, as other kings had been, but was honoured in every possible way.

Ch. 42. At this same time Ildoin, bishop of Lüttich, being expelled from his own see, came into Italy to King Hugh, with whom he was connected by ties of marriage. Hugh received him with all honour, and gave him the bishopric of Verona to supply his personal needs. Soon afterwards it happened that Archbishop Lambert died, and Ildoin was ordained in his place as bishop of Milan. With the aforesaid Ildoin there had come a certain monk named Rather, who because of his piety and his knowledge of the seven liberal arts was made bishop of Verona, of which town Milo, whom we have mentioned above, was then count.

Ch. 43. Meanwhile Wido, marquess of the province of

Tuscany, together with his wife Marozia, began to plot vigorously to secure the expulsion of Pope John. This he did owing to the ill feeling that he bore to the Pope's brother Peter; for as for the Pope himself he honoured him as though he had been his own brother. So it happened that while Peter was staying at Rome Wido had a large number of soldiers secretly assembled there. One day, when the Pope and his brother and a few friends were in the Lateran Palace, Wido's and Marozia's men rushed in upon them and killed Peter before his brother's eyes. They then arrested the Pope and put him into prison, where soon afterwards he died. It is said that they put a pillow over his mouth, and cruelly suffocated him. On his death they appointed as Pope Marozia's own son John, whom the harlot had had by Pope Sergius. Not long after these events Wido died, and his brother Lambert was appointed to his offices.

Ch. 44.   Marozia, who was a fairly shameless harlot, after the death of her husband Wido sent envoys to King Hugh, inviting him to come to her and take the famous city of Rome for himself. But this, she declared, could only be done if Hugh married her.

> Why, why, Marozia, yield to Love's fierce fire?
> Why kisses from your husband's kin desire?
> Like proud Herodias would you know the bed
> Of brothers twain and by them both be led
> In wedlock home? Methinks you have forgot
> The words of John the Baptist – 'Marry not
> Your brother's wife, and put her from you now.'
> The laws of Moses do not this allow.
> Marriage with brothers they permit indeed,
> But only when 'tis done to raise up seed
> For one who had no children ere he died;
> And all men know you as a fruitful bride
> Who to your lord bore offspring. You will say –
> 'Our Lady Venus drunken with love's play
> Cares not for things like these.' 'Tis all too true;
> And like an ox to sacrifice King Hugh
> Came at your summons, hoping to obtain
> Rome for himself and as her lord remain.

> O wicked wench, why seek you thus to bring
> Ruin and trouble on a righteous king?
> Shall crime make you a queen? Nay, God's decree
> Ordains that you from Rome shall driven be.

That this is correct all created things, rational and irrational alike, can now perceive.

Ch. 45. At the entrance to the city of Rome there is a fort, wonderfully constructed and wonderfully strong. At its gates is the most important of all the bridges over the Tiber, which every one must cross in entering or leaving Rome, there being no other way out. But passage is only possible by leave of those who hold the fort. The fort itself, to omit further details, is so high that the church upon its summit, built in honour of the glorious archangel Michael, chief of the heavenly host, is called 'the church of the holy angel in the skies'. Relying on the strength of this fort the king left his troops at some distance and came to Rome with only a few attendants. There he was received with all respect by the Romans, but he turned aside from them to the bed of the harlot Marozia in the aforesaid castle, and at his ease in her impure embrace began to regard the citizens with scorn. Now Marozia had a son named Alberic, whom she had borne to the marquess Alberic. One day, when this youth was pouring out water at his mother's bidding for his stepfather Hugh to wash his hands, the king hit him in the face as a chastisement for not pouring the water in a modest and respectful fashion. Alberic determined to avenge this insult, and getting the Romans together addressed to them the following harangue:– 'The majesty of Rome has sunk to such depths of folly that now she obeys the orders of harlots. Could there be anything viler or more disgraceful than that the city of Rome should be brought to ruin by the impurities of one woman, and that those who were once our slaves, the Burgundians I mean, should now be our masters? If he hit me, his stepson, in the face when he had but just come here as our guest, what do you suppose he will do to you when he has taken root in the city? Are you ignorant of the Burgundians' greed and pride? Consider the very derivation of their name. When the Romans conquered the world they took many of these people captive and bade them build themselves houses outside Rome; from which houses they were soon afterwards forced to expel them as a punishment for their insolence. We are told, therefore, that as in their language a gathering of houses not protected by a wall is called a burgh, these folk were named by the Romans 'Burgundians', that is, people expelled from their burgh. If we prefer the name that nature gave them, they are Gauls of the Allobroges tribe. But I would rather trust my own *sagacité*, that is, intelligence; and I say that 'Burgundian' is another form of 'Gurgulian', and that they are so called either from their arrogant and guttural speech, or, more probably, from the way in which they use their gullets to indulge their greed. As soon as they heard this, all the Romans without hesitation deserted King Hugh and elected Alberic as their liege lord. Then, to prevent Hugh having any time to bring in his soldiers, they began at once to besiege the fort.

Ch. 46. It is plain that all this was part of God's dispensation and that it was His will that Hugh should not under any circumstances hold what he had attempted to win so foully by crime. The king, indeed, was so alarmed that he let himself down by a rope on the side where the fort touched the city wall, and deserting his lady made his escape back to his own men. King Hugh and the aforesaid Marozia being thus expelled, Alberic became sole ruler of Rome, while his brother John ascended the papal throne, the supreme and universal.

Ch. 47. Some people say that Berta, King Hugh's mother, never herself bore a son to her husband the marquess Adalbert but that she foisted Wido and Lambert off upon him, pretending to be with child and procuring the infants secretly from other women. Her purpose, they declare, was to have sons by her side after Adalbert's death, and by their aid to get possession of all her husband's offices. It seems to me however that this tale is a lie invented by King Hugh to cloak his own vices and to escape from *le scandale*, that is, the scandal caused by his improper conduct. An even more probable reason, I think, why the tale was put about is afforded by the circumstances I have now to relate. Lambert, who after his brother Wido's death took control of the march of Tuscany, was a man of warlike spirit ready for every sort of enterprise. King Hugh suspected him of designs on the throne of Italy, and was very much afraid that the Italians would desert him and make Lambert king. Boso for his part, being King Hugh's brother by the same father, was very anxious himself to become marquess of Tuscany, and was lying in wait, ready to entrap Lambert. Accordingly on Boso's advice King Hugh sent a threatening message to Lambert, warning him not to call himself his brother any longer. To that Lambert, who was of a proud and undisciplined temper, instead of replying modestly, as he should have done, returned the following violent answer:— 'The king cannot possibly deny that I am his brother and that we both came to life by the same passage and from the same body. This truth I desire to prove by the ordeal of single combat in the sight of all men.' The king, hearing this, chose a certain youth named Teudin, who challenged Lambert to a duel on this score. But God is just and of righteous judgement, in Him there is no iniquity. To put a stop to any doubt and to reveal the truth to all He decreed that Teudin should be overcome immediately, and Lambert gain the victory. At this result King Hugh was greatly disturbed, but following his counsellor's advice he took Lambert and put him in prison, fearing, if he let him go, that he would rob him of the throne. He then handed over the march of Tuscany to his brother Boso, and soon afterwards put out Lambert's eyes.

Ch. 48. At this time the Italians sent to Burgundy asking Rodulf to come to them. King Hugh learned this and himself sent envoys offering Rodulf all the territory in Gaul which he himself had held before he ascended the Italian throne. Rodulf then gave him his oath that he would never come into Italy. Hugh also won the friendship of the valiant King Henry, whom we have mentioned before, by the gift of many presents, Henry being at that time very famous in Italy since he had subdued the Danes unaided and made them tributary, although they had never before been conquered. They are a wild people living on the shores of the northern ocean and their savage attacks have often brought sorrow to the nobility of many lands. At times they have come up the Rhine with their fleets, and have laid whole districts waste with fire and sword. Once they actually stormed the noble cities of Agrippina, now called Cologne, and Treves, which is some way off the Rhine, together with other towns in Lothair's realm. From them they carried off everything, and what they could not take they burned, even setting fire to the public baths and palaces at Aachen. But we must leave these matters and return to the order of our narrative.

Ch. 49. Arnold, duke of the Bavarians and Carentanians, whom we have mentioned above, being not far from Italy, got an army together and marched down to drive Hugh from the throne. He made his way through the march of Trient, the first in that part of Italy, and arrived at Verona. There he was gladly welcomed by Count Milo and Bishop Rather, who had invited him to come. King Hugh hearing of this collected his troops and advanced against him.

Ch. 50. On approaching Verona Hugh sent his chevaliers, as the people call them, to scour the country, and a battle ensued between them and a large force of Bavarians from the castle of Gossolengo. The Bavarians were completely routed and scarcely a man escaped to tell the news. At this Duke Arnold was greatly disturbed and on the advice of his counsellors determined to leave Italy and take Count Milo back with him to Bavaria, so that when he had recruited a fresh army he might return again in his company.

Ch. 51. Milo was aware of his intention, and distracted by conflicting thoughts was quite at a loss to know what he should do. His past conduct made him afraid to approach King Hugh, while he considered that to be taken off by Arnold to Bavaria was worse than death and as bad as hell fire. In this uncertainty, since he knew that Hugh was easily moved to compassion, he decided to escape from Arnold and make his way to the king. Arnold for his part returned with all possible speed to Bavaria.

Ch. 52. Before he went, however, he stormed the castle of Verona and took back to Bavaria with him Milo's brother and the soldiers who had tried to defend the place. On his departure the city was handed back to King Hugh, and Bishop Rather, being taken prisoner was sent into exile at Pavia. There he wrote a book describing in witty and elegant language the sorrows of his banishment. Those who read his narrative will find in it many polished thoughts suggested by that occasion, which will afford them as much pleasure as benefit.

CONTENTS

BOOK 4

BOOK 4

Ch. 1. Up to this point, reverend father, I have set out my narrative as I heard it from the lips of reputable witnesses. The rest of my story I shall relate from my own personal knowledge; for at this period I held a certain position at court, in that I had won the favour of King Hugh by my sweet voice. He was passionately fond of singing, and in that respect none of the boys who were my contemporaries could surpass me.

Ch. 2. King Hugh, seeing that everything was prospering with him, appointed as his successor his son Lothair, whom he had had by his wife Alda, and secured universal agreement to his choice. This done, he began to consider how he might gain possession of Rome from which he had been ignominiously ejected. Accordingly he collected a large force and set out. But though he devastated the regions and provinces round about in lamentable fashion and made daily attacks on Rome itself, he was not able to discover any method of forcing an entrance.

Ch. 3. At last, hoping to deceive Alberic by guile, he offered him in marriage his daughter Alda, sister of his son King Lothair, promising him that on these terms he should enjoy peace and security as being a member of his family. Alberic accordingly, who was not without sagacity, accepted his daughter as wife, but regarded him still with distrust and refused to satisfy his eager desire for the possession of Rome. It is true that King Hugh would eventually have ensnared and trapped Alberic *avec cet hameau*, that is, with this hook, if he had not been deceived by the treachery of his own men, who did not wish for any long peace between the two rulers. Any of his people that the king meant to chastise always used every effort to escape and take refuge with Alberic, whose apprehension of the king's plans induced him to receive them favourably and give them a place of honour in Rome.

Ch. 4. Meanwhile the Saracens, who were living at Fraxinetum, got a number of men together and advanced as far as Acqui, which is but fifty miles from Pavia. *Leur chef*, that is, their chief, the Saracen Sagittus was one of the worst and most impious of men. But by the grace of God when the battle took place *le misérable*, that is, the wretch, was killed with all his followers.

Ch. 5. About the same time at Genoa, a city in the Cottian Alps eight hundred furlongs from Pavia on the African Sea, a fountain ran copiously with blood, plainly showing that some disaster would soon befall all the inhabitants. In that same year indeed the Africans with a huge fleet arrived there, and taking the people by surprise burst into the city, massacred every one except the children and women, and putting on board ship all the treasures belonging to the city and to God's churches sailed back to Africa.

Ch. 6. At this time, King Hugh's authority being now recognized, Manasses bishop of Arles, who was connected with Hugh by ties of marriage, left the church that had been entrusted to his care, and inspired by ambition made his way to Italy to violate and mangle many of the churches there. King Hugh, hoping to hold his throne more securely if he bestowed the various offices of government upon his own relatives, against all human and divine law handed over to him – or more exactly gave him as a bait – the churches of Verona, Trient and Mantua. But Manasses was not satisfied even with this: he took also the march of Trient, and at the devil's instigation became a soldier and ceased to be a bishop. *Mon saint père*, that is, my holy father, I would fain halt for a moment here, and after giving his own reasons for this conduct flay them, by God's grace, with mine.

Ch. 7. 'Saint Peter,' he says, 'after founding the church at Antioch hastened across the sea to the city of Rome, which then by the greatness of her power was mistress of the whole world. He there, by God's dispensation, founded the holy church which claims universal veneration, handing over his former church, that of Antioch, to his disciple, St Mark the evangelist. But before that he also established the church of Aquileia and made a hasty journey to Alexandria. That this was so we are sure every one knows who has read the Acts of the Apostles.' In answer to this, Manasses, I would have you know that your ideas on these subjects are incorrect, and you must understand that your parents realized the true meaning of your name. Manasses signifies 'the forgetful one' or 'forgetfulness of God'. How could your parents have foretold the future more exactly or more plainly than by giving you this name? You are so self forgetful, I repeat, that you do not even remember that you are a human being. The devil knows the Scriptures, and being himself perverse interprets them perversely, using them not to save but to destroy men. Do you not know that when he impiously attempted to wound Our Lord and Redeemer Jesus Christ with the weapons of temptation, he made evil use of these prophetic words: 'He has given his angels charge over thee, to keep thee: and in their hands they shall bear thee up, lest at any time thou dash thy foot against a stone.' That this was so written and that it refers to Our Lord no one of the faithful doubts. But how treacherously Leviathan brought forward these words of truth you can understand by the reply given by Him who surpasses the understanding not only of men but of angels. 'Thou shalt not tempt', He said, 'the Lord thy God.' You see therefore; and yet you make assertions that are true but full of guile. They are like the reply which the apostate Julian is said to have given to the Christians whom in greed for plunder he had cheated of their property:— 'Your master said, "Provide neither gold nor silver in your purses."' And again:— '*Il est plus aisé qu'un chameau passe par le trou d'une aiguille, qu'il ne l'est qu'un riche entre dans le royaume de Dieu*', that is, 'It is easier for a camel to go through the eye of a needle, than for a rich man to enter into the Kingdom of God.' And also:— 'Whosoever he be of you that forsaketh not all that he hath, he cannot be my disciple.' Come now, can we think that the perversity of these replies of Julian is worse than the foulness of your assertions? What Peter did in the way of righteousness you transfer to the cause of wrong. I for my part believe that you do not understand the Acts of the Apostles, or, what is more probable, that you have never read them. You will find it there plainly written, that the faithful sold their lands and houses and laid the price at the apostles' feet. Everything was in common and no man said that anything was his own: distribution was made to every man according as he had need. Gold is in men's estimation the most precious of all things and to you it is dearer than your own soul. If Peter then refused to touch it, regarding it as pestiferous, how can you justify your assertion that he deserted the church of Antioch and hastily transferred his presence to the church of Rome? If you blatantly declare – it is a villainous lie – that he sought money, I can prove that it was souls to be gained and a glorious martyrdom that he desired. It had been foretold him by his Master, or rather by his Creator and Redeemer, that: 'When thou wast young, thou girdedst thyself and walkedst whither thou wouldest: but when thou shalt be old, thou shalt stretch forth thy hands, and another shall gird thee, and carry thee whither thou wouldest not.' This He said signifying by what death Peter would give glory to God. Again it is said in another place that when after the resurrection Peter asked Our Lord where He was going, He replied: 'To Rome, to be crucified a second time.' Peter came to Rome then, not puffed up with ambition but animated by the spirit of martyrdom, seeking not gold but treasure of souls. How happy, nay how blessed, would you be if your conscience testified that you were such as he! You cannot deny that you sold the bishopric of Verona for a small sum, a thing which we are nowhere told was done by the apostle Peter. By that it is plain that in your desire for gain you have lost all sense both of temporal and spiritual honour. Let this here suffice while I return to my narrative. In its due place by God's favour I will describe how you laid claim to the bishopric of Milan.

Ch. 8.   At that time the caitiff Berengar, under whose tyranny all Italy is now groaning, was known as marquess of Ivrea. King Hugh gave him in marriage his niece Willa, the daughter of his brother Boso, marquess of the province of Tuscany, and Boso's wife Willa. Moreover Anscar, Berengar's brother, son of Adalbert and of Ermengarde, Hugh's sister, was then at the height of his power and confidence.

Ch. 9. In addition to this the hero Tedbald, a close connection of Hugh's by marriage, was marquess of Camerino and Spoleto. He went to the help of the prince of Benevento against the Greeks who had pressed him grievously hard, and attacking them in a regular campaign gained the victory. It happened that he captured a number of the Greeks who had been driven from the country side but were still holding some forts. These men he castrated, saying to the general who commanded them: 'I understand that your holy emperor attaches a special value to eunuchs, and therefore I have hastened to send him a few with my respects, and by God's grace will send him more very soon.'

Ch. 10. Let me here insert the story of a witty, or rather a clever, trick which a certain woman played on this occasion. One day some Greeks in company with the men of the countryside went out from a fortress to fight against the aforesaid Tedbald, and a certain number of them were taken prisoners by him. As he was taking them off to be castrated, a certain woman, fired by love for her husband and very disturbed for the safety of his members, rushed out in a frenzy from the fortress with her hair all flying loose. Tearing her cheeks with her nails until the blood came, she took her stand before Tedbald's tent and began to cry out and wail aloud. At last Tedbald appeared and said to her: 'What is the matter with you, woman, that you are making such a loud and lamentable din.' To that – a pretence of folly is at the proper time the height of wisdom – she replied: 'These are strange and unheard of doings, heroes, to make war against women who cannot attack you back. None of our daughters are descended from the stock of the Amazons. We devote our lives to Minerva's work and are quite ignorant of weapons.' Tedbald then said to her: 'What hero in his right mind ever made war upon women, except in the days of the Amazons?' 'What more cruel war', she answered, 'can you make on women, or what more grievous loss can you inflict upon them, than to seek to deprive their husbands of that member on which the warmth of our bodies depends and in which, most important of all, our hopes of children in the future are centred. By castrating our men you rob them of something which is not theirs but ours. I ask you, did the flocks of sheep and the herds of cattle that you took from me last week bring me as a suppliant to your camp? I willingly agree to give up the animals, but this other loss, so serious, so cruel and so irreparable, I shudder at, I shrink from, I refuse. May all the Gods above protect me from such a calamity!' At this the whole army burst into a guffaw, and her arguments were received with such favour that they earned for her not only the return of her husband intact but also of the beasts that had been driven away. As she was going off with her belongings Tedbald sent a page after her to ask what part of her husband he should remove if he came out again from the fortress to fight against him. 'My husband', she said, 'has a nose, eyes, hands and feet. If he comes out again, let your master remove those parts that belong to him; but let him leave me, his humble servant, what is mine.' Such was the answer she sent back by the messenger, for she realized, by the laughter that her first speech had evoked and by the return of her husband, that she had the favour of the army on her side.

Ch. 11. About that time King Hugh's brother Boso at the instigation of his wife Willa, the most greedy of women, endeavoured most perversely to start a revolt against the king. The plot did not escape Hugh's vigilant eye, and Boso was taken prisoner at once and put in custody. The cause of his downfall was as follows. When Lambert, as we have recorded above, had his eyes put out, Boso became marquess of Tuscany, and his wife Willa was fired with such a passion of greed for gold that not a single noble matron in all the province dared to adorn herself with any jewellery of the slightest value. This Willa had no male children, but she had four daughters, Berta, Willa, Richilda and Gisla. Of these four Willa, fitly married to the Berengar who is still alive, has rendered it possible for her mother not to be the worst woman ever born. I will not describe her conduct in a tedious and winding narrative: from one disgusting scene you will be able to judge how far she went in other matters.

Ch. 12. Willa's husband Boso had a belt of exceptional length and breadth, enriched with a large number of precious gleaming stones. When Boso was caught, the king confiscated his possessions and ordered that for this belt more than for any other of his treasures diligent search should be made. As for Willa, whom he regarded as the criminal responsible for the whole plot, he gave instructions that she should be ignominiously expelled from Italy and sent back to her native land of Burgundy. The most careful scrutiny, however, failed to discover the belt, and when his messengers returned to Hugh with the other articles this was still missing. Thereupon the king cried out to them: 'Go back and cut open his horse's trappings, even the cushioned saddle upon which he rides. If you do not find the belt there, strip the queen of all her clothes and make sure that she has not got it concealed upon her. I know well how cunning and avaricious she is.' The messengers accordingly retraced their steps, and as their search again proved fruitless, in obedience to the king's orders they stripped the queen completely naked. All the honest soldiers turned their eyes away rather than behold such a shameful and unprecedented sight; but one of the servants ventured to look keenly at her and saw a piece of string hanging close by the round and rosy hemispheres of her buttocks. This string the shameless rascal caught and pulled: and lo and behold, the belt made its appearance from the very intimate retreat where it had been hidden. The man, so far from blushing at his disgusting act, burst into a laugh. 'Ha, ha, ha!' he cried, 'we soldiers know something of midwifery. Here is a ruddy youngster for the mistress. I hope he will get on well. What luck it would be for me and how happy I should feel, if my wife would bear me two such pretty dears! I would send them as ambassadors to Constantinople; for if you believe the pedlar's tales the Emperor is always very glad to receive such envoys.'

These jibes so distressed Willa that she burst into tears and revealed to all the secret pain of her heart. But the servant, as is the way with such people, so far from being moved by her distress, was encouraged by it, and to increase the pain of the wound cried out:

> 'What madness, Willa, thus to store up gold
> In the recesses of your private hold!
> Are you a Fury that you have the face
> To use your body as a jewel case?
> No mother e'er on sweeter offspring smiled,
> Though this, methinks, was scarce a ten month child.
> Go on, dear lady, and produce some more,

> And as each darling comes, we'll cry – "Encore".'
> So jeered the rascal, till a captain gruff
> Gripped the knave's neck and said 'Avast that stuff'.

This finished the business: the belt was taken to the king, and the lady was packed off to Burgundy. Whether it was the hider or the searcher who showed the greater lack of decency is a very ticklish question. But it is obvious that both Hugh and Willa were inspired by an excessive love of jewels and gold.

Ch. 13. At this time Rodulf king of the Burgundians died, and as Alda mother of his son King Lothair had just passed away, King Hugh contracted a marriage with Rodulf's widow Queen Berta. He also gave his son Lothair for wife the daughter who had been born to Rodulf and Berta, a lady named Adelaide, charming both by the beauty of her person and the excellence of her character.

To all the Greeks this seems improper; namely that if a father takes a mother to wife and makes with her one body, the son should also be able without sin to join the daughter in marriage with himself.

Ch. 14. Hugh, however, beguiled by the allurements of his many concubines, soon began not only to refuse his aforesaid wife Berta the affection due from a husband, but even heartily to detest her. How justly he was punished by God for this, I shall be glad to describe in the proper place. He had a number of concubines, but for three especially he entertained an ardent and most disgraceful passion. The first called Pezola, a woman of the lowest servile origin, by whom he had a son named Boso, appointed by him after Wido's death as bishop of the church of Piacenza. The second was Roza, daughter of the Walpert whom we have mentioned above as having been beheaded, who bore him a daughter remarkable for her beauty. The third was a Roman named Stephania, who also had by him a son Tedbald, afterwards made archdeacon of Milan with the proviso that on the archbishop's death he should be his successor.

How it was that God did not allow this arrangement to be carried out, the course of my narrative will reveal, if life be granted me. The people in remembrance of the shameless beauty contest gave these three women the names of the three goddesses. Pezola was known as Venus; Roza as Juno, because of her continual bickerings and jealousy of her rival, who in the corruption of this flesh seemed more beautiful than herself; Stephania was called Semele. As the king was not the only man who enjoyed their favours, the children of all three are of uncertain parentage.

Ch. 15. At that time King Henry was taken with a serious illness in the castle of Membleben on the borders of Turingia and Saxony and soon afterwards passed away to his Maker. His body was taken to Quedlinburg in Saxony, a nunnery of pious and high born women situated on the king's own estate, and was laid to rest with all due veneration inside the nunnery chapel. There the venerable Matilda, Henry's wife, consort and kinswoman, still lives, and there, surpassing all wives whom I have ever seen or known, she ceases not to perform the office of the dead in expiation of past offences and to offer to God a living sacrifice. Before her husband came to the throne she bore him a son whom he called Otto, that great monarch, I mean, by whose might the northern and the western countries of our universe are governed, by whose wisdom they are given peace, in whose piety they rejoice, and at whose just severity in judgement they tremble. After his accession she bore two more sons, one called Henry after his father, a youth of gracious wit and prudent counsel, fair and comely of face, mild and watchful of eye. He has but recently passed away and we are still shedding for him streams of tears. The third, called Bruno, was sent by his revered father to do battle for the recovery of Utrecht after the Normans had completely destroyed the church there. However, I will deal with their doings more fully in the proper place. Let me now return to my narrative.

Ch. 16. How prudent was King Henry and how wise may be proved by the fact that he chose as his successor the most capable and the most pious of his sons. Your death threatened destruction to your whole people, most prudent King, if the successor to your regal dignity had not been a man as great as yourself. Therefore I have composed the following lines in honour of you both:

Thou, who the impious didst quell
With fire and sword in days gone by,
Art dead: and now we know too well
How great is our calamity.

But let the people dry their tears
Nor weeps the dear lord who has gone.
To all the world this day appears
The father's image in the son.

Otto shall bring the world beneath
His sway, that peace and concord gives.
All that we lost by Henry's death
Is paid us back while Otto lives.

Gentle and merciful and mild
To all believers is our king.
But to the foemen fierce and wild
Death and destruction he will bring.

Some wars, dear lord, remain to fight,
And then thy fame to heaven will rise
And every man confess thy might
Beneath the stars of northern skies,

And in those lands that take their name
From Hesperus, the evening-born,
Who when he comes with orient flame
Is Lucifer, the star of morn.

Ch. 17.   Before he came to the throne King Otto had married an English lady of high rank, Otwith niece of King Athelstan, and by her had a son named Liutolf. Whenever I remember that son's recent death my bosom is filled with tears. O would that he had never been born, or else had not met so early an end!

Ch. 18.   At this time Henry, King Otto's brother, on the instigation of some perverse advisers took up an attitude of hostility. For he who after winning the glorious honour of creation wished to make himself like to his Creator, by the mouth of his followers stirred up Henry against his brother – nay more, against his king and master – with words like these: 'You were born in the royal state, your brother was not. Do you think that your father acted rightly in preferring him to you? Obviously he did not give due weight to the difference of birth; he was led astray by excessive partiality. Come then, you will find men to help you. Turn your brother off the throne and take it yourself. The regal dignity should be yours, since by God's favour you were born in it.'

Ch. 19.

> Good Saxon prince, why this insane desire
> To mount the throne? 'Tis not thy noble sire
> But God himself forbids, at whose command
> He placed the sceptre in thy brother's hand.
> All things on earth God's ordinance obey;
> He rules the stars, the seasons own His sway.
> God sets up kings, God gives them power to try
> The crimes of men, God gives them victory.
> Thou monstrous serpent, full of guile and spite,
> Wouldst thou once more urge brothers twain to fight
> And at thy word that ancient strife recall?
> On thee, foul fiend, the punishment shall fall.
> For all the wrong that in this world is done
> Thou, wretched traitor, thou shalt pay alone;
> And thy huge frame those fiery chains shall bind
> That are to sinners as their due assigned.
> Begone to thy just place, the flames of hell,
> Nor think that Christians there will burn as well
> For ever by thy side. By grace of heaven
> Forgiveness to the erring soul is given,
> And Jesus' blood avails to wipe away
> The penalty that justly it should pay.

Ch. 20. Count Everard was the man who enticed Henry into this foul and nefarious plot. Up to the time of this first revolt Henry had always rendered due assistance to his brother, his king and overlord, and had used every effort in subduing his enemies. But it is the case, not only with those who are occupied with temporal affairs but even with those who have devoted themselves to eternity and are wrapped in the visions of mystic contemplation, that carelessness sometimes leads to a fall; and as Vegetius Renatus says in his treatise on warfare:– 'a security greater than needful is wont to be especially dangerous'. While Henry was staying in a certain town and not taking any precautions against attack, the aforesaid Everard got a force together and besieged him, and before the king his brother could come to his assistance took the place by storm and carried off Henry with a large amount of treasure to his own lands. The king therefore, anxious to avenge his brother's, or rather his own, disgrace, started a vigorous campaign against Everard and his confederates.

Ch. 21. Everard, it must be said, had seduced Gislebert duke of Lorraine from his loyalty to the king, and with his help put up an active resistance. For though Gislebert had married the king's sister, inspired by hope of gaining the throne he preferred to resist the king rather than do his duty and help him against his rivals. When, however, the confederates saw that even so they could not hold their own, they agreed to a plan, subtle in the eyes of man but foolish in the eyes of God, and addressed Henry as follows:–

Ch. 22. 'If you promise under oath to do what we advise, not only are we ready to release you from captivity but, what is more important, we recognize you as our overlord if you wish to become king.' They said this, not with any idea of putting their words into effect, but in order that they might with his help the more easily beat the king.

Ch. 23. The king had certainly some very strong helpers, namely, Hermann duke of Swabia, Hermann's brother Udo, and Conrad surnamed the Wise. Though these three were bound to Everard by ties of marriage they preferred to die justly, if fate so decreed, with their rightful king rather than to triumph unjustly with their kinsman. Henry accordingly, deceived by the promise made to him, soon collected forces of his own and began with all his might to help the rebels in their struggle against the king. But as it is written 'Iniquity lieth to itself', I would fain pause for a moment and explain how on this occasion iniquity played itself false. Everard had only been able to seduce Gislebert from his allegiance to the king by promising to put him on the throne. Gislebert meant to deceive Henry in the same way; to overcome the king by his help, and then depose him and take the kingship for himself. Everard for his part had quite other intentions. He meant, if he succeeded in beating the king, to rob both his confederates and take the throne. This we may infer from his own words addressed to his wife some time before his death. He was fondling her close when he said: 'Take your pleasure now in a count's arms: you will soon be rejoicing in a king's embrace.' That things turned out otherwise and that iniquity was false to itself is proved by the present state of affairs.

Ch. 24. So then, as we have said, encouraged, or rather entrapped, by this promise Henry collected an army and with Gislebert and Everard prepared to attack the king, while the latter gladly hastened against them, not alarmed by their numbers but trusting in God's protection. That you may know how easy it is for God to conquer a host with a handful of men, and how 'no one shall be saved by the abundance of his own valour', hear the way in which Our Lord repeated a miracle of the past.

The king's soldiers had reached the Rhine at a place called Birten, and had already begun to cross the river, unaware that Henry with his aforesaid confederates was in the near neighbourhood. A few men had landed from the boats and were just able to mount their horses and put on their armour, when with their own eyes they saw the enemies' forces advancing to the attack before they had received any warning of their approach. They therefore addressed one another with these mutual exhortations:— 'The size of this river, as you see, prevents our comrades from coming to our help, and also bars our retreat, even if we wished to retire. We know also full well how ridiculous it would seem, especially among nations of our character, for brave men to surrender to the enemy, escaping death indeed by non-resistance but only winning life at the price of eternal ignominy. The fact that we have no hope of retreat – which is rather a disadvantage to the enemy – and the everlasting shame that we should earn by surrender, both inspire us with confidence; and there is a further motive that urges us to fight, namely the truth and justice of our cause. Even if our earthly habitation be destroyed in resisting unrighteousness, we shall gain in heaven a home not made by hands.' Fired by these words they advanced at full speed and fell upon the ranks of their foes. The king for his part, thinking that his men were not without divine inspiration in showing this courage, since the intervening stream prevented him from helping them with his bodily presence, remembered how the Lord's people had overcome the Amalekites' attack by the prayers of Moses, the servant of God. Accordingly he leaped down from his horse and with all his army burst into tearful prayer, kneeling before the victory-bringing nails that had once pierced the hands of Our Lord and Saviour Jesus Christ and were then fixed upon his spear. What strength the prayers of a righteous man possess, according to Saint James' words, was then plainly revealed. As he prayed, before a single man on his side had fallen, the enemy all turned in flight, some of them not knowing in the least why they were retreating, since their pursuers were so few that they could not see them. Many of them were killed and Henry was struck heavily on the arm. The triple mail of his cuirass prevented the sword from piercing his flesh, but the cruel force of the blow turned the skin completely black. In spite of all his doctors' care the bruise never healed and caused him every year excruciating pain. Indeed it was acknowledged that his death many years later was due to this injury. But as I have made mention of the sacred spear, let me here give an account of how it came into the king's possession.

Ch. 25. Rodulf, king of the Burgundians, who for some years ruled over the Italians, received this spear as a gift from Count Samson. It was of a different appearance from ordinary spears, of a novel shape and constructed in a novel fashion, with apertures on either side of its waist. In front of the thumb pieces two fine cutting edges extend sloping down to the middle of the spear. It is said that it once belonged to Constantine the Great, son of Saint Helena who found the life-giving cross. At the raised part in the middle, which above we called the waist, there are crosses made from the nails that once pierced the hands and feet of Our Lord and Redeemer Jesus Christ. King Henry, who was a God-fearing man and a lover of all sacred things, when he heard that Rodulf possessed this inestimable heavenly treasure, sent envoys to see if he could at any cost acquire it, and so gain for himself an invincible weapon against all enemies, visible and invisible, and make perpetual triumph certain. Rodulf at first declared that he would never give it up, and so Henry, unable to soften him by gifts, did his best to frighten him with threats, swearing that he would lay his whole kingdom waste with fire and sword. But as the gift he sought was that thing whereby God had joined the things of earth to the things of heaven, the corner stone that makes both one, the heart of King Rodulf at last softened and to the just king justly asking for what was justly his he handed over the spear. In the presence of peace there was no room for strife. By Him who was crucified on these nails, passing from Pilate to Herod, the two kings, who had been mutual enemies, were on that day made friends. What love was inspired in Henry's heart by the gift of this inestimable treasure was shown in many ways and especially in this: not only did he honour the giver with presents of gold and silver, but he handed over to him a large district in the province of Swabia. God who sees into men's hearts and knows the purpose of their actions, considering and rewarding not the size of the gift but the giver's good will, showed at this time by certain evidence what a reward He bestowed upon the pious king for his expenditure. With this sign going before him and bringing him victory, Henry routed and put to flight the enemies who had risen up against him. Such was the occasion, or rather such was the will of God, when Henry gained possession of the sacred spear, which on his death he handed down with the inheritance of his throne to his son, of whom we are now speaking. With what veneration Otto has cherished that inestimable gift is shown both by his present victory, and by the admirable generosity of his gifts to God, which we are about to relate. So it was then that King Henry returned home after terrifying and routing his foes, not so much rejoicing in his victory as elated by the proof of God's compassion towards him.

Ch. 26. I would fain pause for a moment and show that this result was not due to chance but to God's directing hand. That will be proved clearer than the light of day if we consider the appearance of Our Lord and Saviour Jesus Christ to the women and disciples after the resurrection. Thomas knew well the faith of Peter and the love of John who at supper leaned on Jesus' bosom; he had heard that they had run to the sepulchre and found nothing but the linen clothes; he was aware that angels had appeared in a vision to the women and assured them that He was still alive. Well and good: perhaps he had considered it women's weakness and refused to believe them. Come, Saint Thomas, say I, even if you do not believe the two disciples who were hastening to the fort of Emmaus, to whom He not only appeared but also expounded the scriptures written concerning Himself, and furthermore, according to His wonted custom, blessed their bread and broke it and gave it to them; still why do you persist in refusing credence to all your fellow disciples to whom He appeared when the doors were shut? Do you remember that your Lord and Teacher, by whose side you promised you would die, foretold all this before His passion? He said: 'Behold, we go up to Jerusalem, and all things that are written by the prophets concerning the Son of man shall be accomplished. For he shall be delivered unto the Gentiles, and shall be mocked, and spitefully entreated, and spitted on; and they shall scourge him and put him to death: and the third day he shall rise again.' Why then do you doubt His resurrection, when you see Him, as He foretold, delivered unto the Gentiles, scourged, spitted on and crucified? Not without reason is it that you insist on touching God with your own hands. Our Lord Himself who before all time assured us our salvation, who knows all things before they happen, had foreseen in His mercy and kindness that many would perish by such an error as this. And so He said: 'Reach hither thy finger and thrust thy hand into my side: and be not faithless but believing.' *Parle, St Thomas*, that is, speak out, St Thomas, and by your doubting save us from any future hesitation. 'My Lord,' said Thomas, 'my Lord and my God.' O doubter worthy of all praise! O waverer to be proclaimed to all ages! If you had not doubted, I shall not so surely believe. If to the heretics, who loudly declared that Our Lord Jesus Christ did not rise again in His true body, we could only have asserted the faith of the believing women and the disciples, they with devilish cunning would have faced us with many arguments. But now when they hear that doubting Thomas handled the body, touched the scars of the wounds, and then, his doubts removed, cried out 'My Lord and my God', those who till then were full of noise seem to become as silent as fishes, knowing that it was true flesh which could be handled and that it was God who entered when the doors were shut. That Thomas doubted was not chance but the divine dispensation.

And so, most pious king, the victory that with your few men you could not have expected was part of the plan of God's providence, wishing to show to mortals how dear to God was he who by his prayers earned so great a triumph with such small forces. Perchance, nay assuredly, you did not yourself know how dear you were to God; that knowledge was given you after He had honoured you with so signal a victory. Holy men do not know, until they have tested it, what virtue they possess and what is their worth when they are set in God's balances. We may infer this from the words spoken by the angel to Abraham when he wished to offer up his son:' 'Stretch not your hand over the child nor do anything to him; now I know that you fear God', that is, I have made you and your posterity to know it. Even before Abraham consented to slay his son, God knew how great was the love that the holy patriarch felt for Him; but he who loved did not know how perfect was his love, until he made it clear as day by the sacrifice of his beloved son. We can prove this statement by the promise that St Peter made: 'Lord, I am ready to go with thee, both into prison and to death.' And Our Lord said to him: 'I tell thee Peter, the cock shall not crow this night, before that thou shalt thrice deny that thou knowest me.' He who made thee, Peter, knew you better than you knew yourself. The faith you profess is, you think, true: but He who knows all things before they happen predicted that you would deny Him thrice. You did not forget that sentence, and when He asked you afterwards if you loved Him, you trusted Him rather than yourself, and declared your love in this modest reply: 'Lord, thou knowest all things; thou knowest that I love thee. In my own consciousness I love thee more than I love myself, save that I love myself in loving thee. But whether this is truth, as I think it is, thou dost know better than I, thou who hast made me to live and fired me with righteous passion to love thee.'

And so, good king, this was done, not to confirm your faith, but for the sake of those weaklings who think that victory depends on numbers and that human affairs are guided by chance. We know that if you had crossed the river with twelve thousand soldiers and gained the victory, you would have imputed your success, not to yourself, but to God. The reason why he decreed that you should win the day by your prayers in spite of your small numbers was that He wished to fire believers with a deeper love of God and also show to those who knew it not how great was the love He felt for you. But now I must leave this subject and return to the order of my narrative.

Ch. 27.   In Alsace there is a castle, called in the language of the country Breisach, which stands on an island in the Rhine, and is furthermore protected by the natural roughness of the locality. In this castle Everard had stationed a number of his soldiers, and by the terror they inspired not only made himself master of a great part of the aforesaid province but also lamentably harassed the king's loyal subjects round about. The good king therefore, considering his people's interests before his own, collected an army and set out for Alsace to lay siege to the aforesaid castle. On his arrival, at the instigation of Frederick, Archbishop of Maintz, who was then with him, a number of the bishops abandoned their tents which they had pitched in a circle round him and began under cover of night to desert their king, secretly retiring to their own cities, while Frederick treacherously stayed behind. The king's soldiers noticing their action addressed the king thus: 'Take thought for your safety, sire, and retire from this district into Saxony. You are well aware that your brother Henry is endeavouring to make war upon you, and if he sees the smallness of your present force, he will fall upon you suddenly without giving you an opportunity to retreat. It would be better therefore to return later with a larger army than to be faced with the alternative of a miserable death or a shameful flight.' The king however was undismayed and answered them, as Judas Maccabeus once answered his men:– 'Nay, nay, do not talk like that. If our time has come, let us die like brave men and not cast a slur upon our good name. It would be better to face death in the cause of righteousness than to escape death and live on in dishonour. If those who resist God's ordinance and hope for aid, not from God but from their own numbers, are content to die in an unrighteous conflict and to go down to eternal punishment in hell, it should give us much greater pleasure to fight with all our strength, since we have the security of fighting for justice, and, if the universal lot of mankind should befall us, we can die in battle without any anxiety for the future. If those who fight for justice were to retreat merely because of their small numbers before they had put things to the test of battle, it would mean that they distrusted God.' By these words not merely did the king dissuade his men from the retreat they contemplated, but fired them at once with vigour for the fray.

Ch. 28. I should like you, excellent father, to give your careful attention to one of the king's deeds; and then you will admire his victory over his own passions even more than his victories over his foes. Even sinners can conquer their adversaries at times, if God permits: but to keep an unshaken courage and to be neither elated by success nor depressed by reverses is only possible when men are perfect. Hear then how amid the tossing storms of life the king founded his ardent faith upon the rock that is Christ. At that time he had with him a certain very wealthy count, whose host of followers formed a glorious part of the king's army. This person, seeing the number of deserters who were every day leaving the royal lines, and considering the outer, not the inner, man, began secretly to revolve these thoughts in his mind:— 'Anything I ask from the king in these troublous times I shall certainly get: a serious attack is threatening us and he is afraid that I shall desert him.' Accordingly he sent messengers, begging to the king to hand over to him the abbey of Lorsch with its rich lands, so that from its possessions he might supply his own and his soldiers' needs. The king, however, who not only had the wisdom of a serpent but was also filled with a dove's simplicity, was quite unable to understand the meaning of this request, and sent the following excuse in reply:— 'I would rather explain in words than by a message, what I think on this subject.' When the count who had sent the messengers heard this, he was filled with boundless joy, thinking that his request was already granted. And so, impatient of delay, he went to the king and asked him to pronounce judgement. To him the king in the presence of the whole army gave the following reply:— 'We must obey God rather than men. What sensible person in his right mind does not see that your request is not a humble petition but has the force of a threat? It is written: "Give not what is sacred to the dogs." And although our teachers say that this must be understood spiritually, I think that I should fairly be giving what is sacred to the dogs if I took away these monastery lands, given by pious souls to men who fight for God, and handed them over to men who are fighting for this world. I call the whole army to witness and solemnly declare in answer to your wanton and unrighteous demand that you shall never receive this nor anything else from me. If it pleases you to join the other traitors in deserting me, the sooner you go the better.' The face is the mirror of the mind: when the count heard this, his blushing cheeks betrayed his mental discomfiture, and falling quickly at the king's feet he confessed his sin and the gravity of his error. Consider therefore the courage wherewith God's athlete crushes both his invisible and his visible foes. Our ancient enemy thought that he had done him no real hurt in persuading so many valiant princes to rise against him and in urging his brother to rob him of his throne. He knew that these were but outward losses, and so he incited the aforesaid count to ask for the inheritance of the saints, in order that the king might the sooner incur God's anger by unjustly handing over to soldiers the wages that belong to the servants of God. In this he failed; and let me now relate the king's marvellous success and how because of his firmness in temptation God Himself fought on his side.

Ch. 29.   That holy man David, speaking in the Lord's person, says: 'If my people had harkened unto me and if Israel had walked in my ways, I would perchance have humbled their enemies to the dust and laid my hand upon those who trouble them.' That this word was fulfilled in the case of the king who harkened unto God and walked in His ways, the account I am going to give will show. When Everard and Gislebert heard that the king was in Alsace, they got together a large army, and having no fear of opposition crossed the Rhine at Andernach, and proceeded to smash up the king's loyal subjects everywhere round about. It must be said that Huto, brother of Hermann duke of Swabia, and Conrad surnamed the Wise, whom we have described above as being still loyal to the king, were in this district. But as their forces were much inferior to the enemy, they feared to engage them. However, at God's command, given not by word of mouth but by inspiration, they followed close behind them as they returned with their load of plunder. After they had gone a little way, a priest met them, who was weeping and wailing aloud. They asked him where he had come from and why he was weeping, and he replied: 'I have just come from those robbers, who have increased the miseries of my poor estate by taking from me the one beast that I possessed.' When the aforesaid Huto and Conrad heard this, they made careful inquiry as to whether he had set eyes on Gislebert and Everard. He told them that almost all the troops with the booty had crossed the Rhine but that the two leaders, alone except for a few picked men, were then taking a meal, curse them! Thereupon Huto and Conrad dashed forward with such speed that, if you had seen them, you would have said they were flying rather than running. To cut a long tale short, Everard was killed by the sword, Gislebert drowned in the Rhine water: there was too much of it for him to swallow, and his breath failing, he gave up the ghost. Not one of their followers escaped: they were all either taken alive or slain by the sword. So you see how the Lord laid His hand upon the king's adversaries, since He knew that he had always walked in His ways.

Ch. 30. While this was going on, the king in Alsace knowing nothing of what had happened had made his preparations to die rather than fly before the foe. It happened accordingly that early one morning he was following his usual custom and mounting his horse to go to church – it was some way off – there to fortify himself with prayer. As he looked in front he saw a man in the distance coming towards him with terrific speed and at once realized that he was the bearer of important news. As the messenger had good tidings to tell, as soon as he saw the king, he gave token of the happy message he had to give by making some preliminary merry gestures. The soldiers therefore, seeing by these signs that he was bringing good news, ran forward on the alert to hear what he had to say. The steady way in which he now began to walk, the manner in which he smoothed his hair and arranged his dress, and the respectful greeting he prepared to give the king, seemed to them as long as a year. The king saw that his men were panting with excitement and that the man's delay was unbearable – 'Come,' said he, 'tell us what you were sent for at once, and invert the usual order by giving us the facts first. Banish this company's fears and fill their hearts with joy: then you may bring out your compliments to myself and indulge in the long preliminaries of a rhetorical prelude. It is what you have to say, not how you say it, that we are this moment expecting. We would rather be made to rejoice by rustic simplicity than left on thorns by Ciceronian wit.' When he heard this, the messenger said outright that Everard and Gislebert had passed away from this life. He wanted to give details, but the king checked him by a gesture and getting down from his horse burst into tearful prayers of gratitude to God. This duty done, he got up and proceeded on his way to church to commend himself to God's protection.

Ch. 31. At this time Bertald, duke of Bavaria, brother of duke Arnold, who was a man of great energy, was very vigorous in supporting the king's cause. So the king, wishing him to share in his present gladness as he had shared in his past tribulations, sent him a messenger the next day to tell him what benefits the Lord had showered upon him. Bertald was not connected with him by any ties of marriage, and therefore to enhance the joyful news the king offered and promised under oath to give him as wife his sister, formerly married to Gislebert, if he could get her. If he could not, he said, he would arrange a marriage for him with Gislebert's and his sister's child, a girl, now almost of marriageable age, whom he had under his control. On hearing this Bertald was immensely delighted, and chose to wait for the young girl rather than take the mother, who had had a husband already.

Ch. 32. Frederick, archbishop of Maintz, at whose instigation some of the bishops had left the king, in order that his treachery, till then concealed, might be plain to all, now openly deserted the king's cause, and about ten days before the death of his aforesaid conspirators came in haste to Maintz and thence passed on without delay to Metz. The king's brother Henry had arranged on the return of Everard and Gislebert to join Frederick there with a large army and to make preparations for a vigorous campaign against the king in Alsace. When the archbishop arrived, however, he was met by a very unexpected and disagreeable piece of news; the two princes, he was told, had been cut off by death and were now no more. These tidings filled him with consternation and he was completely at a loss as to what he should do.

Ch. 33. Meanwhile the king left Alsace and occupied France. In fear of his anger the people of Maintz refused to allow the archbishop to enter the city on his return. So not long after he was taken prisoner by the king's partizans, brought into the royal presence, and sent off to prison in Saxony. There he stayed some time, and then the king's clemency restored him to his former position.

Ch. 34. Henry for his part, terror stricken with fear of the king his brother, determined to take refuge in the castle of Chevremont, a place strong by nature and fortified also by the ingenuity of men. But his sister, Gislebert's widow, learning of this beforehand not only prevented him from so doing, but addressed him thus:– 'Shame on you! Are not the troubles that my husband's death has brought upon me enough for you? Would you shut yourself up in my fort and bring down the king's wrath like a flood upon this country? I will not endure it, I will not suffer it, I will not allow it. I am not so altogether senseless as to let you win your safety at the price of my ruin.'

Ch. 35. When Henry heard this, not knowing what else to do, he took some of the bishops on whose help he had depended, and one day went barefoot to the king. Taking him by surprise he flung himself at his feet and as a suppliant begged for mercy. The king replied: 'Your shameful conduct does not deserve mercy. But as I see you humbled before me, I will not do you any harm.' So he ordered him to go to his French palace of Ingelheim, there to be closely guarded until the bitterness of anger had abated and he could decide on the advice of his wise counsellors what he should do with him.

CONTENTS

BOOK 5

BOOK 5

Ch. 1. It happened, after the death of Everard and Gislebert and the confinement of the king's brother Henry, that when men of rank flocked from every side to congratulate the king, there came also the richest man of the Swabians, Duke Hermann, who after profuse congratulations addressed the king in these terms:—
'It is not unknown to my liege lord that I am immensely rich and that in spite of my broad estates and great wealth I have no children. There is no one except my small daughter to inherit my property when I die. May it please my lord the king, therefore, to allow me to adopt as son his son, the little Liutolf, so that he may be united in marriage with my only children and on my departure derive such glory as the succession to my riches can give.' The proposal pleased the king and his request was granted without delay.

Ch. 2. In this year, as you yourselves know well, there was a great and terrible eclipse of the sun, on the sixth day of the week, at nine o'clock in the morning. On that day your king Abderahamen was overcome in battle by Radamir, the most Christian king of Galicia. Moreover, in Italy for eight nights in succession a comet of wonderful size appeared, drawing after it a very long and fiery trail. This foreshadowed the famine destined soon to follow which by its severity caused lamentable havoc in Italy.

Ch. 3. At that time King Hugh had been shamefully driven from Rome, as we have described, and Alberic was in sole control of the city. King Hugh every year made fierce attacks upon him, laying all the country waste with fire and sword, so that at last he captured from him all the cities except his stronghold of Rome. Even that he would undoubtedly have won either by laying it waste or by bribing the citizens, had not the mysterious sentence of God's justice prevented him.

Ch. 4.   About this period the two brothers Berengar and Anscar became famous in Italy. They were sons of the same father, Adalbert marquess of Ivrea, but they had different mothers. Berengar, as we have said above, was the son of Gisla daughter of King Berengar; Anscar was the son of Ermengarde daughter of Adalbert marquess of Tuscany by Berta daughter of King Hugh. Of these two men Berengar was prudent in counsel and cunning of wit, Anscar was ready for any hazardous enterprise. Indeed King Hugh regarded him with deep suspicion, and thought that he meant to kill him and seize the throne. Accordingly, acting on advice he made him marquess of Spoleto and Camerino after the death of marquess Tedbald, conceiving that the further he knew he was away, the more security he would feel. However, as soon as Anscar got there, being a man impatient by nature, he betrayed at once by his actions all the plans of mischief against the king which his mind had suggested to him.

Ch. 5.   Of all this Hugh was well aware; and after debating what remedy for this annoyance he could find, he called into his presence a Burgundian named Sarlio. To him he said – 'The loyalty of the people of Camerino and Spoleto is something I know well. It is like a reed, which if a man lean upon, it will pierce his hand. Go then and undermine their fidelity with the money I will provide: kill all their affection for Anscar and win them over to yourself. There is no one who can do this better or more easily than yourself. You have the wife of my good nephew Tedbald, the late marquess, and relying on her aid all the people will come over to you.' Sarlio accordingly set out and the people of Camerino and Spoleto did exactly as the king had said they would. So, getting a force of men together, he hastened with all speed to the city where Anscar was living. Hearing of his approach Anscar called to him one of his squires, a man named Wikbert, and addressed him in these words:

The craven Sarlio comes forth to fight
And vainly trusts that numbers give him might.
Up then, with hearts and swords of tempered steel
And let him in red strife your valour feel.
A chosen band, well trained in many a fray,
All warriors bold, is now upon the way
Attending me their lord. Soon you will see
The shining arms that presage victory.

Ch. 6. Wikbert was a man of military experience as well as courage, and when he heard this he replied:– 'Wait and get together as large a force as you can. It is a harzardous thing to engage so numerous an army as his with these few troops. Moreover, if you consider, the men with whom we have to deal are men of valour, as well trained in battle as we are.' Wikbert's advice was good and Anscar had already decided to follow it and by sending messengers in all directions to get an army together, when a certain Arcod, a Burgundian by descent, attacked Wikbert's plan in bitter words:– 'You are like Chremes in the play', he said, 'who in fear of Thraso advised Thais to lock up the house until he should bring helpers from the market place. Thais refused and then, like you, he said:– "It is foolish to allow what you can safely avoid. I prefer to provide against injury rather than to avenge it when it has been done."' To that Wikbert replied:– 'You do well to mention Thraso. At first he was full of windy rage and fury, but when he was faced by the real thing, he posted Syriscus on the right wing and Symalio on the left, and chose for himself a strategic position in the rear. That the Burgundians also are talkative, greedy cowards, no one who knows them doubts. How many stout fights you have waged, and how many you have escaped by running away, the scars on your back declare.'

Ch. 7. Excited by this discussion Anscar and Wikbert hastened to engage Sarlio, as soon as they heard of his approach, although he was in force and they had only a few men. Sarlio had six divisions, three of which he sent against the one that Anscar commanded; he himself remained the other side of the river with the remaining three and awaited events. He was afraid, indeed, that not even his huge numbers could save him if Anscar once set eyes upon him. The battle began at once: Arcod ran away and disappeared: Wikbert, who thought it better to die than retreat, received a mortal wound. When Anscar was trying to find out who of his men had been slain, he was met by Wikbert, covered both with his own and with others' blood, who said to him:–'Two fine divisions are advancing now against us. I earnestly beg and entreat you not to await but rather to refuse their attack. Arcod, as you know, was the prompter of this fray and you see in what fashion he has deserted us. I am at my last gasp and have no more thought of fighting. I only pray God to have mercy on my soul, and not to lay to my charge the crimes I have committed to-day for love of you in sending down so many men to death.' With these words he expired.

Ch. 8. Anscar got together what men he could, and meeting two companies of the enemy leaped forward madly into their midst and dealt destruction all around. A certain Count Hatto was in command of these two divisions, and he now advanced against Anscar with some confidence, since he saw that his spear head was shattered and that he held only the shaft in his hand. Anscar eyed him sternly and cried: 'Are you the perjurer who had no regard for the oath you swore in God's name on the cross and the sacred relics, but deserted me, your liege lord, and went over, like a cowardly turncoat, to that fox Sarlio? Up till now you have only dreamed that "the ghosts are somewhere and the nether realm"; and that there is a river called Cocytus with "black frogs upon the Stygian wave". But now you will very soon find that they are real.' With these words he thrust the pointless spear violently between the other's lips and forced it through the back of his head all bespattered with blood and brains. Then seizing his sword he began to fight stoutly against the crowd who fell upon him. Unaided and without assistance he stood up against the attack of almost a whole army, charging them in all directions, until at last his horse slipped into a ditch and fell on top of its rider with its head down and its legs in the air. Then the enemy rushed in upon him and dispatched him with a shower of missiles. So Anscar died: Sarlio took over the march without opposition, and King Hugh was greatly pleased.

Ch. 9.   While these things were happening the mountain districts that encircle Italy and separate it from the west and north were being cruelly devastated by the Saracens of Fraxinetum; King Hugh accordingly on the advice of his counsellors despatched messengers to Constantinople asking the emperor Romanos to send him some of his Greek fireships, which the Greeks in their own language call chelandia. His idea was himself to march by land and root out the stronghold of Fraxinetum, while the Greeks blockaded the sea side with their fleet, burning the Saracens' ships and completely preventing any reinforcements or supplies of food reaching them from Spain.

Ch. 10.   Meanwhile Berengar, marquess of Ivrea and brother of the aforesaid Anscar, began to plot secretly against the king. Hugh became aware of this, but disguised his wrath and pretended to wish him well. He arranged, however, to get him into his hands and then put out his eyes. His little son Lothair, who was still unaware of his own best interests, got knowledge of this design and being but a child incapable of concealment sent a messenger to Berengar to acquaint him of his father's intention. Berengar thereupon left Italy with all speed and hastened over the Saint Bernard to Duke Hermann in Swabia, telling his wife Willa to come to the same place by another route. When she set out she was with child and very near her time, and yet she got across the Vogelberg. How she was able to cross that rough and pathless mountain on foot I cannot possibly comprehend: it would be miraculous if I did not know that fortune has always been against me. Alas! Lothair did not know the future, nor could he see what a snare he set for himself. In taking thought for Berengar he prepared the loss of his own throne and life. I do not blame Lothair, who erred in childish folly and bitterly repented afterwards: I rather curse that cruel mountain which changed its usual fashion and allowed them an easy passage. I would fain cry out an insult upon it:

Ch. 11.

>   Wicked mountain, once so famed,
>   Never more shalt thou be named

'Pathless': for thou couldst have slain
That foul fiend and didst refrain.
Even when the burning sun
Tells that harvest has begun
And the reaper's sharpened blade
To the ruddy corn is laid;
Even then thy frozen snow
Never passage will allow.
But to-day, when winter's cold
All the countryside doth hold,
Thou dost give an easy way.
If I had my wish, I'ld say –
'Cast the villain from his place
'Mid the hills, and in disgrace
Send him headlong down to hell;
He deserves his sentence well.'
Berengar in safety goes
And his path no danger knows:
For that mountain slays the good
And preserves the devil's brood
Of the savage Moorish crew,
Who their scimitars embrue
In the blood of captives slain
And their food by pillage gain.
Well, I pray the lightning blast
May upon thy rocks be cast,
And that deep to chaos hurled
Thou mayest stay till ends this world!

Ch. 12. When Berengar arrived, Hermann, duke of the Swabians, received him kindly and brought him with all due honours into the presence of the most pious King Otto. With what consideration the king welcomed him, what gifts he bestowed, and what honours he gave, my pen distrusts its power to relate. But the sagacious reader will easily be able to understand from my account what righteousness and courtesy the king displayed, and what a villain Berengar turned out to be.

Ch. 13.   King Hugh, hearing of Berengar's flight, sent envoys to

King Otto, promising to give him any amount of gold and silver that he might decide, if only he would not shelter Berengar or give him any assistance. To them the king made the following reply in explanation of his action:– 'Berengar has sought my protection, not with any idea of overthrowing your master but rather, if possible, of becoming reconciled to him again. If I can help him in this matter with your master, so far from accepting the treasures he offers me, I most willingly give him mine. But when Berengar or any one else implores my clemency and protection, it would be the height of madness to refuse him my aid.' Consider therefore what love and affection the pious king showed to a man, for whom he was willing to spend his own money rather than receive the money that was offered on his account!

Ch. *14.* While these events were taking place, the emperor of Constantinople sent his envoys in company with King Hugh's, telling him that he would supply him with ships and all that he required, if he would give his daughter in marriage to his little grandson, his namesake, son of Constantine. I mean Constantine the son of the Emperor Leo, not Constantine the son of Romanos himself. There were three joint emperors with Romanos, his own two sons, Stephen and Constantine, and Constantine son of the Emperor Leo, with whom we are now concerned. On receiving this message, King Hugh sent envoys again to Romanos, to tell him that he had not any daughters by his lawful wife, but that if he would take one by his concubine he could supply a bride of exceptional beauty. In reckoning a person's nobility the Greeks consider the father's rank and not the mother's; and so Romanos at once equipped his Greek fire ships, sent off handsome presents, and gave instructions for the marriage between the lady and his grandson to take place. My stepfather, a man of weight and distinction, and one full of wisdom, was King Hugh's envoy on this occasion. Therefore it would not be inopportune to insert here the account I have often heard him give of the emperor's wisdom and courtesy and of the manner in which he conquered the Rusii.

Ch. *15.* There is a certain northern people whom the Greek call Rusii, '*les roux*' from the colour of their skins, while we from the position of their country call them Nordmanni, 'northmen'. In the Teuton language 'nord' means north, and 'man' means 'human being', so that Nordmanni is equivalent to 'men of the north'. These people had a king named Igor, who got together a fleet of a thousand ships or more, and sailed for Constantinople. The Emperor Romanos hearing of this was distracted by various thoughts; for his naval forces were either engaged against the Saracens or occupied in guarding the islands. He spent some sleepless nights in reflection while Igor devastated the coast lands, and at last he was informed that there were fifteen old battered galleys in the yards which had been allowed to go out of commission. Thereupon he called *les constructeurs des bateaux*, that is, the ship carpenters, into his presence and said to them:– 'Make haste and get the old galleys ready for service without delay. Moreover, put the fire-throwers not only at the bows but at the stern and both sides as well.' When the galleys had been equipped according to his instructions, he collected his most skilful sailors, and bade them give King Igor battle. So they set out; and when King Igor saw them on the open sea he ordered his men to capture them alive and not kill them. But the merciful and compassionate Lord willed not only to protect His worshippers who pray to Him and beg His aid, but also to give them the honour of victory. Therefore He lulled the winds and calmed the waves; for otherwise the Greeks would have had difficulty in hurling their fire. As they lay, surrounded by the enemy, the Greeks began to fling their fire all around; and the Rusii seeing the flames threw themselves in haste from their ships, preferring to be drowned in the water rather than burned alive in the fire. Some sank to the bottom under the weight of their cuirasses and helmets which they were never to see again; some caught fire even as they swam among the billows; not a man that day escaped save those who managed to reach the shore. For the Rusan ships by reason of their small size can move in very shallow water where the Greek galleys because of their greater draught cannot pass. As the result of this Igor returned to his own country completely demoralized, while the victorious Greeks returned in triumph to Constantinople bringing a host of prisoners with them. These were all beheaded in the presence of King Hugh's envoy, namely my stepfather, by order of Romanos.

Ch. 16. King Hugh having now collected his army sent a fleet across the Gulf of Lyons to Fraxinetum and proceeded thither himself by land. As soon as the Greeks arrived they destroyed all the Saracens' ships with their fire. Moreover the king forced his way into Fraxinetum and compelled the Saracens to retreat to Moors Mountain, where he would have been able to capture them by investment if the circumstance I am about to relate had not prevented him.

Ch. 17. King Hugh was very much afraid that Berengar would collect a force in France and Swabia, and come down upon him and rob him of his throne. So, following bad advice, he sent the Greeks back to their own country and himself concluded a treaty with the Saracens, arranging for them to stay in the mountains that separate Swabia and Italy, and prevent Berengar from passing if he happened to lead an army that way. How many Christian pilgrims on their way to the thresholds of the blessed Apostles Peter and Paul were slain by these heathen under this convention, He alone knows who has their names written in the Book of Life. How unjustly, King Hugh, do you attempt to defend your throne! Herod slew the Innocents to prevent the loss of his earthly kingdom; you, to keep yours, spare guilty men worthy of death. And would that those guilty ones had been allowed to live on condition that they did not afterwards slay the innocent! I think, or more exactly, I believe that you have neither read nor heard the story of Ahab, and how the king of Israel incurred the anger of the Lord by making a truce with Benadab king of Syria and letting a man go who deserved death. It was one of the sons of the prophets who said to Ahab: 'Thus saith the Lord: "Because thou hast let go out of thy hand a man whom I appointed to utter destruction, therefore thy life shall go for his life, and thy people for his people."' And so it happened. But what disasters you brought upon yourself by this act, my pen will more suitably describe at the proper season.

Ch. 18. At the time when Berengar fled from Italy, he was accompanied by one of his vassals, a man of noble birth named Amedeus, who, as was shown later, was not inferior to Ulysses himself in cunning and audacity. The valiant King Otto was prevented by various reasons from supplying Berengar with men; and furthermore King Hugh kept him quiet by the immense sums of money he gave him every year. Accordingly the aforesaid Amedeus went to Berengar and addressed him thus:— 'It is not unknown to you, my lord, how hateful King Hugh has made himself to all the Italians by the harshness of his rule, especially seeing that he gives every position of importance to the sons of his concubines or to the Burgundians, and that there is not one Italian noble to-day who has not either been driven from the country or deprived of all his dignities. The only reason that they do not concert a revolt against the king is that they lack a leader. So if some one amongst us were to go there in disguise and find out their wishes, he would doubtless be able to hatch a plot which would be all to our advantage.' To this Berengar replied:— 'No one can do this more easily, or more effectually than yourself.' So Amedeus disguised himself and joined some poor folk who were going on a pilgrimage to Rome. Thus under pretext of a Roman visit he got into Italy, met the Italian princes, and found out what they variously desired. But he did not show himself to them all in the same guise: for one he darkened his skin, for another he had rosy cheeks, for a third his face was covered with spots. At last it got to the king's ears that he was in Italy, for 'rumour is a hot-foot jade and to swiftness owes her strength', and orders were given that diligent search should be made for him. Amedeus then befouled his beautiful long beard with pitch and changed the colour of his golden hair by the help of black dye, and so, with dirty face and limping gait, appeared among the beggars who took their food in the king's presence. He actually faced Hugh naked and received from him a cloak to wear, listening meanwhile to all that the king was saying about himself and Berengar. Then, after having carefully investigated the whole position, he returned to his master; but not this time with the pilgrims, as he had come. The king had given orders to the guards at the frontier barriers to allow no one to pass until they had thoroughly satisfied themselves as to his identity. Amedeus heard of this and got across the frontier by rough trackless country where no guards were set; and so reached Berengar bringing with him exactly the news that he wished to hear.

Ch. 19. At this time King Hugh made peace with the Hungarians, giving them ten pecks of money. He then exacted hostages and expelled them from Italy, supplying them with a guide to show them the road to Spain. The reason that they never got to that country and to the city of Cordoba, where your king has his lodging, was that for three days they had to traverse a waterless district, barren with drought. Thinking that they and their horses would die there of thirst, they beat to death the guide that Hugh had given them and went back quicker than they came.

Ch. 20. At this same time King Hugh sent his daughter Berta, whom he had had by the courtesan Pezola, to Constantinople to be married to the little Romanos, son of Constantine Porphyrogenitus, the ceremony being performed by Sigefred, the venerable bishop of Parma. The imperial power was then held by the elder Romanos and his two sons Constantine and Stephen. Next to Romanos however in order of precedence came Constantine, son of the emperor Leo, whose little son by Helena, the elder Romanos' daughter, married the aforesaid Berta, whose name was changed by the Greeks to Eudoxia. These four then were joint emperors, when the two brothers Stephen and Constantine, without the knowledge of Constantine son of the emperor Leo, prepared to play *un mauvais tour*, that is, a nasty trick upon their father Romanos. They were weary of his strict control which did not allow them to do anything that they wished. So, listening to bad advice, they began to consider how they might deprive him of the throne.

Ch. 21. The palace at Constantinople surpasses both in beauty and in strength all the fortresses I have ever seen, and it is moreover guarded constantly by a great crowd of soldiers. It is the custom to open the gates to everyone soon after daybreak, but at nine o'clock the signal 'mis' is given and all have to leave, entrance being then forbidden until three o'clock in the afternoon. In this palace Romanos lived in state in the finest room, *le salon d'or*, that is, the golden chamber, handing over the rest of the palace to his son-in-law Constantine and his two sons Stephen and Constantine. These two latter, discontented, as we have said, with their father's just severity, collected a large force in their apartments, and fixed upon a date when they should dethrone their father and become themselves sole rulers. The longed for day arrived, and when everyone, as usual, had left the palace, Stephen and Constantine got their men together and fell upon their father. They got him out of the palace without the citizens knowing anything of it, and after giving him the monastic tonsure sent him off to philosophize in an island near by, where a congregation of monks were pursuing their studies. Very soon, however, the voice of loud rumour made itself heard in the city. People began to cry out that Romanos was dethroned, others that his son-in-law Constantine had been murdered. In a moment the whole multitude flocked to the palace. Loud mutinous cries of 'Constantine' were raised, and so at the request of Stephen and Constantine, the popular favourite went to that side of the palace where the vast space of the Zucanistrion stretches and put his dishevelled head through the lattice. His appearance quieted the popular disturbance and the crowd had to return home: but all this of course was very annoying to the two brothers. 'What good is it that our father has abdicated', they said, 'if we have to endure another master, who is not our father? It would be more tolerable and more honourable for us to submit to a paternal despotism that to a stranger's tyranny. Moreover, foreigners as well as his own people came flocking to this fellow's aid. Bishop Sigefred, King Hugh's envoy, with his fellow-countrymen from Amalfi, Rome and Caieta, was here, prepared to help him and destroy us.'

Ch. 22.   Thereupon they filled their rooms again with armed men, as they had done for their father. The commander of these troops was Diavolinus, who after having prompted the brothers now betrayed them. He found Constantine bent over his books and addressed him thus: 'Your longstanding rule of righteous conduct keeps you in ignorance of the dangers which threaten you at the hands of Stephen and Constantine, your brothers and enemies. If you realized the fate they have prepared for you, you would be taking measures now to save your life. Your wife's brothers have collected an armed force and have them now shut up in their own apartments, and they intend, not to drive you from the palace as they did their father, but to murder you within its walls. Their opportunity will come three days from now, when they intend to invite you to a banquet. When you attempt to take your seat in the centre, as is your highness' custom, a blow will be struck upon a shield, the soldiers will burst out from the room, and your life will end in bloodshed. If you want a proof of what I say, I can give you plain evidence this very moment. In the first place I can show you the concealed soldiers through a hole in the wall; and secondly, what is more important for your safety, I hand you now the keys of the doors.' At this Constantine said: 'Well, as you have revealed to me this treacherous plot, tell me next how I may baffle it. My life is dear to me, but I shall take even greater pleasure in piously repaying your services.' Then Diavolinus said: 'You are not unaware that the Macedonian guards are both sturdy fighters and devoted to yourself: send for them and fill your own rooms with troops without letting Stephen and Constantine know. When the day appointed for the banquet comes and the dispute for pride of place begins, give the signal I told you of by striking upon a shield. Their men will not be able to get out to help them, while your guards will leap upon them unexpectedly and make them prisoners. It will be a surprise attack and perfectly easy. Then you can send them across the water with their heads duly tonsured to philosophize in the monastery close by, where they sent their and your wife's father. Your enterprise will be favoured by God's rightful judgement, consideration for which did not prevent them from sinning against their father, although it has guarded you from offence.' That God's just verdict was in this matter fulfilled is proclaimed to-day by Europe and Asia and Africa. On the appointed day, when under pretence of friendship the brothers had invited Constantine to a banquet and a disturbance was beginning over pride of place, a blow was struck upon a shield, as we have said, and the Macedonians made their unexpected appearance. The two brothers Stephen and Constantine were at once arrested, had their heads tonsured, and were sent off to philosophize in the neighbouring island to which they had despatched their father.

Ch. 23. When their father Romanos heard of their arrival, he rendered thanks to God and with a glad face came to meet them outside the monastery door. 'O happy hour', he cried, 'that has compelled your majesties to visit my humble estate. The affection which drove me from the palace, I suppose, has not allowed your filial love to remain there any longer. What a good thing it was that you sent me here some time first. My brothers and fellow soldiers in Christ give all their time to philosophy, and they would not have known how to receive emperors if they did not have in me an expert in imperial etiquette. Here is boiled water for you colder than the Gothic snows: here are soft beans, greenstuff and fresh cut leeks. There are no fishmonger's delicacies to cause illness; that is rather brought about by our frequent fasts. Our modest abode has no room for a large and extravagant company; but it is just large enough for your majesties who have refused to desert your father in his old age.' I need not say, for you can well believe how modestly Stephen and Constantine cast down their eyes while their father was indulging in these sarcasms and how unwillingly they entered the monastery. Then Romanos with arms extended flung himself before the base of the altar and poured forth this tearful prayer:—

Ch. 24.

> O Christ, with Father and the Spirit one,
> Word of the Father, whence the Light hath shone
> On this dark world, and to our mortal eyes
> He hath revealed His heavenly mysteries.
> Look on the creature that thy goodness made,
> And let me not by Satan be betrayed
> Whom thou didst ransom with thy sacred blood.
> I pray thee, Saviour; let my strength hold good
> To tread the world's vain strife beneath my feet
> And still resolve the tempter foul to cheat
> Who seeks to spoil our happiness. I crave
> No power on earth if I salvation have.
> And thanks to thee I see them overthrown
> Who took their father's empire for their own.

Ch. 25. After this Stephen and Constantine were kept constantly under close guard; but their father submitted to his lot with equanimity. We are told by reliable witnesses that when the brothers reproached him for weeding beans he replied:— 'It is a more glorious kingdom to serve the humble needs of God's servants than to rule over the proud sinners of this world.'

Ch. 26. Meanwhile Berengar by request left Swabia with a few attendants and made his way through Fair Valley to Italy. He there pitched camp close to the fortress known as The Ant's Nest, which Manasses, archbishop of Arles and Trient and usurper of the bishoprics of Verona and Mantua, had at that time, as we have said before, entrusted to the care of his clerk Adelard. Berengar saw that neither siege train nor attack by storm were of any use against this stronghold, but knowing Manasses' ambition and his *fatuité*, that is, his shallow boastfulness, he asked for an interview with Adelard and addressed him thus:— 'If you put this fort in my hands and bring over your master Manasses to my side, when I gain kingly power I will give him the rank of archbishop of Milan and make you bishop of Como. And that you may believe my promise, I hereby confirm my offer by oath.' When Manasses heard of this from Adelard, not only did he order him to hand over the fort to Berengar but he invited all the Italians to join his side.

Ch. 27. So Rumour, 'hot-foot jade, surpassing swift, who from her speed draws strength', very soon announced to all men the coming of Berengar, and people began to leave Hugh and attach themselves to the invader. The first to do so was Milo, the powerful count of Verona. Hugh suspected him and had set guards secretly to keep him under watch. He pretended not to notice and one evening prolonged a banquet till midnight. Then, when all heavy with sleep and the wine god had given their weary limbs to rest, he stole away attended only by his shield bearer and hastened to Verona. Thence he sent messengers to Berengar and offered him the town as a base of firm resistance to Hugh. It must be allowed that it was not disloyalty which thus severed him from his king: the latter had inflicted upon him some slights which he could not endure any longer. His lead was followed by Wido, bishop of Modena, who had not been injured in any way but coveted the great abbey of Nonantola, which he afterwards got into his hands. He not only deserted Hugh but brought a number of others with him. Hugh, hearing of this, collected his forces and attacked his castle of Vignola, an attack that may truthfully be called as useless as it was valiant, as the following will show. While he was occupied there Berengar left Verona and at the invitation of Archbishop Arderic hastened to Milan. This news brought Hugh in sad depression to Pavia.

Meanwhile all the chief men in Italy began to leave Hugh's ill starred fortunes and to join the needy Berengar. I call a man needy, not when he possesses nothing, but when he finds that nothing is ever sufficient. The unprincipled and greedy find their possessions always uncertain and dependent on chance and they ever seek more. No one among them is satisfied with what he has and they should be considered as beggarly paupers rather than as rich men of wealth. They alone are rich and possess a fruitful and a lasting estate, who are content with their lot and think what they have is enough. To have no desires is real wealth: not to be fond of buying things is the best of incomes. Let us confess the truth. Which is the richer, the man who wants or the man who has more than sufficient? The man who needs or the man who has abundance? The man who finds that the greater his possessions the more they need to protect them, or the man who can rely on his own strength? To be satisfied with one's fortunes is the greatest and most certain riches. On this topic let this suffice. My eager pen must now return to Berengar, at whose appearance all men thought that the golden age had come again and cried out –
'O happy age that has produced such a man as this.'

Ch. 28. While he was busy at Milan, distributing the high offices of Italy to his adherents, King Hugh sent his son Lothair to present himself to Berengar and the whole nation, asking them, as they were getting rid of him as not being to their taste, to welcome his innocent son for the love of God and make him compliant with their wishes. Then, while Lothair made his way to Milan, Hugh left Pavia with all his money and prepared to abandon Italy and go to Burgundy. One thing however stopped him. When Lothair prostrated himself before the cross in the church of the blessed confessor Ambrose and the blessed martyrs Gervasius and Protasius, the people were seized with compassion for him, and raising him up proclaimed him as king, while they also sent a messenger immediately after Hugh, promising that he should rule over them again. This proposal, or rather this trick, was

Berengar's sole invention and was in accordance with the cunning wherewith he was stuffed full. He did not mean either of them to be king, but he wanted, as was seen later, to prevent Hugh from getting away and calling in the Burgundians or some other people against him by the help of his immense wealth.

Ch. 29. At this time a certain Joseph was bishop of Brescia, a man of good repute, young in years but old in wisdom. As he was of upright character, Berengar, with his usual piety, deprived him of his see, and appointed Antony, who is still alive, in his place, without either holding a council or consulting with the other bishops. Moreover he did not appoint Adelard to the see of Como, as he had sworn to do, but out of affection for the archbishop of Milan chose a certain Waldo as bishop. What a good appointment that was is shown in outward signs and in people's groans, by the decrease of the congregation, the cutting down of vines, the stripping of bark from trees, the knocking out of eyes, and the constant repetition of quarrels. As for Adelard, he made him bishop of Reggio.

Ch. 30. He intended to expel Boso, Hugh's bastard, from the see of Piacenza and Liutefred from Pavia, but for a monetary consideration he let them alone, pretending that he acted out of love of God. How immense then was the joy in Italy! 'Another David has come' men cried; and in their blindness said that he was greater than Charlemagne. For though the Italians had accepted Hugh and Lothair as kings again and Berengar was nominally only a marquess, in the reality of power he was king, and the other two, if kings in name, were actually held as less important than counts. Why say more? My parents were so allured by Berengar's reputation and by his fame for courtesy and generosity that they put me into his service, and at very great expense got me appointed as his private secretary responsible for all state despatches. I served him faithfully for years and he repaid me – O shame! – in the fashion that I shall describe in due season. His conduct would almost have driven me to despair if I had not found many others as companions in misfortune. To him those beautiful words apply:– 'The wings of the ostrich are like the wings of the hawk and the heron. When the time has come, she

lifteth her wings on high, and scorneth the horse and his rider.'
While Hugh and Lothair were with us, he, the huge greedy
ostrich, though not really good, yet seemed good. But when they
were deposed and everyone put him upon the throne, how then he
lifted his wings and scorned us all I am going to relate, not so
much in words as in sighs and groans. But let us leave this now and
return to the order of my narrative.

Ch. 31.   King Hugh, being unable to escape God's punishment
or get the mastery over Berengar, left Lothair behind under
Berengar's protection, pretending that he was his friend, and
taking all his money with him hastened back to Provence.
Whereupon Raimond prince of the Aquitanians came to him and
in consideration of a large sum offered himself as his vassal,
declaring under oath that he would be his loyal supporter. He
promised moreover that he would collect his forces, march into
Italy, and crush Berengar; a laughable offer which the worthless
character of his people rendered ridiculous. However, even if he
could have been of any help, his proposal could not have been put
into effect; for soon afterwards at the Lord's summons King Hugh
took the way of all flesh, leaving his money to his niece Berta,
widow of Boso Count of Arles. This lady, after a short interval the
aforesaid Raimond, a fellow even more filthy than the filthy
people he ruled, got for his wife, although competent judges of
beauty vigorously assert that he was quite unworthy of her bed or
even of one kiss from her lips.

Ch. 32.   It was at this time that Berta's sister Willa, wife of
Berengar, incurred the charge of unchastity. Her conduct was not
only known to the chamberlains and other officials of the court,
but was the common talk of all the tradesmen of the town. She
had in her service as chaplain a priestling named Dominic, a
fellow of short stature and swarthy complexion, boorish, hairy,
intractable, rough, shaggy, wild, uncouth, fond of mad strife,
with a wanton tail like appendage, and no regard for right. To his
teaching Willa had entrusted her two daughters Gisla and
Girberga, that they might imbibe from him a sound knowledge of
literature. Taking advantage of the facetious lessons, which the
hairy, unwashed priest gave to the girls, the mother won his

favourable notice by gifts of costly robes and delicate food. Every one was surprised that a woman generally so ungracious, grasping and detestable should suddenly show herself so generous in this one case. But the word of truth which says: 'There is nothing hidden which shall not be revealed, nothing secret which shall not be made known', did not allow men to wonder for long. One night this hairy creature according to his wont was on his way to his mistress' bed when a dog came on the scene, woke up the sleepers in the adjoining rooms with his fierce barking, and gave the priest several severe bites. The whole household jumped out of bed, seized the intruder, and asked him where he was going; but his mistress anticipated any excuse on his part by crying –'The villain was after my maids.' Thereupon the miserable priest, thinking that it would be better for him to back up the lady, whined:– 'I confess; that is the truth.' His mistress after this began to plot against his life and offered a reward to anyone who would kill him. But as all her people were God-fearing men, she could not get her plan executed, and at last some gossip on the subject reached Berengar's ears. Then Willa had recourse to soothsayers and sorcerers, hoping that their charms would help her. Whether success was due to their incantations or to Berengar's weakness I do not know: at any rate her husband gave way and of his own accord put his head into the conjugal halter. So the priest was castrated for having whinnyed after his lady's maids and dismissed from her service: the lady herself received more than ever of Berengar's affection. Those who turned the priest into a eunuch declared there was good reason for the love his mistress bore him: his tool, they discovered, was worthy of Priapus himself.

Ch. 33.   About this time Taxis, king of the Hungarians, came into Italy with a large army, and was paid ten pecks of money by Berengar, who got the amount not from his own purse but by making a collection from the churches and poor folk. Indeed his action was not due to any regard for the people; he used the opportunity to get a large sum of money together. In this he was successful enough. Every person of either sex, adults and babes at the breast, had to pay one gold coin each. By mixing bronze coins with the gold he made up ten pecks: the rest of the money together with all that he took from the churches he kept for himself.

CONTENTS

BOOK 6

BOOK 6

Ch. 1. If it were not that the Lord had prepared a table in my sight against those who trouble me, the character of my fortunes to-day would call for a tragedy rather than a history from my pen. I cannot describe by what calamities I have been buffeted in my painful journeyings, and my outer man would prefer to sit down and weep rather than write words on paper. But my inner man is strengthened by the Apostle's ordinance:— 'he glories in tribulations of this kind; knowing that tribulation worketh patience; and patience, experience; and experience, hope; and hope maketh not ashamed; because the love of God is shed abroad in our hearts by the Holy Ghost which is given unto us.' So let the outer yield to the inner man, and so far from shrinking from his misfortunes, let him rather rest content in them. If he concentrates on his writing and describes how some rise and some fall on fortune's wheel, he will feel less acutely the troubles that now beset him. Let him rejoice at fortune's mutability: he need fear no worse grief — that is impossible, unless he were to die or lose a limb — and let him always be expecting a turn for the better. If fortune changes his present state, she will bring him the happiness that he lacks and banish the sorrow that he has. So let him go on writing and add the true story that follows to his previous narrative.

Ch. 2. After the death of King Hugh in Provence the fame of Berengar spread abroad in many lands, and especially among the Greek peoples. By virtue of his abilities he was the chief man in Italy, while Lothair was king only in name. So Constantine, who after the downfall of Romanos and his sons had become emperor at Constantinople, hearing that in actual power Berengar was

superior to Lothair, sent him a letter by the hand of a certain
Andreas, who from his functions had the title of 'prefect of the
guard'. In this letter he said that he was very desirous of a visit
from an envoy of Berengar's, that the latter on his messenger's
return might know with what affection he was regarded. He also
wrote him another letter on Lothair's behalf, commending him to
his care and begging him to be faithful in administering the realm,
to whose governance by God's favour he had been appointed.
Constantine indeed had no small regard for Lothair's welfare and
made it a subject of scrupulous thought, owing to the affection he
felt for his son's wife who was Lothair's sister.

Ch. 3. Accordingly, Berengar, who was a man stuffed full of
cunning, began to consider whom he could best send without
contributing anything himself to the expense of the long journey.
He therefore sent for my stepfather, under whose care I was then
living, and addressed him thus:– 'What a boon it would be to me
if your stepson knew Greek!' My stepfather replied: 'I would
spend half my estate to give him that knowledge.' 'Nay,' said
Berengar, 'you need not spend one hundredth part of it. The
emperor of Constantinople begs me in this letter to send an envoy
to his court. As far as courage goes, no one could be better than
your stepson, and on the score of eloquence no one could be more
satisfactory than he will be. And I need not tell you how easily
there he will imbibe the learning of Greece, he who in his youth
has drunk so deep of Latin knowledge.' At this my stepfather was
fired by hope, contributed all the expenses of the journey, and sent
me off, the bearer of handsome gifts, to Constantinople.

Ch. 4. On the first of August I left Pavia and sailing down the
Po arrived in three days at Venice. There I met a Greek envoy, the
eunuch Salemo, chamberlain of the palace, who had just returned
from Spain and Saxony. He was anxious to sail for Constantinople and was taking there with him an envoy from my
present master, who was then king and is now emperor. This man,
who was the bearer of costly presents, was a rich merchant of
Maintz called Liutefred. Finally we left Venice on the twenty-fifth
of August and reached Constantinople on the seventeenth of

September. It will be a pleasant task to describe the marvellous and unheard of manner of our reception.

Ch. 5. Next to the imperial residence at Constantinople there is a palace of remarkable size and beauty which the Greeks call Magnavra, the letter v taking the place of the digamma, and the name being equivalent to 'Fresh Breeze'. In order to receive some Spanish envoys, who had recently arrived, as well as myself and Liutefred, Constantine gave orders that this palace should be got ready and the following preparations made.

Before the emperor's seat stood a tree, made of bronze gilded over, whose branches were filled with birds, also made of gilded bronze, which uttered different cries, each according to its varying species. The throne itself was so marvellously fashioned that at one moment it seemed a low structure, and at another it rose high into the air. It was of immense size and was guarded by lions, made either of bronze or of wood covered over with gold, who beat the ground with their tails and gave a dreadful roar with open mouth and quivering tongue. Leaning upon the shoulders of two eunuchs I was brought into the emperor's presence. At my approach the lions began to roar and the birds to cry out, each according to its kind; but I was neither terrified nor surprised, for I had previously made enquiry about all these things from people who were well acquainted with them. So after I had three times made obeisance to the emperor with my face upon the ground, I lifted my head, and behold! the man whom just before I had seen sitting on a moderately elevated seat had now changed his raiment and was sitting on the level of the ceiling. How it was done I could not imagine, unless perhaps he was lifted up by some such sort of device as we use for raising the timbers of a wine press. On that occasion he did not address me personally, since even if he had wished to do so the wide distance between us would have rendered conversation unseemly, but by the intermediary of a secretary he enquired about Berengar's doings and asked after his health. I made a fitting reply and then, at a nod from the interpreter, left his presence and retired to my lodging.

Ch. 6. It would give me some pleasure also to record here what I did then for Berengar, so that all may recognize what affection I showed to him and what recompense I have received from him for my services. The Spanish envoys and the aforesaid Liutefred, who represented my present master who was then King Otto, had brought handsome gifts from their masters to the emperor Constantine. I for my part had brought nothing from Berengar except a letter and that was full of lies. I was very greatly disturbed and shamed at this and began to consider anxiously what I had better do. In my doubt and perplexity it finally occured to me that I might offer the gifts, which on my own account I had brought for the emperor, as coming from Berengar, and trick out my humble present with fine words. I therefore presented him with nine excellent cuirasses, seven excellent shields with gilded bosses, two silver gilt cauldrons, some swords, spears and spits, and what was more precious to the emperor than anything, four carzimasia; that being the Greek name for young eunuchs who have had both their testicles and their penis removed. This operation is performed by traders at Verdun, who take the boys into Spain and make a huge profit.

Ch. 7. Three days after I had presented my gifts the emperor summoned me to the palace and personally invited me to dinner with him, after the banquet bestowing a handsome present on myself and my attendants. As the opportunity has occurred to describe the appearance of the emperor's table, particularly on a feast day, and also the entertainments that are given there, I think it best not to pass the matter over in silence but to give an account.

Ch. 8. There is a palace near the Hippodrome looking north-wards, wonderfully lofty and beautiful, which is called 'Decanneacubita', 'The house of the nineteen couches'. The reason of its name is obvious: 'deca' is Greek for ten, 'ennea' for nine, and 'cubita' are couches with curved ends; and on the day when Our Lord Jesus Christ was born according to the flesh nineteen covers are always laid here at the table. The emperor and his guests on this occasion do not sit at dinner, as they usually do, but recline on couches: and everything is served in vessels, not of silver, but of gold. After the solid food fruit is brought on in three golden bowls, which are too heavy for men to lift and come in on carriers covered over with purple cloth. Two of them are put on the table in the following way. Through openings in the ceiling hang three ropes covered with gilded leather and furnished with golden rings. These rings are attached to the handles projecting from the bowls, and with four or five men helping from below, they are swung on to the table by means of a moveable device in the ceiling and removed again in the same fashion. As for the various entertainments I saw there, it would be too long a task to describe them all, and so for the moment I pass them by. One, however, was so remarkable that it will not be out of place to insert an account of it here.

Ch. 9. A man came in carrying on his head, without using his hands, a wooden pole twenty-four feet or more long, which a foot and a half from the top had a crosspiece three feet wide. Then two boys appeared, naked except for loin cloths round their middle, who went up the pole, did various tricks on it, and then came down head first, keeping the pole all the time as steady as though it were rooted in the earth. When one had come down, the other remained on the pole and performed by himself, which filled me with even greater astonishment and admiration. While they were both performing their feat seemed barely possible; for, wonderful as it was, the evenness of their weights kept the pole up which they climbed balanced. But when one remained at the top and kept his balance so accurately that he could both do his tricks and come down again without mishap, I was so bewildered that the emperor himself noticed my astonishment. He therefore called an interpreter, and asked me which seemed the more wonderful, the boy who had moved so carefully that the pole remained firm, or the man who had so deftly balanced it on his head that neither the boys' weight nor their performance had disturbed it in the least. I said that I did not know which I thought *plus merveilleux* that is, more wonderful; and he burst into a loud laugh and said he was in the same case, he did not know either.

Ch. 10. I do not think that I ought to pass over in silence another strange and wonderful sight that I saw there. In the week before the feast Vaiophoron, which we call the Feast of Palms, the emperor makes a payment in gold coins to his vassals and to the different officers of his court, each one receiving a sum proportionate to his office. As I wished to be present at the ceremony, the emperor bade me attend it. The procedure was as follows. A table was brought in, fifteen feet long and six feet broad, which had upon it parcels of money tied up in bags, according to each man's due, the amount being written on the outside of the bag. The recipients then came in and stood before the king, advancing in order as they were called up by a herald. The first to be summoned was the marshall of the palace, who carried off his money, not in his hands but on his shoulders, together with four cloaks of honour. After him came the commander in chief of the army and the lord high admiral of the fleet. These being of equal rank received an equal number of money bags and cloaks, which they did not carry off on their shoulders but with some assistance dragged laboriously away. After them came twenty-four controllers, who each received twenty-four pounds of gold coins together with two cloaks. Then followed the order of patricians, of whom every one in turn was given twelve pounds of gold and one cloak. As I do not know how many patricians there are, I do not know the total amount that was paid; but every one received an equal share. After them came a huge crowd of minor dignitaries; knights of the sword of the first, second and third class, chamberlains, treasury and admiralty officials. Some of these received seven pounds of gold, others six, five, four, three, two and one, according to their rank. I would not have you think that this was all done in one day. It began on the fifth day of the week at six o'clock in the morning and went on till ten, and the emperor finished his part in the proceedings on the sixth and seventh day. Those who take less than a pound receive their share, not from the emperor, but from the chief chamberlain during the week before Easter. While I was standing and marvelling at the proceedings the emperor sent his chancellor to me and asked me how the ceremony pleased me. 'It would please me', I replied, 'if it did me any good. When Dives was in torment the rest that he saw Lazarus enjoying would have pleased him, if it had come his way. As it did not, how, pray, could it have pleased him?' The emperor smiled in some confusion, and motioned me to come to him. He then presented me with a large cloak and a pound of gold coins; a gift which he willingly made and I even more willingly accepted.

LIBER DE REBUS GESTIS OTTONIS
A Chronicle of Otto's Reign

A CHRONICLE OF OTTO'S REIGN

Ch. 1. Berengar and Adalbert were reigning, or rather raging, in Italy, where, to speak the truth, they exercised the worst of tyrannies, when John, the supreme pontiff and universal pope, whose church had suffered from the savage cruelty of the aforesaid Berengar and Adalbert, sent envoys from the holy church of Rome, in the persons of the cardinal deacon John and the secretary Azo, to Otto, at that time the most serene and pious king and now our august emperor, humbly begging him, both by letters and a recital of facts, for the love of god and the holy apostles Peter and Paul, whom he hoped would remit his sins, to rescue him and the holy Roman church entrusted to him from their jaws, and restore it to its former prosperity and freedom. While the Roman envoys were laying these complaints, Waldpert, the venerable archbishop of the holy church of Milan, having escaped half-dead from the mad rage of the aforesaid Berengar and Adalbert, sought the powerful protection of the above mentioned Otto, at that time king and now our august emperor, declaring that he could no longer bear or submit to the cruelty of Berengar and Adalbert and Willa, who contrary to all human and divine law had appointed Manasses Bishop of Arles to the see of Milan. He said that it was a calamity for his church thus to intercept a right that belonged to him and to his people. After Waldpert came Waldo Bishop of Como, crying out that he also had suffered a like insult at the hands of Berengar, Adalbert and Willa. With the apostolic envoys there also arrived some members of the laity, among them the illustrious marquess Otbert, asking help and advice from his most sacred majesty Otto, then king now emperor.

Ch. 2. The most pious king was moved by their tearful complaints, and considered not himself but the cause of Jesus Christ. Therefore, although it was contrary to custom, he appointed his young son Otto as king, and leaving him in Saxony collected his forces and marched in haste to Italy. There he drove Berengar and Adalbert from the realm at once, the more quickly inasmuch as it is certain that the holy apostles Peter and Paul were fighting under his flag. The good king brought together what had been scattered and mended what had been broken, restoring to each man his due possessions. Then he advanced on Rome to do the same again.

Ch. 3. There he was welcomed with marvellous ceremony and unexampled pomp, and was anointed as emperor by John the supreme bishop and universal pope. To the church he not only gave back her possessions but bestowed lavish gifts of jewels, gold and silver. Furthermore Pope John and all the princes of the city swore solemnly on the most precious body of Saint Peter that they would never give help to Berengar and Adalbert. Thereupon Otto returned to Pavia with all speed.

Ch. 4. Meanwhile Pope John, forgetful of his oath and the promise he had made to the sacred emperor, sent to Adalbert asking him to return and swearing that he would assist him against the power of the most sacred emperor. For the sacred emperor had so terrified this Adalbert, persecutor of God's churches and of Pope John, that he had left Italy altogether and had gone to Fraxinetum and put himself under the protection of the Saracens. The righteous emperor for his part could not understand at all why Pope John was now showing such affection to the very man whom previously he had attacked in bitter hatred. Accordingly he called together some of his intimates and sent off to Rome to inquire if this report was true. On his messengers' arrival they got this answer, not from a few chance informants, but from all the citizens of Rome:– 'Pope John hates the most sacred emperor, who freed him from Adalbert's clutches, for exactly the same reason that the devil hates his creator. The emperor, as we have learned by experience, knows, works and loves the things of God: he guards the affairs of church and state with his sword, adorns them by his virtues, and purifies them by his laws. Pope John is the enemy of all these things. What we say is a tale well known to all. As witness to its truth take the widow of Rainer his own vassal, a woman with whom John has been so blindly in love that he has made her governor of many cities and given to her the golden crosses and cups that are the sacred possessions of St Peter himself. Witness also the case of Stephana, his father's mistress, who recently conceived a child by him and died of an effusion of blood. If all else were silent, the palace of the Lateran, that once sheltered saints and is now a harlot's brothel, will never forget his union with his father's wench, the sister of the other concubine Stephania. Witness again the absence of all women here save Romans: they fear to come and pray at the thresholds of the holy apostles, for they have heard how John a little time ago took women pilgrims by force to his bed, wives, widows and virgins alike. Witness the churches of the holy apostles, whose roof lets the rain in upon the sacrosanct altar, and that not in drops but in sheets. The woodwork fills us with alarm, when we go there to ask God's help. Death reigns within the building, and, though we have much to pray for, we are prevented from going there and soon shall be forced to abandon God's house altogether. Witness the women he keeps, some of them fine ladies who, as the poet says, are as thin as reeds by dieting, others everyday buxom wenches. It is all the same to him whether they walk the pavement or ride in a carriage and pair. That is the reason why there is the same disagreement between him and the holy emperor as there is of necessity between wolves and lambs. That he may go his way unchecked, he is trying to get Adalbert, as patron, guardian and protector.'

Ch. 5. When the envoys on their return gave this report to the emperor, he said:– 'He is only a boy, and will soon alter if good men set him an example. I hope that honourable reproof and generous persuasion will quickly cure him of these vices; and then we shall say with the prophet:– "This is a change which the hand of the Highest has brought."' He added:– 'The first thing required by circumstances is that we dislodge Berengar from his position on Montefeltro. Then let us address some words of fatherly admonition to the lord pope. His sense of shame, if not his own wishes, will soon effect a change in him for the better. Perchance if he is forced into good ways, he will be ashamed to get out of them again.'

Ch. 6. This done, the emperor went on board ship and sailed down the Po to Ravenna. Thence he advanced to Montefeltro, sometimes called St Leo's Mountain, and besieged the fort in which Berengar and Willa had taken refuge. Thereupon the aforesaid Pope John sent Leo, then the venerable chief notary of the holy Roman church and now in that same see successor to Saint Peter chief of the apostles, together with Demetrius, one of the most illustrious of the Roman princes, as envoy to the holy emperor. By their mouths he declared that it was not surprising if in the heat of youth he had hitherto indulged in childish follies; but now the time had come when he would fain live in a different fashion. He also cunningly alleged that the holy emperor had sheltered two of his disloyal subordinates, Bishop Leo and the cardinal deacon John, and that he was now breaking his sworn promise by letting them take an oath of allegiance not to the Pope but to the Emperor. To the envoys the emperor gave this answer: 'I thank the pope for the change and improvement in his ways that he promises. As for the violation of pledges that he charges me with, judge yourselves if the accusation be true. We promised to restore all the territory of Saint Peter that might fall into our hands: and for that reason we are now striving to drive Berengar with all his household from yonder fort. How can we restore this territory to the pope, if we do not first wrest it from the hands of violent men and bring it under our control? As for Bishop Leo and the cardinal deacon John, his disloyal subordinates, whom he accuses us of having welcomed, we have neither seen them in these days nor welcomed them. The lord pope sent them to Constantinople to do us damage, and on their way, we are told, they were taken prisoners at Capua. We are also informed that with them was arrested a certain Saleccus, a Bulgarian by birth and an Hungarian by training, who is an intimate friend of the lord pope, and also a reprobate named Zacheus, a man quite ignorant of all literature sacred or profane, whom the lord pope has recently consecrated as bishop, with the intention that he should preach to the Hungarians a campaign against us. We would not have believed that the lord pope would have acted thus, whoever told us; but his letter, sealed with leaden seals and bearing his signature, compels us to think that it is true.'

Ch. 7. This done, the emperor sent Landohard the Saxon bishop of Minden and Liudprand the Italian bishop of Cremona to Rome in company with the pope's envoys, to satisfy the lord pope that no blame attached to him. Furthermore the righteous emperor bade the soldiers of their guard to prove the truth of his words in single combat if the pope refused to believe him. The aforesaid bishops Landohard and Liudprand came before the lord pope at Rome, and although they were received with all due honour they saw clearly with what scorn and indifference he was prepared to treat the holy emperor. They explained everything in order, as they had been told to do, but the pope refused to be satisfied either with an oath or with a single combat and persisted in being obdurate. Still, a week later he craftily sent John, Bishop of Narni, and Benedict, cardinal deacon, back to the lord emperor with his envoys, thinking that by their tricks he could delude a man whom it is exceptionally difficult to deceive. Before they got back, however, Adalbert at the pope's invitation had left Fraxinetum and reached Civita Vecchia; whence he set out for Rome and there, so far from being repudiated by the pope, as he should have been, received from him an honourable welcome.

Ch. 8. While these things were going on, the fierce heat of the dog days kept the emperor away from the hills of Rome. But when the sun had entered the sign of the Virgin and brought a temperate change, he collected his forces, and at the secret invitation of the Romans drew near to the city. Yet why do I say 'secret', when the greater part of the Roman princes forced their way into the castle of St Paul and giving hostages invited the holy emperor to enter. Why make a long tale? When the emperor pitched his camp in the vicinity, the pope and Adalbert made their escape together from Rome. The citizens welcomed the holy emperor and all his men into their town, promising again to be loyal and adding under a strong oath that they would never elect or ordain a pope except with the consent and approval of the august Caesar Otto the lord emperor and his son King Otto.

Ch. 9. Three days later at the request of the bishops and people of Rome a synod was held in the church of St Peter, attended by the emperor and the Italian archbishops. The deacon Rodalf acted in place of Ingelfred patriarch of Aquileia, who had been seized by a sudden sickness in that city; Waldpert came from Milan, Peter from Ravenna; Archbishop Adeltac and Landohard, bishop of Minden, represented Saxony; Otker, bishop of Spires, France. The Italian bishops were Hubert of Parma, Liudprand of Cremona, Hermenard of Reggio; the Tuscans, Conrad of Lucca, Everard of Arezzo, the bishops of Pisa, Sienna, Florence, Pistoia, Peter of Camerino, the bishop of Spoleto; the Romans, Gregory of Albano, Sico of Ostia, Benedict of Porto, Lucidus of Gavio, Theophylact of Palestrina, Wido of Selva Candida, Leo of Velletri, Sico of Bieda, Stephen of Cervetri, John of Nepi, John of Tivoli, John of San Liberato, Romanus of Ferentino, John of Norma, John of Veroli, Marinus of Sutri, John of Narni, John of Sabina, John of Gallese, the bishops of Civita, Castellana, Alatri, Orte, John of Anagni, the bishop of Trevi, Sabbatinus of Terracina. There were also present: Stephen cardinal archpriest of the parish Balbina, Dominic of the parish Anastasia, Peter of the parish Damasus, Theophylact of the parish Chrysogonus, John of the parish Equitius, Peter of the parish Pamachius, Adrian of the parish Calixtus, John of the parish Caecilia, Adrian of the parish Lucina, Benedict of the parish Sixtus, Theophylact of the parish Four Crowned Saints, Stephen of the parish Sabina, Benedict cardinal archdeacon, John deacon, Bonofilius chief cardinal deacon, George second cardinal deacon, Stephen assistant, Andrew treasurer, Sergius chief warden, John sacristan, Stephen, Theophylact, Adrian, Stephen, Benedict, Azo, Adrian, Romanus, Leo, Benedict, Leo, Leo, Leo notaries, Leo chief of the school of singers, Benedict subdeacon in charge of the offertories, Azo, Benedict, Demetrius, John, Amicus, Sergius, Benedict, Urgo, John, Benedict subdeacon and steward, Stephen arch-acolyte with all the acolytes and district deacons. Representing the princes of Rome were Stephen son of John, Demetrius Meliosi, Crescenti de Caballo Marmoreo, John Mizina, Stephen de Imiza, Theodore de Rufina, John de Primicerio, Leo de Cazunuli, Rihkard, Pietro de Canapanaria, and Benedict with his son

Bulgamin. The commoner Peter, also called Imperiola, together with the whole body of Roman soldiery was in attendance.

Ch. 10. When all had taken their seats and complete silence was established, the holy emperor began thus: 'How fitting it would have been for the lord pope John to be present at this glorious holy synod. I ask you, holy fathers, to give your opinion why he has refused to attend this great gathering, for you live as he does and share in all his interests.' Thereupon the Roman bishops and the cardinal priests and deacons together with the whole populace said:– 'We are surprised that your most holy wisdom deigns to ask us this question: even the inhabitants of Iberia and Babylonia and India know the answer to it. John is not now even one of those who come in sheep's clothing and within are ravening wolves: his savageness is manifest, he is openly engaged in the devil's business, and he makes no attempt at disguise.' The emperor replied:– 'It seems to us right that the charges against the pope should be brought forward seriatim, and that the whole synod should then consider what course we should adopt.' Thereupon the cardinal priest Peter got up and testified that he had seen the pope celebrate mass without himself communicating. John bishop of Narni and John cardinal deacon then declared that they had seen the pope ordain a deacon in a stable and at an improper season. Benedict cardinal deacon with his fellow deacons and priests said that they knew the pope had been paid for ordaining bishops and that in the city of Todi he had appointed a bishop for ten years. On the question of his sacrilege, they said, no inquiries were necessary; knowledge of it was a matter of eyesight not of hearsay. As regards his adultery, though they had no visual information, they knew for certain that he had carnal acquaintance with Rainer's widow, Stephana his father's concubine, the widow Anna, and his own niece, and that he had turned the holy palace into a brothel and resort for harlots. He had gone hunting publicly: he had blinded his spiritual father Benedict who died of his injuries: he had caused the death of cardinal subdeacon John by castrating him: he had set houses on fire and appeared in public equipped with sword, helmet and cuirass. To all this they testified; while everyone, clergy and laity alike, loudly accused him of drinking wine for love of the devil. At dice, they said, he asked the aid of Jupiter, Venus, and the other demons; he did not celebrate matins nor observe the canonical hours nor fortify himself with the sign of the cross.

Ch. 11. When he had heard this, as the Romans could not understand his native Saxon tongue, the emperor bade Liudprand bishop of Cremona to deliver the following speech in the Latin language to all the Romans. Accordingly he got up and began thus: 'It often happens, and we know it by experience that men set in high positions are besmirched by the foul tongue of envy: the good displease the bad, even as the bad displease the good. For this reason we still regard as doubtful the charge against the pope which the cardinal deacon Benedict read out and communicated to you, and we are uncertain whether it originated from zeal for righteousness or from impious envy. Therefore, unworthy as I am, by the authority of the position that has been granted me I call upon you all by the Lord God, whom no one, even if he wishes, can deceive, and by his holy mother the pure virgin Mary, and by the most precious body of the chief of the apostles, in whose church this is now being read, cast no foul words against the lord pope nor accuse him of anything that he has not really done and that has not been witnessed by men on whom we can rely.' Thereupon the bishops, the priests, the deacons, the rest of the clergy, and the whole Roman people cried out as one man:— 'If Pope John has not committed all the shameful crimes that the deacon Benedict read out to us and done things even worse and more disgusting than those, may the most blessed Peter, whose verdict closes the gates of heaven against the unworthy and opens them for the righteous, never free us from the chains of our sins: may we be held fast in the bonds of anathema and at the last day be set on the left hand with those who said to the Lord God: "Depart from us, we would have no knowledge of thy ways." If you do not give us credence, at least you ought to believe the army of our lord the emperor, against whom the pope advanced five days ago, equipped with sword, shield, helmet and cuirass. It was only the intervening waters of the Tiber that saved him from being taken prisoner in that garb.' Then the holy emperor said:— 'There are as many witnesses to that as there are fighting men in our army.' So the holy synod pronounced: 'If it please the holy emperor, let a letter be sent to the lord pope, that he come here and purge himself from all these charges.' Thereupon a letter was sent to him as follows:—

Ch. 12. 'To the supreme pontiff and universal pope lord John, Otto, august emperor by the grace of God, together with the archbishops and bishops of Liguria, Tuscany, Saxony and France, sends greeting in the name of the Lord. When we came to Rome in god's service and inquired of your sons, the Roman bishops, cardinal priests and deacons, and the whole body of the people besides, concerning your absence, and asked them what was the reason that you were unwilling to see us, the defenders of your church and your person, they brought out such foul and filthy tales about you that we should be ashamed of them, even if they were told about actors. That your highness may not remain in complete ignorance we set down some of them briefly here: for though we would fain give them all seriatim, one day is not enough. Know then that you are charged, not by a few men but by all the clergy and laity alike, of homicide, perjury, sacrilege and of the sin of unchastity with your own kinswoman and with two sisters. They tell me too something that makes me shudder, that you have drunk wine for love of the devil, and that in dice you have asked the help of Jupiter, Venus and the other demons. Therefore we earnestly beg your paternal highness not to refuse under any pretence to come to Rome and clear yourself of all these charges. If perchance you fear the violence of a rash multitude, we declare under oath that no action is contemplated contrary to the sanction of the holy canons.'

Ch. 13. After reading this letter, the pope sent the following reply: 'Bishop John, servant of God's servants, to all the bishops. We hear say that you wish to make another pope. If you do, I excommunicate you by Almighty God, and you have no power, to ordain no one or celebrate mass.'

Ch. 14. When this answer was read in the holy synod, the following clergy, who had been absent at the previous meeting, were present: from Lorraine, Henry Archbishop of Trèves; from Aemilia and Liguria, Wido of Modena, Gezo of Tortona, Sigulf of

Piacenza. The synod returned the following reply to the lord pope:— 'To the supreme pontiff and universal pope lord John, Otto, august emperor by the grace of God, and the holy synod assembled at Rome in God's service, send greeting in the Lord's name. At our last meeting of the sixth of November we sent you a letter containing the charges made against you by your accusers and their reasons for bringing them. In the same letter we asked your highness to come to Rome, as is only just, and to clear yourself from these allegations. We have now received your answer, which is not at all of a kind suited to the character of this occasion but is more in accordance with the folly of rank indifference. There could be no reasonable excuse for not coming to the synod. But messengers from your highness ought certainly to have put in an appearance here, and assured us that you could not attend the holy synod owing to illness or some such insuperable difficulty. There is furthermore a sentence in your letter more fitting for a stupid boy than a bishop. You excommunicated us all if we appointed another bishop to the see of Rome, and yet gave us power to celebrate the mass and ordain clerical functionaries. You said:— "You have no power to ordain no one." We always thought, or rather believed, that two negatives make an affirmative, if your authority did not weaken the verdict of the authors of old. However, let us reply, not to your words, but to your meaning. If you do not refuse to come to the synod and to clear yourself of these charges, we certainly are prepared to bow to your authority. But if — which Heaven forbid! — under any pretence you refrain from coming and defending yourself against a capital charge, especially when there is nothing to stop you, neither a sea voyage, nor bodily sickness, nor a long journey, then we shall disregard your excommunication, and rather turn it upon yourself, as we have justly the power to do. Judas, who betrayed, or rather who sold, Our Lord Jesus Christ, with the other disciples received the power of binding and loosing from their Master in these words:— "Verily I say unto you, Whatsoever ye shall bind on earth shall be bound in heaven: and whatsoever ye shall loose on earth shall be loosed in heaven." As long as Judas was a good man with his fellow disciples, he had the power to bind and loose. But when he became a murderer for greed and wished to destroy all men's lives, whom then could he loose that was bound or bind that was loosed save himself, whom he hanged in the accursed noose?' This letter was written on the twenty-second day of November and sent by the hand of the cardinal priest Adrian and the cardinal deacon Benedict.

Ch. 15. When these latter arrived at Tivoli, they could not find the pope: he had gone off into the country with bow and arrows, and no one could tell them where he was. Not being able to find him they returned with the letter to Rome and the holy synod met for the third time. On this occasion the emperor said: 'We have waited for the pope's appearance, that we might complain of his conduct towards us in his presence: but since we are now assured that he will not attend, we beg you earnestly to listen to an account of his treacherous behaviour. We hereby inform you, archbishops, bishops, priests, deacons, clerics, counts, judges and people, that Pope John being hard pressed by Berengar and Adalbert, our revolted subjects, sent messengers to us in Saxony, asking us for the love of God to come to Italy and free him and the church of St Peter from their jaws. We need not tell you how much we did for him with God's assistance: you see it to-day for yourselves. But when by my help he was rescued from their hands and restored to his proper place, forgetful of the oath of loyalty which he swore to me on the body of St Peter, he got Adalbert to come to Rome, defended him against me, stirred up tumults, and before my soldiers' eyes appeared as leader in the campaign equipped with helmet and cuirass. Let the holy synod now declare its decision.' Thereupon the Roman pontiffs and the other clergy and all the people replied: 'A mischief for which there is no precedent must be cauterized by methods equally novel. If the pope's moral corruption only hurt himself and not others, we should have to bear with him as best we could. But how many chaste youths by his example have become unchaste? How many worthy men by association with him have become reprobates? We therefore ask your imperial majesty that this monster, whom no virtue redeems from vice, shall be driven from the holy Roman church, and another be appointed in his place, who by the example of his goodly conversation may prove himself both ruler and benefactor, living rightly himself and setting us an example of like conduct.' Then the emperor said: 'I agree with what you say;

nothing will please me more than for you to find such a man and to give him control of this holy universal see.'

Ch. 16.   At that all cried with one voice:– 'We elect as our shepherd Leo, the venerable chief notary of the holy Roman church, a man of proved worth deserving of the highest sacerdotal rank. He shall be the supreme and universal pope of the holy Roman church, and we hereby reprobate the apostate John because of his vicious life.' The whole assembly repeated these words three times, and then with the emperor's consent escorted the aforesaid Leo to the Lateran Palace amid acclamations, and later at the due season in the church of St Peter elevated him to the supreme priesthood by holy consecration and took the oath of loyalty towards him.

Ch. 17.   When this had been arranged the most holy emperor, hoping that he could stay at Rome with a few men and not wishing the Roman people to be burdened with a great army, gave many of his soldiers leave to return home. John, the so-called pope, hearing of this and knowing how easily the Romans could be bribed, sent messengers to the city, promising the people all the wealth of St Peter and the churches, if they would fall upon the pious emperor and the lord pope Leo and impiously murder them. Why make a long tale? The Romans encouraged, or rather ensnared by the fewness of the emperor's troops and animated by the promised reward, at once sounded their trumpets and rushed in hot haste upon the emperor to kill him. He met them on the bridge over the Tiber, which the Romans had barricaded with waggons. His gallant warriors, well trained in battle with fearless hearts and fearless swords, leaped forward among the foe, like hawks falling on a flock of birds, and drove them off in panic without resistance. No hiding place, neither basket nor hollow tree trunk nor filthy sewer, could protect them in their flight. Down they fell, and as usually happens with such gallant heroes, most of their wounds were in the back. Who of the Romans then would have escaped from the massacre, had not the holy emperor yielded to the pity, which they did not deserve, and called off his men still thirsting for the enemies' blood.

Ch. 18. After they were all vanquished and the survivors had given hostages, the venerable pope Leo fell at the emperor's feet and begged him to give the hostages back and rely on the people's loyalty. At the request of the venerable pope Leo the holy emperor gave back the hostages, although he knew that the Romans would soon start the trouble I am about to relate. He also commended the pope to the Romans' loyalty, a lamb entrusted to wolves; and leaving Rome hastened towards Camerino and Spoleto where he had heard that Adalbert was to be found.

Ch. 19. Meanwhile the women, with whom the so-called pope John was accustomed to carry on his voluptuous sports, being many in numbers and noble in rank, stirred up the Romans to overthrow Leo, whom God and they themselves had chosen as supreme and universal pope, and bring John back again into Rome. That they did; but by the mercy of God the venerable pope Leo escaped from their clutches and with a few attendants made his way to the protection of the most pious emperor Otto.

Ch. 20. The holy emperor was bitterly grieved at this insult, and to avenge the expulsion of the lord pope Leo and the foul injuries done by the deposed John to the cardinal deacon John and the notary Azo, one of whom had his right hand cut off, and the other his tongue, two fingers and his nose, he got his army together again and prepared to return to Rome. But before the holy emperor's forces were all assembled, the Lord decreed that every age should know how justly Pope John had been repudiated by his bishops and all the people, and how unjustly afterwards he had been welcomed back. One night when John was disporting himself with some man's wife outside Rome, the devil dealt him such a violent blow on the temples that he died of the injury within a week. Moreover at the prompting of the devil, who had struck the blow, he refused the last sacraments, as I have frequently heard testified by his friends and kinsmen who were at his death bed.

Ch. 21. At his death the Romans, forgetful of the oath they had taken to the holy emperor, elected Benedict cardinal deacon as pope, swearing moreover that they would never abandon him but would defend him against the emperor's might. Thereupon the emperor invested the city closely and allowed no one to get out with a whole skin. Siege engines and famine completed the work, and finally in spite of the Romans he got possession of the city again, restored the venerable Leo to his proper place, and bade Benedict the usurper to appear before him.

Ch. 22.   Accordingly the supreme and universal pope the lord Leo took his seat in the church of the Lateran and with him the most holy emperor Otto, together with the Roman and Italian bishops, the archbishops of Lorraine and Saxony, the bishops, priests, deacons and the whole Roman people whose names will be given later. Before them appeared Benedict, the usurper of the apostolic chair, brought in by the men who had elected him and still wearing the pontifical vestments. To him the cardinal archdeacon Benedict addressed the following charge: 'By what authority or by what law, O usurper, are you now wearing this pontifical raiment, seeing that our lord the venerable pope Leo is alive and here present, whom you and we elected to the supreme apostolic office when John had been accused and disowned? Can you deny that you swore to our lord the emperor here present that you and the other Romans would never elect nor ordain a pope without the consent of the emperor and his son King Otto?' Benedict replied:– 'Have mercy upon my sin.' Then the emperor, revealing by his tears how inclined he was to mercy, asked the synod not to pass hasty judgement upon Benedict. If he wished and could, let him answer the questions and defend his case: if he had neither the wish nor the power but confessed his guilt, then let him for the fear of God have some mercy shown to him. Thereupon Benedict flung himself in haste at the feet of the lord pope Leo and the emperor, and cried out: 'I have sinned in usurping the holy Roman see.' He then handed over the papal cloak and gave the papal staff which he was holding to pope Leo, who broke it in pieces and showed it to the people. Next the pope bade Benedict to sit down on the ground and took from him his chasuble and stole. Finally he said to all the bishops: 'We hereby deprive Benedict, usurper of the holy Roman apostolic chair, of all pontifical and priestly office: but, by reason of the clemency of the lord emperor Otto, by whose help we have been restored to our proper place, we allow him to keep the rank of deacon, not at Rome but in exile, which we now adjudge against him.'

DE LEGATIONE
CONSTANTINOPOLITANA
The Embassy to Constantinople

THE EMBASSY TO CONSTANTINOPLE

That the Ottos, the invincible august emperors of the Romans and the most noble Adelaide the august empress, may always flourish, prosper and triumph, is the earnest wish, desire and prayer of Liudprand bishop of the holy church of Cremona.

Ch. 1. What was the reason that you did not receive my previous letters or messengers the following account will explain. On the fourth of June we arrived at Constantinople, and after a miserable reception, meant as an insult to yourselves, we were given the most miserable and disgusting quarters. The palace where we were confined was certainly large and open, but it neither kept out the cold nor afforded shelter from the heat. Armed soldiers were set to guard us and prevent my people from going out, and any others from coming in. This dwelling, only accessible to us who were shut inside it, was so far distant from the emperor's residence that we were quite out of breath when we walked there – we did not ride. To add to our troubles, the Greek wine we found undrinkable because of the mixture in it of pitch, resin and plaster. The house itself had no water and we could not even buy any to quench our thirst. All this was a serious 'Oh dear me!', but there was another 'Oh dear me' even worse, and that was our warden, the man who provided us with our daily wants. If you were to seek another like him, you certainly would not find him on earth; you might perhaps in hell. Like a raging torrent he poured upon us every calamity, every extortion, every expense, every grief and every misery that he could invent. In our hundred and twenty days not one passed without bringing to us groaning and lamentation.

Ch. 2.   On the fourth of June, as I said above, we arrived at Constantinople and waited with our horses in heavy rain outside the Carian gate until five o'clock in the afternoon. At five o'clock Nicephorus ordered us to be admitted on foot, for he did not think us worthy to use the horses with which your clemency had provided us, and we were escorted to the aforesaid hateful, waterless, draughty stone house. On the sixth of June, which was the Saturday before Pentecost, I was brought before the emperor's brother Leo, marshal of the court and chancellor; and there we tired ourselves with a fierce argument over your imperial title. He called you not emperor, which is Basileus in his tongue, but insultingly Rex, which is king in ours. I told him that the thing meant was the same though the word was different, and he then said that I had come not to make peace but to stir up strife. Finally he got up in a rage, and really wishing to insult us received your letter not in his own hand but through an interpreter. He is a man commanding enough in person but feigning humility: whereon if a man lean it will pierce his hand.

Ch. 3.   On the seventh of June, the sacred day of Pentecost, I was brought before Nicephorus himself in the palace called Stephana, that is, the Crown Palace. He is a monstrosity of a man, a dwarf, fat-headed and with tiny mole's eyes; disfigured by a short, broad, thick beard half going gray; disgraced by a neck scarcely an inch long; piglike by reason of the big close bristles on his head; in colour an Ethiopian and, as the poet says, 'you would not like to meet him in the dark'; a big belly, a lean posterior, very long in the hip considering his short stature, small legs, fair sized heels and feet; dressed in a robe made of fine linen, but old, foul smelling, and discoloured by age; shod with Sicyonian slippers; bold of tongue, a fox by nature, in perjury and falsehood a Ulysses. My lords and august emperors, you always seemed comely to me; but how much more comely now! Always magnificent; how much more magnificent now! Always mighty; how much more mighty now! Always clement; how much more clement now! Always full of virtues; how much fuller now! At his left, not on a line with him, but much lower down, sat the two child emperors, once his masters, now his subjects. He began his speech as follows:—

Ch. 4. 'It was our duty and our desire to give you a courteous and magnificent reception. That, however, has been rendered impossible by the impiety of your master, who in the guise of a hostile invader has laid claim to Rome; has robbed Berengar and Adalbert of their kingdom contrary to law and right; has slain some of the Romans by the sword, some by hanging, while others he has either blinded or sent into exile; and furthermore has tried to subdue to himself by massacre and conflagration cities belonging to our empire. His wicked attempts have proved unsuccessful, and so he has sent you, the instigator and furtherer of this villainy, under pretence of peace to act *comme un espion*, that is, as a spy upon us.'

Ch. 5. To him I made this reply: 'My master did not invade the city of Rome by force nor as a tyrant; he freed her from a tyrant's yoke, or rather from the yoke of many tyrants. Was she not ruled by effeminate debauchers, and what is even worse and more shameful, by harlots! Your power, methinks, was fast asleep then; and the power of your predecessors, who in name alone are called emperors of the Romans, while the reality is far different. If they were powerful, if they were emperors of the Romans, why did they allow Rome to be in the hands of harlots? Were not some of the holy popes banished, others so distressed that they could not procure their daily supplies nor money wherewith to give alms? Did not Adalbert send insulting letters to your predecessors, the emperors Romanos and Constantine? Did he not rob and plunder the churches of the holy apostles? Who of your emperors, led by zeal for God, troubled to punish so heinous a crime and bring back the holy church to its proper state? You neglected it, my master did not. From the ends of the world he rose, and came to Rome, and drove out the ungodly, and gave back to the vicars of the holy apostles all their power and honour. Those who afterwards rose against him and the lord pope, as being violators of their oath, sacrilegious robbers and torturers of their lords the popes, in accordance with the decrees of such Roman emperors as Justinian, Valentinian, Theodosius etc., he slew, beheaded, hanged, or exiled. If he had not done so, he himself would be an impious, unjust, cruel tyrant. It is a known fact that Berengar and Adalbert became his vassals and received the kingdom of Italy with a golden sceptre from his hand and that they promised fealty under oath in the presence of your servants, men still alive and now dwelling in this city. At the devil's prompting they perfidiously broke their word, and therefore he justly took their kingdom from them, as being deserters and rebels. You yourself would have done the same to men who had sworn fealty and then revolted against you.'

Ch. 6. 'But', said he, 'there is one of Adalbert's vassals here, and he does not acknowledge the truth of this.' 'If he denies it', I replied, 'one of my men, at your command, will prove to him tomorrow in single combat that it is so.' 'Well,' said he, 'he may, as you declare, have acted justly in this. Explain now why he attacked the borders of our empire with war and conflagration. We were friends and were thinking by marriage to enter into a partnership that would never be broken.'

Ch. 7. 'The land', I answered, 'which you say belongs to your empire, is proved by race and language to be part of the kingdom of Italy. The Lombards held it in their power, and Louis, emperor of the Lombards or Franks, freed it from the grip of the Saracens with great slaughter. For seven years also Landulf, prince of Benevento and Capua, held it under his control. Nor would it even now have passed from the yoke of slavery to him and his descendants, had not your emperor Romanos bought at a great price the friendship of our King Hugh. It was for this reason also that he made a match between King Hugh's bastard daughter and his own nephew and namesake. I see now that you think it shows weakness in my master, not generosity, when after winning Italy and Rome he for so many years left them to you. The friendly partnership, which you say you wished to form by a marriage, we hold to be a fraud and a snare: you ask for a truce, but you have no real reason to want it nor we to grant it. Come, let us clear away all trickeries and speak the plain truth. My master has sent me to you to see if you will give the daughter of the emperor Romanos and the empress Theophano to his son, my master the august emperor Otto. If you give me your oath that the marriage shall take place, I am to affirm to you under oath that my master in grateful return will observe to do this and this for you. Moreover he has already given you, his brother ruler, the best pledge of friendship by handing over Apulia, which was subject to his rule. I, to whose suggestion you declare this mischief was due, intervened in this matter, and there are as many witnesses to this as there are people in Apulia.'

Ch. 8. 'It is past seven o'clock,' said Nicephorus 'and there is a church procession which I must attend. Let us keep to the business before us. We will give you a reply at some convenient season.'

Ch. 9. I think that I shall have as much pleasure in describing this procession as my masters will have in reading of it. A numerous company of tradesmen and low-born persons, collected on this solemn occasion to welcome and honour Nicephorus, lined the sides of the road, like walls, from the palace to Saint Sophia, tricked out with thin little shields and cheap spears. As an additional scandal, most of the mob assembled in his honour had marched there with bare feet, thinking, I suppose, that thus they would better adorn the sacred procession. His nobles for their part, who with their master passed through the plebeian and barefoot multitude, were dressed in tunics that were too large for them and were also because of their extreme age full of holes. They would have looked better if they had worn their ordinary clothes. There was not a man among them whose grandfather had owned his tunic when it was new. No one except Nicephorus wore any jewels or golden ornaments, and the emperor looked more disgusting than ever in the regalia that had been designed to suit the persons of his ancestors. By your life, sires, dearer to me than my own, one of your nobles' costly robes is worth a hundred or more of these. I was taken to the procession and given a place on a platform near the singers.

Ch. 10. As Nicephorus, like some crawling monster, walked along, the singers began to cry out in adulation: 'Behold the morning star approaches: the day star rises: in his eyes the sun's rays are reflected: Nicephorus our prince, the pale death of the Saracens.' And then they cried again: 'Long life, long life to our prince Nicephorus. Adore him, ye nations, worship him, bow the neck to his greatness.' How much more truly might they have sung:– 'Come, you miserable burnt-out coal; old woman in your walk, wood-devil in your look; clodhopper, haunter of byres, goat-footed, horned, double-limbed; bristly, wild, rough, barbarian, harsh, hairy, a rebel, a Cappadocian!.' So, puffed up by these lying ditties, he entered St Sophia, his masters the emperors following at a distance and doing him homage on the ground with the kiss of peace. His armour bearer, with an arrow for pen, recorded in the church the era in progress since the beginning of his reign. So those who did not see the ceremony know what era it is.

Ch. 11.   On this same day he ordered me to be his guest. But as he did not think me worthy to be placed above any of his nobles, I sat fifteenth from him and without a table cloth. Not only did no one of my suite sit at table with me; they did not even set eyes upon the house where I was entertained. At the dinner, which was fairly foul and disgusting, washed down with oil after the fashion of drunkards and moistened also with an exceedingly bad fish liquor, the emperor asked me many questions concerning your power, your dominions and your army. My answers were sober and truthful; but he shouted out:– 'You lie. Your master's soldiers cannot ride and they do not know how to fight on foot. The size of their shields, the weight of their cuirasses, the length of the swords, and the heaviness of their helmets, does not allow them to fight either way.' Then with a smile he added: 'Their gluttony also prevents them. Their God is their belly, their courage but wind, their bravery drunkenness. Fasting for them means dissolution, sobriety, panic. Nor has your master any force of ships on the sea. I alone have really stout sailors, and I will attack him with my fleets, destroy his maritime cities and reduce to ashes those which have a river near them. Tell me, how with his small forces will he be able to resist me even on land? His son was there: his wife was there: his Saxons, Swabians, Bavarians and Italians were all there with him: and yet they had not the skill nor the strength to take one little city that resisted them. How then will they resist me when I come followed by as many forces as there are

> Corn fields on Gargarus, grapes on Lesbian vine,
> Waves in the ocean, stars in heaven that shine?'

Ch. 12. I wanted to answer and make such a speech in our defence as his boasting deserved; but he would not let me and added this final insult: 'You are not Romans but Lombards.' He even then was anxious to say more and waved his hand to secure my silence, but I was worked up and cried: 'History tells us that Romulus, from whom the Romans get their name, was a fratricide born in adultery. He made a place of refuge for himself and received into it insolvent debtors, runaway slaves, murderers and men who deserved death for their crimes. This was the sort of crowd whom he enrolled as citizens and gave them the name of Romans. From this nobility are descended those men whom you style 'rulers of the world'. But we Lombards, Saxons, Franks, Lotharingians, Bavarians, Swabians and Burgundians, so despise these fellows that when we are angry with an enemy we can find nothing more insulting to say than – "You Roman!" For us in the word Roman is comprehended every form of lowness, timidity, avarice, luxury, falsehood and vice. You say that we are unwarlike and know nothing of horsemanship. Well, if the sins of the Christians merit that you keep this stiff neck, the next war will prove what manner of men you are, and how warlike we.'

Ch. 13. Nicephorus, exasperated by these words, commanded the long narrow table to be removed and then calling for silence with his hand ordered me to return to my hateful abode, or, to speak more truly, to my prison. There two days later, as a result of my indignation as well as of heat and thirst, I fell seriously ill. Indeed there was not one of my companions who, having drunk from the same cup with me, did not fear that his last day was approaching. Why, I ask, should they not sicken? Their drink instead of good wine was brackish water; their bed was not hay, straw, or even earth, but hard marble; their pillow was a stone; their draughty house kept out neither heat nor rain nor cold. Salvation herself, to use a common expression, if she had poured all her favours on them, could not have saved them. Weakened therefore by my own tribulations and those of my companions I called in our warden, or rather my persecutor, and by prayers and bribes induced him to take the following letter to the emperor's brother:

Ch. 14. 'Bishop Liudprand to Leo, chancellor and marshal of the palace. If his serene highness the emperor intends to grant the request for which I came, then the sufferings I am now enduring shall not exhaust my patience: my master however must be informed by letter and messenger that my stay here is not useless. On the other hand, if a refusal is contemplated, there is a Venetian merchantman in harbour here just about to start. Let him permit me as a sick man to go on board, so that, if the time of my dissolution be at hand, my native land may at least receive my corpse.'

Ch. 15. Leo read my letter and gave me an audience four days later. In accordance with their rule their wisest men, strong in Attic eloquence, sat with him to discuss your request, namely, Basil the chief chamberlain, the chief secretary, the chief master of the wardrobe, and two other dignitaries. They began their discourse as follows: 'Tell us, brother, the reason that induced you to take the trouble to come here.' When I told them that it was on account of the marriage which was to be the ground for a lasting peace, they said:— 'It is unheard of that a daughter born in the purple of an emperor born in the purple should contract a foreign marriage. Still, great as is your demand, you shall have what you want if you give what is proper: Ravenna, namely, and Rome with all the adjoining territories from thence to our possessions. If you desire friendship without the marriage, let your master permit Rome to be free, and hand over to their former lord the princes of Capua and Benevento, who were formerly slaves of our holy empire and are now rebels.'

Ch. 16. To this I answered:— 'Even you cannot but know that my master rules over Slavonian princes who are far more powerful than Peter king of the Bulgarians who has married the daughter of the emperor Christopher.' 'Ah,' said they, 'but Christopher was not born in the purple.'

Ch. 17. 'As for Rome,' I went on, 'for whose freedom you are so noisily eager; who is her master? To whom does she pay tribute? Was she not formerly enslaved to harlots? And while you were sleeping, nay powerless, did not my master the august emperor free her from that foul servitude? Constantine, the august emperor who founded this city and called it after his name, as being ruler of the world made many offerings to the holy Roman apostolic church, not only in Italy, but in almost all the western kingdoms as well as those in the east and south, in Greece, Judæa, Persia, Mesopotamia, Babylonia, Egypt, Libya, as his own special regulations testify, preserved in our country. In Italy, in Saxony, in Bavaria, and in all my master's realms, everything that belongs to the church of the blessed apostles has been handed over to those holy apostles' vicar. And if my master has kept back a single city, farm, vassal or slave, then I have denied God. Why does not your emperor do the same? Why does he not restore to the apostolic church what lies in his kingdoms and thereby himself increase the richness and freedom which it already owes to my master's exertions and generosity?'

Ch. 18. 'He will do so', said the chief chamberlain Basil, 'when Rome and the Roman church shall be so ordered as he wishes.' Then said I:– 'A certain man having suffered much injury from another, approached God with these words:– "Lord, avenge me upon my adversary." To whom the Lord said: "I will do so on the day when I shall render to each man according to his works." "How late that day will be!" the man replied.'

Ch. 19. At that everyone except the emperor's brother burst into laughter. Then they broke off the discussion and ordered me to be taken back to my detestable dwelling place and to be carefully guarded until the day of the holy apostles, a feast which all religious persons duly observe. At the ceremony the emperor commanded me, though I was very ill at the time, together with the Bulgarian envoys who had arrived the day before, to meet him at the church of the holy apostles. After some verbose chants had been sung and the mass celebrated, we were invited to table, where I found placed above me on my side of the long narrow board the Bulgarian envoy. He was a fellow with his hair cut in Hungarian fashion, girt about with a brazen chain, and, as I fancy, just admitted into the Christian faith: the preference given to him over me was plainly meant as an insult to you, my august masters. On your account I was despised, rejected and scorned. I thank the Lord Jesus Christ, whom you serve with all your heart, that I have been considered worthy to suffer insults for your sake. However, my masters, I considered that the insult was done to you, not to me, and I therefore left the table. I was just going indignantly away when Leo, the emperor's brother, marshal of the court, and Simeon the chief secretary came after me, howling: 'When Peter king of the Bulgarians married Christopher's daughter, a mutual agreement was sworn to on both sides, to the effect that envoys of the Bulgarians should with us be preferred, honoured and esteemed above the envoys of other nations. What you say is true: the Bulgarian envoy over there has his hair cut short, he has not washed himself, and his girdle consists of a brass chain. But nevertheless he is a patrician and we are definitely of opinion that it would be wrong to give a bishop, especially a Frankish bishop, the preference over him. We have noticed your show of indignation and we are not going to allow you to return to your lodgings, as you suppose; we shall force you to take food with the emperor's servants in an inn.'

Ch. 20.   My mental anguish was so unparalleled that I could not answer them back but did what they ordered, judging that table no fit place for me, seeing that there a Bulgarian envoy was preferred, I will not say to myself personally, that is, to Bishop Liudprand, but to your representative. But my indignation was appeased by a handsome present! The sacred emperor sent me one of his most delicate dishes, a fat goat, of which he himself had partaken, richly stuffed with garlic onion and leeks, and swimming in fish sauce. I wish, sires, that you could have had it on your table. The sight of it, I am sure, would have banished any incredulity you have felt concerning the sacred emperor's luxurious ways.

Ch. 21.   When eight days had passed and the Bulgarians had left the city, Nicephorus, thinking that I esteemed his table highly, compelled me in spite of my ill health to dine with him again in the same place. The patriarch with several other bishops was present, and before them he propounded to me many questions concerning the Holy Scriptures, which, under the inspiration of the sacred spirit, I elegantly answered. Finally, wishing to make merry over you, he asked what synods we recognized. Those of Nicæa, Chalcedon, Ephesus, Carthage, Antioch, Ancyra, and Constantinople, I replied. 'Ha, ha,' said he, 'you have forgotten to mention Saxony. If you ask me, the reason why our books do not mention it either is that the Christian faith there is too young to have been able to reach us.'

Ch. 22. I answered: 'On that member of the body where the malady has its seat a cautery must be used. All the heresies have emanated from you and among you have flourished; by our western peoples they have been either strangled or killed. Synods have often been held at Rome and Pavia, but I do not count them here. It was a Roman cleric, he whom you call Dialogus, who afterwards became the universal Pope Gregory, that freed the heretic Eutychius, patriarch of Constantinople, from his error. Eutychius said, and not only said but in his teachings, sermons and writings proclaimed that at the Resurrection we should put on not the real flesh that we have here, but a certain fantastic substance of his own imagination. The book that set forth this heresy was burned in the interests of orthodoxy by Gregory. Moreover, Ennodius, Bishop of Pavia, was sent here, that is, to Constantinople, by the patriarch of Rome, to deal with a certain other heresy, which he repressed and restored the orthodox catholic doctrine. As for the Saxon people, since they received the holy baptism and the knowledge of God, they have not been stained by any heresy which rendered a synod necessary for its correction; of heresies we have had none. You declare that our Saxon faith is young, and I agree. Faith in Christ is always young and not old among people whose faith is seconded by works. Here faith is old, not young; works do not accompany it, and by reason of its age it is held in light esteem like a worn-out garment. I know for certain of one synod held in Saxony where it was enacted and decreed that it was more seemly to fight with the sword than with the pen, and better to face death than to fly before a foe. Your own army is finding that out now.' And in my own mind I said: 'May it soon find out by experience how warlike our men are.'

Ch. 23. He ordered me that same afternoon to attend him on his return to the palace, although I was so weak and changed that the women who before when they met me used to call out in admiration 'Holy Mother', now, pitying my misery, beat their breasts with their hands and cried: 'Oh, the poor sick man.' I hope that what I prayed for him as he approached me may happen; and I hope, sires, that what I prayed for you in your absence with hands lifted up to heaven may be granted also. Still, he made me laugh heartily; and you may well believe it, for though he is such a pygmy, he was riding a restless horse without a bridle, a very small man on the very big beast. My mind pictured to itself one of those dolls which your Slavonians tie on to a foal's back, allowing it then to follow its mother unbridled.

Ch. 24.   After this I was taken back to the five lions who were my fellow-citizens and housemates in the aforesaid hateful house, and for the next three weeks received no visits nor held any conversation with anyone but my companions. I pictured to myself that Nicephorus meant never to let me go, and my boundless depression so brought on illness after illness that I should have died had not the Mother of God by her prayers won my life from the Creator and His Son. This was shown to me in a true, not an imagined, vision.

Ch. 25.   During these three weeks Nicephorus was staying outside Constantinople at a place called 'The Fountains', and thither he bade me come. I was so ill that even sitting, and much more standing, was a burden; but he compelled me to stand before him with uncovered head, a thing which was very wrong in my weak health. He then said: 'The envoys of your master King Otto who were here before you last year promised me under oath – and the wording of the oath is extant – that they would never in any way cause scandal in our empire. Do you want a greater scandal than that he should call himself emperor and claim for himself provinces belonging to our empire? Both these things are intolerable; and if both are insupportable, that especially is not to be borne, nay, not to be heard of, that he calls himself emperor. If you will confirm their undertaking our majesty will straightway let you go enriched with a full purse.' This he said, not because he thought that you would keep such an engagement, even if I were foolish enough to make it, but because he wanted to have in hand something which in the future he might bring forward to his own glory and our discredit.

Ch. 26.   To him I gave this answer: 'My most holy master, a man of wisdom and full of the spirit of God, foreseeing this demand and fearing lest I might transcend the bounds he set for me, gave me written instructions which he also signed with his own seal lest I should contravene them.' – What I relied on in saying this, my august master, is known to you.– 'Let those instructions be produced, and whatever they order I will confirm by oath. But as regards anything that our former envoys promised, swore or wrote without their master's authority, in the words of Plato: "the responsibility rests with the chooser, the god is free from blame."'

Ch. 27.   When this topic was finished we came to the matter of the most noble princes of Capua and Benevento, whom he calls his slaves and is troubled by an inward pain on their account. 'Your master', said he, 'has taken my slaves under his protection. If he will not let them go and restore them to their former servitude, he will forfeit my friendship. They themselves demand to be taken into our empire again; but our empire refuses their request, so that they may learn by experience how dangerous it is for slaves to skulk away from their masters and try to escape from servitude. It would be more seemly for your master to hand them over as a friend than to have to give them up against his will. They shall indeed learn, if life be granted me, what comes of cheating your lord and failing in your duty as a slave. Even now, I think, they are feeling what I say; my soldiers across the sea are putting my words into effect.'

Ch. 28.   To this he would not allow me to reply. I was anxious to go away, but he ordered me to return to his table. His father sat with him, a man, it seemed to me, a hundred and fifty years old. For him, as for his son, the Greeks cry out in hymns of praise, or rather of blatant folly, 'May God multiply your years.' We may infer from this how senseless the Greeks are, how fond of such windy talk, how apt at flattery, and how greedy. Not merely is he an old man, but he has one foot in the grave; and yet they pray for him something that they know for certain nature will not allow. The old tombstone himself rejoices that they are asking on his behalf for what he knows God will not grant, something that, if God did grant it, would be a curse, and not a blessing. Nicephorus, for his part, takes pleasure in being hailed as 'Prince of Peace' and 'Morning Star'. To call a weakling strong, a fool wise, a pygmy a giant, a black man white, a sinner a saint, is not praise, believe me, but contumely. And he who takes more pleasure in false attributes than in real is exactly like those birds whose sight is blinded by the light of day and illumined by the shades of night.

Ch. 29.   But I must return to my subject. At this meal – a thing that he had not done before – he ordered a homily of St John Chrysostom on the Acts of the Apostles to be read aloud. After the reading was ended, I asked for permission to return to you; but though he nodded affirmatively, he told my persecutor to take me back to my housemates and fellow citizens, the lions. This was done, and I had no further audience with him until the twentieth day of July, being kept under close guard, lest I might in conversation chance upon news of his movements. Meanwhile he ordered Grimizo, Adalbert's envoy, to be brought to him, and gave him instructions to return to Italy with an imperial expeditionary force. This consisted of twenty-four fire-ships, two filled with Russian troops, and two with Galatians; I do not know if he sent any more, I did not see them. The bravery of your soldiers, my masters and august emperors, needs no encouragement from the thought of their enemies' weakness, although this has often been the case with other nations, the feeblest of whom, lacking comparatively all strength, have frequently routed this Greek courage and made it pay them tribute. Just as it would not frighten you if I were to describe them as valiant heroes cast in the mould of the great Alexander, so I am not going to fire your spirits when I tell you of their weakness, real as it is. I would have you believe me, and you will believe me, I know, when I say that you with four hundred of your men would slaughter the whole expedition if there were no ditches or walls in the way. As general of this force – to make a mock of you, I think – he has appointed a man of sorts – I say of sorts because the fellow has ceased to be a male and has not been able to become a female. Adalbert has sent word to Nicephorus that he has eight thousand men at arms and that with the help of the Greek army they can rout or destroy you. He has also asked your rival to send him some money, so that he may urge his men the more eagerly to the fray.

Ch. 30.   Now, my masters, 'learn the wiles of the Greeks, and from one crime know them all'. Nicephorus gave the slave, to whom he had handed over this higgledy-piggledy hireling host, a considerable sum of money, to be disposed of as follows. If Adalbert should join him, as he had promised, with seven thousand men at arms and more, then he was to distribute it as a donative amongst them. Adalbert's brother Cona with his and the Greek army was to attack you, but Adalbert was to be kept under close guard at Bari until his brother should return victorious. If, however, Adalbert did not bring with him the seven thousand men promised, the instructions were that he should be seized, bound and handed over to you on your arrival; moreover that the money originally destined for him should be paid into your hands. What a warrior! What loyalty! He wishes to betray the man for whom he prepares a defender; he prepares a defender for him whom he wishes to destroy. He is loyal to neither, disloyal to both. He does what he did not need to do; he needed to do what he has not done. But so be it! He has acted as becomes a Greek! I must return to my subject.

Ch. 31.   On the nineteenth of July he sent off his motley fleet, I viewing the spectacle from my detestable abode. The next morning, that being the day on which these flippant Greeks celebrate the ascension of the prophet Elijah with stage plays, he ordered me again to attend upon him, and said: 'Our imperial majesty is thinking of leading an army against the Assyrians, not, as your master does, against followers of Christ. Last year I meant to do so, but hearing that your master intended to invade the territory of our empire, we let the Assyrians go and wheeled round sharp upon him. His envoy, the Venetian Dominic, met us in Macedonia, and with much labour and exertion, tricked us into returning, since he affirmed with an oath that your master would never think of such a thing, much less do it. Return therefore now'

– when I heard that I said 'Thank God' to myself – 'and give this, and this message to your master. If he satisfies my requirements, you may come back.'

Ch. 32. To him I gave this reply: 'Were your most sacred majesty to bid me fly to Italy, my master assuredly would fulfil all your majesty's wishes, and I should return rejoicing to you.' With what purpose I said this did not, alas, escape him. He nodded his head with a smile, and as I was bowing to the earth in homage and preparing to take my leave bade me wait outside and have dinner with him, a dinner which smelt strongly of garlic and onions and was filthy with oil and fish sauce. On this day by urgent prayers I induced him graciously to accept a present from me, a thing which before he had frequently refused to do.

Ch. 33. While we were sitting at table, a table which had length without breadth and was covered over for a rod's breadth but was practically bare down its length, he made merry over the Franks, including the Germans as well as the Latins under that name, and asked me to tell him where the chief city of my bishopric was situated and in what name it rejoiced. 'It is called Cremona', I replied, 'and it is quite close to Po, the king of all Italian rivers. As your majesty is preparing in haste to send your war galleys to that country, let me reap some advantage from having already made your acquaintance. Grant Cremona the blessings of peace, and of your grace allow it existence, seeing that resistance to you is impossible.' The cunning rogue saw that I was speaking ironically, and lowering his eyes promised he would do what I asked. He swore furthermore by the virtue of his sacred majesty that no harm should come to me and that his galleys would convey me speedily and safely to the harbour of Ancona. On this he took his oath, striking his breast with his fingers.

Ch. 34. But mark how foul was his perjury. His conversation took place on Monday, the twentieth of July, and for the next nine days I received no supplies from him at all. This too was at a time when the famine at Constantinople was so severe that three gold pieces were insufficient to provide one meal for my twenty-five attendants and our four Greek guards. On the fourth day of that week Nicephorus left Constantinople to march against the Assyrians.

Ch. 35. On the fifth day his brother summoned me and addressed me thus: 'His sacred majesty has gone forth, and at his orders I have remained at home to-day. Tell me then now if you desire to see his sacred majesty or if you have anything to say which you have not as yet brought forward.' To that I said: 'I have no reason for asking an interview with his sacred majesty nor have I anything fresh to say. My one request is that in accordance with his sacred majesty's promise I be conveyed on his war galleys to the harbour of Ancona.' On hearing this – the Greeks are always ready to swear by the head of another – he began to swear that he would carry out the promise by the head of the emperor, by his own life and by his children – may God's protection for them be suited to the truth of his words! I asked him: 'When?' and he replied: 'As soon as the emperor has gone; the admiral of the fleet, who has sole control in naval matters, will see to your business directly after his majesty's departure.' Deceived by this hope I went away from him rejoicing.

Ch. 36. Two days later, however, on the Saturday Nicephorus bade me attend him at Umbria, a place eighteen miles distant from Constantinople. He there addressed me thus: 'I thought that you, as a man of rank and honour, had come here to fulfil my wishes and establish a perpetual friendship between me and your master. Since by reason of the hardness of your heart you are unwilling to do this, at least bring about one thing, which you can with perfect justice arrange. Promise me that your master will give no help to the princes of Capua and Benevento, my slaves, whom I am arranging to attack. As he offers me nothing that is his, let him at least give up what is mine. It is a known fact that their fathers and their grandfathers paid tribute to our empire, and my imperial forces will see to it that they themselves soon do the same.' To that I answered: 'These princes are men of high nobility and my master's vassals. If he sees an army of yours attacking them, he will send them such a force as will annihilate your expedition and take the two oversea provinces from you.' Then, swelling like a toad with anger, he cried: 'Go away. By my life, and by my parents who begat me to be the man I am, I will soon give your master other things to think about than protecting rebellious slaves.'

Ch. 37. I was just leaving him when he bade me sit down to dinner with the interpreter; and summoning the brother of the two princes and Bysantius of Bari, ordered them to vomit gross insults against yourselves and against the Latin and German nations. On my departure, however, from the disgusting meal they sent messengers to me secretly and swore that their yelpings were not voluntary but due to the emperor's wishes and threats. Nicephorus himself at the same dinner, asked me if you had parks and if in your parks you had wild asses and other animals. When I told him you had parks and animals in the parks, but no wild asses, he said: 'I will take you into our park and you will be surprised both at its size and at the wild asses it contains.' I was accordingly taken to a park which was fairly large and hilly and full of bushes, but not at all picturesque. I was riding along with my hat on when the marshal of the palace saw me and sent his son in haste to say that it was not permitted for any one to wear a hat in the emperor's presence and that I must put on a bonnet. I answered: 'Women with us wear bonnets and hoods when they are out riding, men wear hats. You have no right to compel me to change the custom of my country here, seeing that we allow your envoys when they come to us to keep to their ways. They wear long sleeves, bands, brooches, flowing hair, and tunics down to their heels, both when they ride or walk or sit at table with us; and what to all of us seems quite too shameful, they alone kiss our emperors with covered heads.' And then I said to myself: 'May God forbid it in the future.' 'Well', said he, 'you must go back.'

Ch. 38. As I was doing so I met their so-called wild asses, in a herd with some roe deer. But why, I ask, wild asses? Our tame ones at Cremona are just like them. Their colour and shape are the same; both have long ears, both are equally melodious when they begin to bray; they are alike in size and in swiftness, and wolves find each kind equally delicious. When I saw them I said to the Greek who was riding with me: 'I never saw the like in Saxony.' 'Ah', he replied, 'if your master be compliant to his sacred majesty, he will give him many such; and it will be no small glory for him to possess something that none of his illustrious predecessors had even seen.' But believe me, my august masters, my brother and fellow bishop Antony can supply beasts quite as good as these – witness the market at Cremona – and his walk the streets not as wild asses but as tame ones, and instead of roaming idle they carry loads upon their backs. However, when my companion told Nicephorus what I had said, he sent me two wild goats and gave me permission to go. On the following day he himself set out for Syria.

Ch. 39. Pray now mark why he led his army against the Assyrians. The Greeks and Saracens have certain writings which they call The Visions of Daniel; I should call them Sibylline Books. In them is found written how many years each emperor shall live; what crisis will occur during his reign; whether he shall have peace or war and whether fortune will smile upon the Saracens or not. According to these prophecies the Assyrians in the time of the present emperor Nicephorus will not be able to resist the Greeks, but Nicephorus himself will only live for seven years. After his death an emperor will rise worse than he – only I fear that none such can be found – and more unwarlike; in whose time the Assyrians shall so prevail that they will bring under their rule all the country as far as Chalcedon, which is not far from Constantinople. Both peoples pay serious heed to these dates; and so now for one and the same reason the Greeks are pressing vigorously forward and the Saracens in despair offer no resistance, awaiting the time when they will attack and the Greeks in turn not resist.

Ch. 40. A certain Sicilian bishop named Hippolytus wrote similarly concerning your empire and our people – I call 'our people' all those who are under your rule – and I pray that what he wrote about these present times may turn out true. His other prophecies, as I have heard from those who know his books, have all been fulfilled. One of his many sayings may be here mentioned. He says that in these days the writing shall be fulfilled – 'The lion and his whelp shall together exterminate the wild ass.' The Greeks interpret this as follows. Leo – that is, the Emperor of the Romans or the Greeks – and his whelp – the king, namely, of the Franks – shall together in these days drive out the wild ass – that is, the

African king of the Saracens. But their interpretation does not seem to me to be true. The lion and his whelp differ in size, but are of one nature, species, and kind; and to the best of my knowledge it seems irrational to make the lion the emperor of the Greeks and his whelp the king of the Franks. Both these rulers are men, as the lion and his whelp are both animals; but they differ from one another in character as much – I will not say as one species differs from another – but as rational beings differ from those devoid of reason. The whelp differs from the lion only in age; the form is the same, the fury is the same, the roar the same. The king of the Greeks has long hair and wears a tunic with long sleeves and a bonnet; he is lying, crafty, merciless, foxy, proud, falsely humble, miserly and greedy; he eats garlic, onions and leeks, and he drinks bath water. The king of the Franks, on the other hand, is beautifully shorn, and wears a garment quite different from a woman's dress and a hat; he is truthful, guileless, merciful when right, severe when necessary, always truly humble, never miserly; he does not live on garlic, onions and leeks nor does he spare animals' lives so as to heap up money by selling instead of eating them. You have heard the difference: do not accept the Greek interpretation; it either refers to the future, or it is not true. It is impossible that Nicephorus, as they falsely say, should be the lion and Otto the whelp, and that they together should exterminate anyone. 'Sooner shall the Parthians and the Germans traverse one another's lands and in exile drink the one from the Arar and the other from the Tigris', than that Nicephorus and Otto should join in friendship and confirm a treaty of union.

Ch. 41. You have heard the Greek interpretation; now hear that of Liudprand, bishop of Cremona. I say – and not merely do I say but I affirm – that if the writing is to be fulfilled in these days, the lion and his whelp are the father and the son, Otto and Otto, unlike in nothing, only differing in age; and they shall together at this time exterminate the wild ass Nicephorus; who not unsuitably is compared to a wild ass by reason of his vain and empty boastings and his incestuous marriage with his mistress and fellow god-parent. If this wild ass be not exterminated by our lion and his whelp – namely by Otto and Otto, father and son, the august emperors of the Romans – then that which Hippolytus wrote will not be true. The Greek interpretation mentioned above must be entirely discarded. O blessed Jesus, eternal God, Word of the Father, who dost speak to us, unworthy as we are, not by voice but by inspiration, mayest Thou decree no other interpretation of this sentence than mine. Command that our lion and his whelp exterminate and humble this wild ass in his mortal life, so that at the Day of the Lord his soul may be saved, returning to its proper place and making submission to his masters the emperors Basil and Constantine!

Ch. 42. Astronomers also make the same pronouncement as this in relation to yourselves and Nicephorus. It is truly wonderful. I have spoken with a certain astronomer who exactly described to me your figure and habits, and those, sire, of your august namesake; and also told me everything that has happened to me in the past as though it had happened that day. There was not a single friend or enemy, whom I thought of asking him about, whose appearance figure and habits he could not describe. He foretold every disaster that has occurred to me on this journey. Even though everything else he said prove false, I pray that one thing be true – I mean, what he foretold you would do to Nicephorus. O may it come to pass! O may it come to pass! Then I shall feel that all the wrongs I have suffered are as nothing.

Ch. 43. The aforesaid Hippolytus writes also that not the Greeks but the Franks shall crush the Saracens. Encouraged by this prophecy the Saracens three years ago engaged in battle in Sicilian waters near Scylla and Charybdis with the patrician Manuel, nephew of Nicephorus. They overcame his immense forces, and taking Manuel prisoner killed him and hung up his headless corpse. As for his fellow-admiral, a gentleman who was of neither gender, they disdained to put him to death; they put him in chains and after he was wasted by long years of imprisonment they sold him for a price which no sane man would have given for a creature of his kind. Encouraged by this same prophecy they soon afterwards attacked the general Exacontes with equal resolution, and putting him to flight completely destroyed his army.

Ch. 44.   Another reason also compelled Nicephorus to lead his army against the Assyrians at this moment. By the will of God this year a famine had so wasted all the Greek territory that one gold piece did not purchase two of our Pavian measures of corn; and this in the very realm of plenty. This misfortune, in which field mice played their part, Nicephorus increased by collecting for himself at harvest time all the available corn and paying the wretched owners a very low price for it. In the Mesopotamian district, where there was an absence of mice, the crops were abundant, and the amount of corn he got from there equalled the amount of the sands of the sea. As the result of this mean transaction famine raged shamefully everywhere, and so he brought together eighty thousand men under pretence of a military expedition, and for one whole month went on selling for two gold pieces what he had bought for one. These, my master, are the reasons which compelled Nicephorus to lead his forces against the Assyrians just at this moment. And what forces! They are not really men; they are dummies; their tongues are saucy, but 'cold are their hands in war.' Nicephorus did not look for quality in them, but only for quantity. How dangerous this will be for him he will learn to his sorrow, when his unwarlike host, relying only on its size, shall be put to flight by a handful of our men who have both knowledge and appetite for fighting.

Ch. 45.   When you were besieging Bari, not more than three hundred Hungarians laid hands on five hundred Greeks near Thessalonica and hauled them off into Hungary. Their success induced two hundred Hungarians in Macedonia, not far from Constantinople, to attempt a similar feat; but forty of them, retiring carelessly along a narrow pass, were taken prisoners. These men Nicephorus has released from prison, and dressing them in the most costly garments has made them his bodyguard and defenders, to go with him against the Assyrians. What sort of an army it is you can infer from this fact: the chief officers come from Venice and Amalfi!

Ch. 46.   But I must resume my story and tell you what happened to me next. On the twenty-seventh of July at Umbria, outside Constantinople, I received permission from Nicephorus to return to you. On my arrival at Constantinople, however, I was told by the patrician Christopher, the eunuch who represented Nicephorus there, that I could not start just then. The Saracens were holding the sea, he said, and the Hungarians the land; I should have to wait till they retired. Both of his statements, alas, were lies! The next thing was that guards were set to prevent myself and my companions from leaving our house. The poor of Latin speech who came to me for alms they seized and slew or put in prison. They would not allow our Greek interpreter to go out, even to buy supplies; and so our cook had to go, although he knew no Greek and could only speak to the vendor, when he bought from him, with signs on his fingers or nods of his head instead of words. He bought for four shillings about as much food as the interpreter got for one. Some of my friends sent me spices, bread, wine and fruit; they flung everything on the ground and drove the messengers away with their backs loaded with blows. Had not God's pity prepared before me a table against my adversaries, I should have had to accept the death they devised for me. But He who permitted me to be thus tried, mercifully gave me power to endure. Such were the trials and tribulations I suffered at Constantinople from the fourth of June until the second of October, a period of one hundred and twenty days.

Ch. 47.   To increase my calamities, on the day of the Assumption of the Virgin Mary the holy mother of God, an ill-omened embassy came from the apostolic and universal Pope John with a letter asking Nicephorus 'the emperor of the Greeks' to conclude an alliance and firm friendship with his beloved and spiritual son Otto, 'august emperor of the Romans'. If you ask me why these words, and manner of address, which to the Greeks seem sinful audacity, did not cost the bearer his life and overwhelm it even before they were read, I cannot answer. On other points I have often shown a fine and copious flow of words; on this I am as dumb as a fish. The Greeks abused the sea, cursed the waves, and wondered exceedingly how they could have transported such an iniquity, and why the deep had not opened to swallow up the ship. 'The audacity of it!' they cried, 'to call the universal emperor of the Romans, the one and only Nicephorus, the great, the august "emperor of the Greeks", and to style a poor barbaric creature "emperor of the Romans!" O sky? O earth! O sea! What shall we do with these scoundrels and criminals? They are paupers, and if we kill them we pollute our hands with vile blood; they are ragged, they are slaves, they are peasants; if we beat them we disgrace not them but ourselves; they are not worthy of our gilded Roman scourge, or of any punishment of that kind. Would that one of them were a bishop and the other a marquess! Then we would sew them in a sack, and after giving them a sound beating with rods and plucking out their beards and hair we would throw them into the sea. As for these fellows, their lives may be spared; but they shall be kept in close custody until Nicephorus, the sacred emperor of the Romans, be informed of these insults.'

Ch. 48. When I heard of this I considered them happy in their poverty, myself unhappy in my riches. At home my own desire excused my lack of wealth; in Constantinople fear taught me that I had the gold of Crœsus. Poverty had always seemed burdensome; but then it appeared light, acceptable, desirable; in any case desirable, since it saved its votaries from death, its followers from the whip. But since at Constantinople alone poverty thus defends its children, may it there alone be cherished!

Ch. 49. The pope's envoys were therefore put in prison and the offensive letter sent to Nicephorus in Mesopotamia. No one returned with an answer from him until the twelfth of September, and then I was not informed of its purport. Two days later, that is, on the fourteenth of September, by dint of prayers and bribes, I secured permission to adore the cross that gives us life and salvation. Amid the noisy crowd some persons approached me unnoticed by my guards and cheered my sad heart with words of furtive consolation.

Ch. 50. On the seventeenth of September, however, though I was but half way between life and death, I was summoned to the palace. The patrician eunuch Christopher with three other officials was there, and when I arrived he rose to his feet and gave me a courteous reception. Their discourse began as follows: 'The pallor of your face, the emaciation of your whole body, the unusual length of your hair and beard, all reveal the immense pain that is in your heart because the date of your return to your master has been delayed. But be not angry with the sacred emperor, we pray, nor yet with us. The cause of your delay is this. The Pope of Rome – if indeed he may be called pope when he has held communion and ministry with Alberic's son, the apostate, the adulter, the sacrilegious – has sent a letter to our most sacred emperor, worthy of himself and unworthy of Nicephorus, calling him emperor of "the Greeks", and not "of the Romans" *Certainement* this has been done at your master's instigation.'

Ch. 51. 'What's this I hear!' said I to myself. 'I am lost. Assuredly now I shall be marched off straight into court.' 'Listen', they continued, 'we know you mean to tell us that the pope is the most stupid of men.' 'I do not say so', interposed I. 'Listen! The silly blockhead of a pope does not know that the sacred Constantine transferred to this city the imperial sceptre, the senate, and all the Roman knighthood, and left in Rome nothing but vile slaves, fishermen, confectioners, poulterers, bastards, plebeians, underlings. He never would have written this letter if your king had not suggested it; and how dangerous for both of them it will be, unless they come to their senses, the immediate future will show.' 'But the pope', said I, 'in his noble simplicity thought that in writing thus he was honouring the emperor, not insulting him. We know, of course, that Constantine the Roman emperor came here with the Roman knighthood and called the city he founded by his own name. But as you have changed your language, customs and dress, the most holy pope thought that the name of the Romans, like their dress, would displease you. If life be granted him, he will make this plain in his future letters. Their superscription shall be this: "John, the Roman pope, to Nicephorus, Constantine and Basilius, the great and august emperors of the Romans".' Mark, pray, why I said this.

Ch. 52. Nicephorus came to his high place on the throne by perjury and adultery. Since the welfare of all Christians is a matter of anxiety to the pope of Rome, let the lord pope send to Nicephorus a letter like in all respects to those sepulchres which without are whited, within are full of dead men's bones. Let him in that letter show him how by perjury and adultery he has obtained the rule over his masters; let him then invite him to a synod, and if he will not come, let him be smitten with the papal anathema. If the superscription be not as I have said, the letter will never reach him.

Ch. 53. Now let me return to my narrative. When the aforesaid princes heard my undertaking about the address on the letter, they said, not suspecting any guile: 'We thank you, sir bishop; it becomes your wisdom to act as mediator in these important matters. You are the only one of the Franks for whom we now feel any esteem. But when at your bidding they have corrected their mistakes, we will love them also. As for yourself, when you return to us, you shall not go away unrewarded.' 'If ever I return here of my own accord', I said to myself, 'may Nicephorus give me a crown and a golden sceptre!' 'But tell us', they continued, 'does your most sacred master wish to confirm friendship with the emperor by a marriage treaty?' 'When I came here, he wished it', I replied, 'but during my long stay here he has received no letter from me, and he thinks that you have made a *faux pas* and put me in prison as a captive. He is burning with rage, like a lioness robbed of her whelps, and will not rest until he has taken vengeance in just wrath. He hates the idea of a marriage and is only anxious to pour out his anger upon you.' 'If he tries to do that', they answered, 'neither Italy will protect him, nor his native land of Saxony, that poverty-stricken country where the people dress in skins. With our money, which gives us power, we will rouse the whole world against him, and we will break him in pieces like a potter's vessel, which when broken cannot be put into shape again. And since we think that you have bought some cloaks in his honour, we order them now to be produced. Those that are fit for you shall be marked with a leaden seal and left in your possession; those that are prohibited to all nations, except to us Romans, shall be taken away and their price returned.'

Ch. 54. Thereupon they took from me five very valuable pieces of purple cloth; considering yourselves and all the Italians, Saxons, Franks, Bavarians, Swabians – nay, all nations – as unworthy to appear abroad in such ornate vestments. How improper and insulting is it that these soft, effeminate creatures, with their long sleeves and hoods and bonnets, idle liars of neither gender, should go about in purple, while heroes like yourselves, men of courage, skilled in war, full of faith and love, submissive to God, full of virtues, may not! 'But where is your emperor's word?' I said. 'Where is the imperial promise? When I said farewell to him, I asked him up to what price he would allow me to buy vestments in honour of my church. He replied, "By any that you like and as many as you like." In thus fixing quality and quantity he clearly did not make a distinction, as if he had said, "excepting this and that". His brother Leo, the marshal of the palace, can bear me witness; so can the interpreter Euodisius, and John and Romanus. I can testify to it myself, for even without the interpreter I understood what the emperor said.' 'But these stuffs are prohibited,' they replied, 'and when the emperor spoke as you say he did he could not imagine that you would ever dream of such things as these. As we surpass all other nations in wealth and wisdom, so it is right that we should surpass them in dress. Those who are unique in the grace of their virtue should also be unique in the beauty of their raiment.'

Ch. 55. 'Such garments can hardly be called unique,' I said, 'when with us street walkers and conjurors wear them.' 'Where do you get them from?' they asked. 'From Venetian and Amalfian traders', I replied, 'who by bringing them to us support life by the food we give them.' 'They shall not do so any longer', they answered. 'They shall be searched, and if any cloth of this kind be found on them, they shall be punished with a beating and have their hair clipped close.' 'In the time of the Emperor Constantine, of blessed memory,' I said, 'I came here not as bishop but as deacon, not sent by an emperor or king but by the Marquess Berengar. I then bought many more vestments of greater value than those I have bought now, and they were not inspected, and scrutinized by the Greeks, nor yet stamped with a leaden seal. Now, having become a bishop by the mercy of God and being sent as envoy by the magnificent emperors, Otto and Otto, father and son, I am treated with ignominy; my vestments are marked after the manner of the Venetians, and any of them that seem of value are taken from me, although they are being transported for use in the church entrusted to my care. Are you not weary of insulting me, or rather, my masters, for whose sake I am thus scorned? Is it not enough that I was given into custody, tortured by hunger and thirst, and not allowed to return to them, but detained here until now? Must you also, as one final insult to them, rob me of things that are honestly mine? At least only take away what I purchased; leave me what was presented as a gift by friends.' To that they replied: 'The emperor Constantine was a mild man, who always stayed in his palace, and by peaceful methods won the friendship of all the world. The Emperor Nicephorus on the other hand shuns the palace as if it were the plague. We call him a man of contention and almost a lover of strife; he does not win people's friendship by offering them money, he subdues them to his sway by terror and the sword. And that you may realize in what esteem we hold your royal masters, we shall treat gifts and purchases in the same way: every purple vestment you have acquired must be returned to us.'

Ch. 56. Having done and said these things, they gave me a letter written and sealed with gold to bring to you; but even that in my opinion was not worthy of your greatness. They brought also another dispatch sealed with silver and said: 'We think it improper for your pope to receive a letter from our emperor. But the marshal of the court, the emperor's brother, sends him an epistle which is good enough for him – by you and not by his pauper envoys – and warns him that unless he comes to his senses he will find that he is completely ruined.'

Ch. 57. After I had received the letters they bade me farewell and sent me off with many sweet and loving kisses. But as I went they despatched another message, right worthy of themselves but not of me, to the effect that they would supply horses for myself and my suite but not for my baggage. Consequently, to my great and natural annoyance, I had to give my guide a present worth fifty gold pieces as an extra fee. I had no other means of repaying Nicephorus for his misconduct; so I wrote the following verses upon the wall of my hateful house and also upon a wooden table:

> Trust not the Greeks; they live but to betray;
> Nor heed their promises, whate'er they say.

If lies will serve them, any oath they swear,
And when it's time to break it feel no fear.
This lofty marble house with windows wide,
That has no well and cannot shade provide
Against the sun, but lets in cold and heat,
Was for four summer months my sole retreat.
I, Liudprand, from far Cremona came
To the great town that bears Constantine's name,
A messenger of peace, when my great lord,
The Emperor Otto, had with fire and sword
Gone up to conquer Bari, and in haste
Wrought havoc and laid all the country waste.
He yielded to my prayers, the victory won,
For lying Greece had promised to his son
Her princess as a bride. Ah, would that she
Had not been born nor this land e'er seen me!
And then I should not have endured the spite
Of him who now refuses to unite
His stepchild with our prince. The time draws near
When Mars, by Furies driven, will appear
And banish Peace, unless God bars his way,
Fair Peace, for whom the whole world sighs to-day.
And if he comes, all blame I shall decline:
The fault, Nicephorus, the fault is thine.

Ch. 58. After writing these lines, on the second of October, I went on board my boat and left the city that was once so rich and prosperous and is now such a starveling, a city full of lies, tricks, perjury and greed, rapacious, avaricious, vain-glorious. My guide was with me and after forty-nine days of ass-riding, walking, horse-riding, fasting, thirsting, sighing, weeping and groaning, I arrived at Naupactus, which is a city of Nicopolis. There my guide deserted me after putting us on two small ships and committing us to two imperial messengers who were to bring me by sea to Otranto. Their commission, however, did not give them the right of obtaining supplies from the Greek princes, who everywhere treated them with scorn, and we fed them rather then they us. How often in my indignation did I not think of Terence's line:

Those whom you have sent to help us need themselves a
helper too.

Ch. 59. On the twenty third of November then I left
Naupactus, and in two days reached the river Phidari, my
companions not remaining on the ships, which could not hold
them, but walking along the shore. From where we were on the
Phidari we could see Patras eight miles away on the opposite
coast. This place of apostolic suffering, which we had visited with
our prayers on our way up to Constantinople, we now omitted — I
confess my fault — to visit with prayers a second time. My
unspeakable longing to return to you, my august lords and
masters, and my desire to see you again was the cause of my
weakness; indeed, if it had not been for that desire I think I should
have died there and then.

Ch. 60. A south wind rose up against me, madman that I was,
disturbing the sea to its lowest depths by its gusts. It did this for
several days and nights in succession and on the thirtieth of
November, the day of Andrew's passion, I realized that my sin
was the cause of the trouble. Trouble taught me wisdom. We were
suffering terribly from hunger. The people of the country were
planning to murder us and seize our goods. The sea was raging
fiercely and prevented our escape. So, turning to the church before
my eyes, I said with tears and lamentation: 'O holy apostle
Andrew, I am the servant of thy fellow-fisherman, brother, and
fellow apostle Simon Peter. It was not from distaste or from pride
that I avoided the place of thy passion; I was tormented by love for
my august masters and by their command to return home. If my
sin has stirred thee to wrath, let the merit of my august masters
incline thee to mercy; thou hast nothing to bestow on thy brother;
bestow something on the emperors who show their love for thy
brother by clinging to Him who knows all things. Thou knowest
with what labour and toil, with what vigils and at what cost they
have saved the Roman church of thy brother Apostle Peter from
the hands of the ungodly, and have enriched, honoured and
exalted it, and restored it to its proper condition. If my works have
brought me into danger, let their merits save me; and let not those
whom thy aforesaid brother in the faith and in the flesh, Peter the

chief apostle of the apostles, wishes to rejoice and prosper, have cause for sorrow in this matter, sorrow, I mean, for myself, who am their envoy!'

Ch. 61. Truly, my masters and august emperors, this is not flattery, nor do I sew pillows under my arms. The thing, I repeat, is true. After two days through your merits the sea grew calm and became so tranquil that when our sailors deserted us we sailed the ship ourselves the hundred and forty miles to Leucas, suffering no danger or discomfort, except a little difficulty at the mouth of the river Achelous, where its strong current is beaten back by the sea waves.

Ch. 62. How, most mighty emperors, will you repay God for all that He did for you in my case? I will tell you. This is God's will and demand; and although He can do it without your help, He wishes you to be His instruments in this matter. He himself gives what is offered to Him, and He keeps what He claims from us in order to crown His work. Attend to me then, pray. Nicephorus, who loves to harm all churches, out of the abundant envy he feels towards you has ordered the patriarch of Constantinople to raise the church of Otranto to the rank of an archbishopric, and not to allow the divine mysteries throughout Apulia and Calabria to be celebrated in Latin, but to have them celebrated in Greek. He says that the former popes were merchants who sold the Holy Spirit, whereby all things are vivified and ruled, which fills the world, which knows the Word, which is co-eternal and consubstantial with God the Father and His Son Jesus Christ, without beginning, without end, continually true, which is not valued at a price, but is bought by the clean of heart for as much as they deem it worth. So Polyeuctus, the patriarch of Constantinople, has written to the Bishop of Otranto, giving him power under this authority to consecrate bishops in Acerenza, Tursi, Gravena, Matera and Tricarico, all sees which evidently belong to the jurisdiction of our apostolic Pope. But why need I say that, when the church of Constantinople itself is properly subject to our holy catholic and apostolic church of Rome? We know, nay, we have seen that the Bishop of Constantinople only wears the pallium by permission of our holy father. But when the godless Alberic, filled by cupidity not in drops but in torrents, laid claim to the city of Rome and held the apostolic Pope like a slave in his dwelling, the emperor Romanos made his own son, the eunuch Theophylactus, patri- arch. Knowing Alberic's cupidity, he sent him handsome presents and got a letter despatched to the patriarch Theophylactus in our pope's name, giving him and his successors authority to wear the pallium without further papal permission. The result of that shameful transaction has been the growth of the custom whereby not only the patriarchs but all the Greek bishops now wear the pallium. How absurd that is goes without further remark. It is therefore my proposal that a sacred synod should be held to which Polyeuctus shall be summoned. If he be unwilling to come and refuse canonically to amend the above stated faults, then let that be done which the sacred canons decree. Do you, most mighty emperors, continue the work you have begun; if Nicephorus will not obey us, when we proceed to convict him canonically, see to it that he hears from you, whose armies the old corpse does not dare to face. This, I say, is what the apostles, our masters and fellow- soldiers, wish us to do. The Greeks must not hold Rome a place of no account, because Constantine left it; it must rather receive especial love, veneration, and respect, inasmuch as the apostles, the holy teachers Peter and Paul, came there. May what I have written on this matter suffice until by the grace of God and the holy apostles' prayers I escape from the hands of the Greeks and return to you. I hope then it will not weary me to say what it irks me now to write. Now let me return to my subject.

Ch. 63.   On the sixth of December we came to Leucas, where, as by all the other bishops, we were most unkindly received and treated by the bishop who is a eunuch. In all Greece – I speak the truth and do not lie – I found no hospitable bishops. They are both poor and rich; rich in gold chains wherewith they gamble recklessly; poor in servants and utensils. They sit by themselves at a bare little table, with a ship's biscuit in front of them, and instead of drinking their bath water they sip it from a tiny glass. They do their own buying and selling; they close and open their doors themselves; they are their own stewards, their own ass- drivers, their own 'capones' – aha, I meant to write 'caupones', but the thing is so true that it made me write the truth against my will – as I say, they are 'capones', that is, eunuchs, which is against canon law; and they are also 'caupones', that is, innkeepers, which is again uncanonical. It is true of them to say:

> Of old a lettuce ended the repast:
> To-day it is the first course and the last.

If their poverty imitated that of Christ, I should judge them happy in it. But their reason is sordid gain and the accursed hunger for gold. May God be merciful to them. I think that they act thus because their churches are tributary to the state. The bishop of Leucas swore to me that his church had to pay Nicephorus a hundred gold pieces every year, and the other churches the same, more or less according to their means. How unjust this is is shown by the enactments of the holy patriarch Joseph. At the time of the famine he made all Egypt pay tribute to Pharaoh, but the land of the priests he allowed to be exempt.

Ch. 64.   Leaving Leucas then on the fourteenth of December and sailing the ship ourselves – for the crew, as we said above, had run away – on the eighteenth we arrived at Corfu. There, even before we left the ship, we were met by a certain captain called Michael, a Chersionite from Cherson. He was a gray-haired man, jovial looking and of merry conversation; but, as it afterwards proved, a devil in heart, as God showed to me even then by clear signs, if only I had had the wit to understand them. At the very moment when he was giving me the kiss of peace, which in his heart he did not mean, all the great island of Corfu trembled; and not only once but three times on the same day it trembled to its base. Moreover, four days later, on the twenty-second of December, while I was breaking bread at table with the man who was treading me under foot, the sun, ashamed of his disgraceful conduct, hid the rays of his light and suffering an eclipse that terrified Michael but did not change him.

Ch. 65.   I will explain what I did for him in the way of friendship and what I received from him in recompense. On my way up to Constantinople I gave his son the costly shield, gilded and wonderfully ornamented, which you, my august masters, had given me with the other presents I was to bestow upon my Greek friends. On this occasion returning from Constantinople I gave the father a very expensive cloak; and this is all the thanks I got. Nicephorus had written that at whatever hour I should arrive he should put me on a fast galley and send me on to the chamberlain Leo. He did not do this, but kept me there for twenty days, I, not he, paying for my food; until at last a messenger came from the aforesaid chamberlain Leo, rating him for delaying me. Unable to endure my reproaches, lamentations and sighs he went away and handed me over to a fellow so utterly sinful and bad that he did not even allow me to buy supplies until I gave him a caldron worth a pound of silver. After twenty days I got away, but the man who had had my caldron ordered the ship's captain, after passing a certain promontory, to put me ashore and let me die of hunger. He did this because he had turned over my cloaks to see if I had any purple cloth concealed, and I had refused to give him the one he wanted. O you Michaels, you Michaels, where have I ever found so many of you together and such ones! The fellow at Constantinople who had charge of me was a Michael, and he handed me over to a rival Michael, bad to worse, rascal to rogue. My guide was also called Michael, a simple man indeed, but one whose saintly simplicity harmed me almost as much as did the others' perversity. But from the hands of these puny Michaels I fell into yours, O monstrous Michael, half-hermit, half-monk. I tell you and I tell you truly; the bath water will not avail you, which you drink so assiduously for the love of St John the Baptist. Those who seek God falsely never merit to find him.

INDEX OF PERSONS

Liudprand's spelling of proper names varies. The index adopts one form for convenience: e.g. Adalbert for Adalbertus, Adelbertus, Adelpertus